Farmcall Fatality

Abby Deuel

Published by
Deuel Veterinary Services PC
via Createspace

Library of Congress Cataloging-in-Publication Data

Deuel, Abby

Farmcall Fatality (Book 1 Mandy Bell DVM Mystery Series)

ISBN 9781500278984

This book is dedicated with love to Alfred H. Deuel, my father

Happy Birthday Dad

RIP 6/19/50 – 4/13/10

About the Author

Abby Deuel is a practicing veterinarian in a small town in the Midwest. She worked in the Dairy farming industry in New Zealand before attending vet school there. After graduating and practicing as a mixed animal vet in the North Island of New Zealand, she moved back to America. Deuel served as a relief vet for several years, until she set up her own practice.

While she pulls from real life experiences for some of the cases and characters for this series, everything is fictional. The only exception is that she too has a Border collie named Lyle that continues to serve as inspiration for upcoming books as well as a constant companion.

Chapter One

Mandy rolled into the sleepy Midwestern town of Crestview in her thirty-four-foot RV on a crisp Sunday evening in Fall. Her Border collie, Lyle, was asleep in the passenger seat. Normally Lyle had her head out the window trying to herd the oncoming traffic with her cunning, working-dog eyes. The journey from Arizona to Illinois had taken about three days of solid driving, and she was fresh out of enthusiasm.

"Second building on the left," she read from her tattered, leather-bound Moleskin notebook.

She turned off and pulled the RV behind the clinic. There wasn't anywhere obvious to hook up a 50amp connection and the cool autumn air was divine so Mandy powered down the generator. Lyle bounced out of her seat, ready for a stretch. Also in need of restoring circulation to her feet after the drive, Mandy switched out of her driving slippers for her dusty, soft leather work boots. Of course, Lyle immediately found the cattle chute and sheep races behind the clinic. Even though she had never actually worked with stock herself, her genes were from a long line of sheep dogs from which she inherited the natural inclination. Lyle was eagerly sniffing through all of the chutes and paddocks, presumably hoping to find the source of the sheep dung.

"Come on in, girl," Mandy called to Lyle and together they entered the back entrance of the clinic using the key that had been sent to her PO Box out in Arizona.

Mandy's plan was to use the following week to look around the veterinary clinic and start getting it ready to sell. Her classmate from vet school, Anna, had died suddenly leaving the clinic and her house to Mandy in her will. Anna was an only child from elderly parents who had passed away several years ago. Mandy wasn't aware of any other relatives of Anna's. Anna and Mandy had been best friends for years. Although Mandy didn't really have any ties to where she'd driven from, she wasn't the sort to nest. She had been living in an RV for the last fourteen years, traveling across America as she saw fit. Being a veterinarian in such a vast country meant that she was never short on work or adventure. Mandy had never made the trip before despite Anna's many previous invitations. It felt wrong to finally be seeing it under these circumstances.

Not one to dwell on sad things, Mandy recalled the day she met Anna. They were all sitting in the lecture theater on the very first day of vet school, pleased as punch that they had been accepted into such an esteemed program. Everyone had a brand new set of notebooks and pens lined up on their desk for the occasion. Two people burst in through the side door, interrupting the riveting tale of the role of digestive enzymes from the plump, grey-haired physiology professor, Dr. Crisp. They announced that the lecture would resume the next day and an activity would ensue.

"Everyone must remove their shoes and socks. Form a single-file line and start making your way out the front door of the theater. Leave all of your belongings. We will lock the door as you leave," announced one of the interrupters.

They all did as they were told and found themselves led through
an obstacle course of tires filled with mud, cow dung, milk, and
other animal-related gooey substances. Water balloons were
thrown, silly string was sprayed. Each student received a
mouthful of "drench" from a cattle drench gun. The idea was to
expose them to the wonders that would be part of the world of
veterinary medicine.

The induction took place on the main concourse of the university
and by this time a crowd had gathered to watch the new vet class
lose a little of the arrogance they came to school with that day.
They were all starting to see the humor in the situation when
someone shouted.

"Look up!"

There was a string of shoes hanging from the eighth floor
window that resembled those that the students had been wearing
earlier. Simultaneously, a new barrage of water balloons
followed by flour fell on the crowd of students. Not knowing the

rules of the building, a few students ran to the entrance of the building to rescue the suicidal shoes and escape the dropping balloons. However, they were stopped by a professor who informed them that they could not enter a hospital with inappropriate footwear, particularly none at all. Dejected, the vet students put their heads together. Someone had the bright idea of going back to the original lecture theater to see if there were any shoes left behind. That building wasn't in the hospital so the footwear rule would not apply.

Indeed, a single shoe from every pair sat under the desks. Thinking quickly, they started trying to pair up shoes of similar sizes. Lo and behold, Mandy and Anna had the same shoe size and Anna got the task of wearing one of each to gain access to the vet tower and rescue the rest of the shoes. From that day on, Anna and Mandy became close throughout the trials and tribulations of vet school.

Smiling at the memory of their friendship, Mandy took a deep breath and entered the clinic. Since Anna had passed recently, the clinic had not been left long. Cabinets were stocked full and the daily appointment diary was all ready to go on the desk. The clinic served a small, rural community where everyone seemed to have an animal of some sort. The majority of clients were farmers with cattle, some sheep, and horses to help move the stock. Everyone had a dog or a whole pack of dogs and a barn cat or two. Anna had said that there was always something coming in to keep her busy.

As Mandy wandered around the clinic, she imagined Anna walking these very steps. Just then she heard a loud noise from the back of the clinic. She found Lyle with her nose in a container of dog food, enjoying a late afternoon snack. Mandy remembered that in all of her business to get here, she hadn't fed Lyle her lunch. Although Lyle was five years old now, she was such an active dog who, without three meals, started to get a bit sluggish in the afternoon. She found a bowl for Lyle and set it down in the dog run area.

"Here you go girl, sorry I forgot about lunch. I'm pretty

famished myself," she said. While Lyle was eating, she thought she may as well find a level spot for the RV and settle in for the night.

Mandy had a walk around the clinic's back paddock to find a place to call home for the next little while. She had become an expert at scouting out the best level area with good wind protection and access to morning and afternoon sun. Mandy had decided long ago that as long as you have the ability to choose your locale to hang your hat at night, you may as well put some thought into it. She found a great spot under the oak tree. She put the RV parking brake on and lowered the hydraulic feet. Then, she opened the door to the book case and pressed the switch to bring out the lounge slide, doubling the main room of the RV. She went down the hall to the bedroom and flicked the switch to extend the bedroom slide out. That was much better, she thought. An RV is pretty small without the slides out.

This was her third RV. She had first bought one when she lived in Montana and was going camping every weekend. After a while, she found herself living in it more than her apartment so she decided to go full time. She loved the lifestyle of having her whole house already packed up and ready to go. Most weekends, she went exploring new areas with Lyle. She had enough space to sleep six, though she rarely had any visitors. The first RV she had was smaller and the bathroom too minimal. Now, she had upgraded to a larger model with one large lounge slide and one in the bedroom. She had all the modern conveniences, an oven, a dishwasher, a washer/dryer, a fridge/freezer, and a tub. There was plenty of storage for essentials without encouraging clutter. She also had a compact barbecue, a few lounge chairs for outside, and a hammock and stand. In less than twenty minutes, she could park and set up her whole life in a completely new place. Behind the RV she towed her trusty Jeep. Mandy had given herself a Jeep as her graduation present because it lent to the life she wanted to lead. She could take the doors right off and let the dog fur and dirt whip right out the side while driving. It had served her well all of these years. She had no intention of upgrading.

With the house squared away, Mandy went back in to get Lyle. It was going to be an interesting week and she better get some dinner started. Lyle was curled up on the bean bag chairs in the corner of the clinic lobby. There was a box of children's toys and books under the table near the bean bags. Lyle had always liked children, presumably because they matched her high octane energy and often gave her tasty morsels when their adult counterparts were not watching.

Mandy opened the door to the RV and Lyle bounded up the four steps to take her throne in the Lazy-boy chair by the door. From this spot, she could see through most of the windows to be sure that no animals or humans could pass by without receiving a good once over with her intelligent eyes. Mandy pulled out some left over beans from the night before so she whipped up some burritos. Being in the Southwest meant she had had access to all sorts of wonderful burrito additives, and luckily, she had stopped off at a road-side stand to get tomatoes and avocados.

She had cleverly stock-piled a few items for her stay in the land of casseroles and dressing: The Midwest. As a side dish, Mandy put together a fresh spinach salad with a pineapple and cucumber salsa.

After living in an RV for so long, Mandy was an expert at making meals in small spaces and not using many dishes. She rinsed the dishes to be ready when she had a full load and went outside to let Lyle run. Lyle jumped out of the RV with a tennis ball in her mouth. She dropped it by Mandy's feet and backed up with her head still facing Mandy. Her lips caught on her upper teeth, giving her a puffy lip look and her eyes were wide with intensity. She stood, not moving a muscle, waiting in anticipation. Mandy picked up the ball and threw it, sending Lyle running like a greyhound. Lyle caught the ball on the first bounce and returned it to Mandy's feet. Although this could go on for days, Mandy brought Lyle back inside and decided to go for an after dinner stroll to explore. She put her boots back on and sauntered up the main drag of town, leaving Lyle to nap.

There wasn't much to this little town, she had noticed when she drove in, a car garage on the left, a small grocery store on the right, and just up the road a variety store. There was a florist, funeral home, church, a cafe, a hardware store, a gas station, and a doctor's office with a post office incorporated. In keeping with a Midwest town, the railroad passed through it to service the grain silos from local farmers' fields. Anna had told Mandy all about this town and how devoted to working the land it was. Now Mandy could see if for herself.

The last building on the left in town was the Inn and also the only business open this late on a Sunday. The door was the old saloon style door although this was far from the Wild West. Through the window, she could see that there were a few people playing pool and another few looking at the juke box. She decided to enter to have something to warm her up from the brisk air. The carpet was well worn in the path from the bar to the tables and back. She followed the path many others had taken and ordered a nice light, cold beer with a lime. Not usually a drinker, she thought when in Rome... She needed to start collecting information to help her sell the clinic.

"Here you go, Mandy," the bartender said when he handed it to her. She was taken by complete surprise and spit out the beer she had just sipped. "It's a small town, nothing happens without everyone knowing about it, you'll see," he said.

"Cheers," Mandy said.

"Don't be scared, Mandy, none of us bite around here. They outlawed that at least ten years ago," said a bronzed man with gray stubble and bear-sized hands. He chuckled.

Feeling a little vulnerable, Mandy took a stool by the window and sipped her beer. A Cher song came on the jukebox so she figured that maybe this town is a little more inviting than it first looks.

It wasn't long before a few of the locals came over to satisfy a little harmless curiosity about the new arrival.

"Found everything ok? Anna kept a nice house so you should

feel right at home," said a man in a shredded pair of Carharts and a red flannel shirt.

"Yep, I live in an RV so I just parked it up behind the clinic. I haven't been to the house yet," replied Mandy.

"I'm Billy. I farm hogs out west of the town. Don't be shy around here. We are a whole town of friendly folks. And we sure did love Anna. So, a friend of hers is a friend of ours. Such a shame to lose her. It was so sudden."

"It was a shock to me. We had spoken on the phone just days before she passed. She said she had a mild headache but who would have thought it would be a fatal aneurysm? At least she was living the life she had always wanted when she passed," Mandy said. "That's the best we can all hope for - to die doing what we love."

"True indeed. Let me know if there is anything I can do to help your transition here," said Billy.

"Will do, thanks," said Mandy, through a smile.

Chapter Two

When she finished her beer, she left a tip on the table and walked back to the RV, looking in the windows of the shops along the way. She saw her reflection in the window of the florist. Her wildly curly brown hair was in top form. Mandy was always battling with it to keep from expanding beyond any acceptable style. In fact, even when she was a kid, the problem had been embarrassing. In second grade, the kid behind her had told his mom that he couldn't see the board. The mother had written a note to the teacher and poor Mandy was asked to wear her hair back so little Toby could see the lessons on the blackboard. Ever since then, Mandy had tried all sorts of hairstyles. The only real cure was living somewhere really dry and hoping the lack of humidity would keep the frizz at bay. Even out in the desert, her hair had been fluffy. In the Midwest, it was blossoming into its full glory of curls. She had worn it down today and, after seeing it in the window, she pulled a bandanna out of her leather satchel and tried to tie it back.

She strolled along the main street, stopping to look at the town map in front of the post office. The whole main area was one street long. She had lived in a number of small towns her life and she found they all had their charm to them. From the map, she could see that there were cattle yards for a weekly stock sale just at the edge of town. "I bet that is an experience," she thought out loud.

The plaque above the map explained that Crestview had received its name because of the hill to the north that provided an outlook point from which to see the whole town. The generally flat terrain of the area meant that a hill became a landmark back in the pioneer days. The name Crestview had stuck through hundreds of years of maps featuring the tallest hill for miles around. Mandy decided that the name suited the town now that she was finally seeing it in person. Anna's descriptions had made it seem like a storybook village, devoid of many of the unpleasant aspects of more populated areas. Mandy meandered down the street, soaking up the ambiance of her late friend's stomping ground.

Arriving back at the clinic, Mandy was ready for a good night's sleep. She opened the door to the RV and climbed the three stairs up to the lounge. Lyle was curled up in the bedroom but came out to greet her with her shiny new Wilson tennis ball. Lyle dropped the ball at Mandy's feet and backed up, ready to catch the ball.

"I'm too tired to fetch tonight," Mandy said, "but I promise that we can go for a walk tomorrow."

Mandy opened the door to the bathroom and brushed her teeth. A green ball appeared at the doorway. Lyle slowly backed up from where she had placed the ball, waiting patiently for Mandy to recount her earlier statement.

"It's time for bed. Fetch will have to wait for morning," Mandy said to Lyle.

As if comprehending, Lyle leaped onto the bed and rolled herself into a little ball with her head on the pillow and her tail tucked under her front paws.

"That's more like it," Mandy said. She changed into her well-worn flannel pajamas and tucked herself into bed. Mandy pulled a map out from her bedside shelf and opened it up. Traveling was just as much a favorite pastime for her as falling asleep looking at a map of her new surrounds. She had kept track of everywhere she had been and enjoyed perusing the detailed maps of the States to see where she needed to fill any holes. She hadn't been here before, so it was at least exposing her to a new part of America. She had one of those maps that had National and State Parks in green. There was lots of green around this area. Mandy figured once she had the clinic squared away, she would explore for weekend camping spot. She drifted off, pondering if there were any fishing spots in the vicinity.

In the morning, Mandy got dressed in her favorite pair of jeans and an old wool button up shirt. It wasn't very cold out. She figured she would prepare for any type of weather that might strike in Fall and wool was her trustiest garment. Today would be the day to finally see Anna's clinic in all of its glory. She was

a little nervous about it, butterflies fluttering in her stomach.

She walked down the hall of the RV to the kitchen area and fixed

herself some oatmeal and coffee to get the day started on the

right foot. She filled Lyle's bowls with food and fresh water.

She sat down at the dining nook to eat her modest breakfast. The

radio was on and golden oldies was the current selection. Mandy

tried to find another station but it seemed that there was either

country or oldies. She had listened to country the whole way

here yesterday. For some reason, when driving across America

where reception is patchy, the default station available is always

country. Mandy enjoyed the story-telling quality of country

music, wondering when that had phased out of music. As

"Sixteen Tons" hummed from the stereo, Mandy rinsed out the

dishes and added them to the dishwasher. Almost a full load, she

thought. Lyle had finished her breakfast and was ready to play

again.

"I wish I had as much energy as you sometimes," Mandy said to

Lyle. "I did promise you some exercise this morning."

Mandy opened the cupboard above the stairs and dug out Lyle's walking harness. A traditional collar would not contain Lyle's enthusiasm for life, especially if Lyle spotted a squirrel. The first time Lyle had ever seen a squirrel, in fact, she was unattended in the bedroom of the RV. They were parked in the Carolinas somewhere and Mandy was outside starting a fire for the night. Mandy saw the squirrel fluff its tail and scurry up a tree. The picturesque nature scene was quickly replaced with a Border collie leaping through the glass window, landing at the foot of the tree. Her nose had been sliced open by a shard of glass from the window and was bleeding profusely. Meanwhile, the squirrel was flirting with Lyle's curiosity by jumping from branch to branch just out of reach. As a veterinarian, Mandy got the situation under control but learned a valuable lesson about Lyle and squirrels.

"Sit," Mandy said. "Paw," she said and Lyle obediently handed her left paw to Mandy. This way, Mandy could place the harness over Lyle's foot and head and fasten it over the shoulders. Lyle didn't stop moving very often. However, she was more than willing to stop to let Mandy put the harness on because she knew that meant that they were going somewhere. Lyle was a lucky dog. She went with Mandy everywhere and over the years had been more places than many people. She had been hiking in the mountains, skiing, fishing, and even went tubing on a river once in Texas.

As Mandy's constant companion, they had a great relationship. However, Mandy had learned after the first time she took Lyle fishing with her that perhaps that was one activity a dog shouldn't be allowed to enjoy. They had been parked on a river in Arkansas and Mandy was just casting her fly out. Mandy was learning how to fly fish and was just at the stage where the fly was getting caught in a tree or shrub one out of every three casts, instead of every cast. Lyle was lying in the sun on the bank, watching Mandy. Unfortunately, there were some bubbles in the water just below the bank. Lyle really didn't have much control when she saw something that came and went like a bubble. She dove in after the bubbles, digging in the current to try to capture one. Meanwhile, her long curly tail had caught on the line and Mandy was desperately trying to keep the fly from getting caught in her hair. Lyle kept bouncing and jumping on the bubbles, which made more of them. Alas, the fly did get caught in Mandy's hair and she lost balance and fell in an icy cold springfed pool. No amount of yelling could deter the fun-loving Lyle from her newfound game. The line was in knots, Mandy was soaked, but Lyle was happy as could be. Finally untangled, Mandy took a moment to catch her breath, perching on a rock. Lyle found a stick and dropped it at Mandy's feet as if nothing has ever happened. That was the last time Lyle went on a fishing trip.

With the harness on, Lyle and Mandy headed down the road for an early morning walk. Nothing was open yet and there was no activity to speak of. Mandy liked this time of the day because it was so peaceful that she could hear herself think. As they walked a few leaves blew along the pavement. The town was decorated for Halloween with little murals of pumpkins and witches in the windows. Halloween was one of Mandy's favorite holidays because she loved to eat the little bite-sized candies that always appeared in full force in the grocery stores.

She also enjoyed dressing Lyle up for the occasion. Last year, Lyle was a frog, complete with a lily pad beneath her and a fly suspended above her head. This year, she had been working on fashioning a bumble bee outfit for Lyle. Although Lyle was a long and lanky dog, she seemed to fit into children's clothing really easily. Plus, as long as someone was playing fetch with her, she didn't mind how Mandy dressed her. Mandy's sewing skills were not prize winning. However, she was capable of altering costumes for Lyle as long as she kept the concepts simple.

They had walked the whole length of town without seeing a single person. At the edge of town, they turned around to see the chief's car pull over beyond them. Someone got out and faced her and Lyle. On his breast pocket was a name badge that read Chief Larry Pullman.

"Can I help you, ma'am?" the chief asked, as he readjusted his rigid gray hat with a black brim and police medallion. His uniform was starched and press to perfection. The shiny black shoes completed the look of someone who meant business. However, the uniform was a few sizes too small so his less than firm love handles made a nice ledge above his belted waist.

"No, I just drove in last night and thought I would take a walk through town," Mandy said.

"I'm Larry, the chief and this is Gerald, my assistant," pointing to the occupant of the passenger seat.

"You can call me Gerry," he interjected. He was every bit as tone as the chief was flabby. His face was framed by a square jaw with a Roman nose sitting in the midst of his bronzed skin.

"I'm - ," but before Mandy could finish, Larry interjected.

"Mandy, right? We figured you would be in town soon. The

town has been in a bit of shock since Anna's passing. We knew she had put in her will that a classmate of hers would be coming in to take over. Have you found everything you need?"

"I think so. It's a pretty standard small town," Mandy said.

"You'd be surprised. When things get going around here, we sure do know how to put a smile on your dial. Who's the pooch?" asked Gerry.

"Lyle, but she's a girl," said Mandy.

"Well hello Lyle, but she's a girl!" said Gerry. "What kind of name is Lyle anyway?"

"She's named after Lyle Lovett, the…"

"We know who Lyle Lovett is," interrupted Gerry. "You'll fit right in. We better go check on the shops before they open for the day. Let us know if you need anything. We might see you later on."

Mandy watched as the chief's car turned to the back alley of the main street. She hadn't been very friendly with cops before. In fact, whenever she saw one on the road, she immediately got very nervous. She wasn't the sort to break laws or anything, but something always made her uneasy around cops.

Lyle and Mandy arrived back to the clinic and noticed lights on in the reception area. When they went inside, there was a woman on the phone.

"That sounds pretty serious, Mrs. Price. I think we need to have a look at little Suzie. Can you come in at, say, 8:30? Great, I will write you in the book and we'll see you then," said the woman and then she hung up the phone.

"Hi Mandy, how was your trip? Here's a cup of tea. Milk and sugar, I hope that's ok. I've marked out 12 to 1 for your lunch hour like Anna used to take. If you want to change it, let me know. That was Mrs. Price on the phone. It looks like Suzie got into the chocolate again. She'll be right over. And who's this lovely little dog?" she said as she gave Lyle a pat. Lyle was sitting like a perfect lady at the woman's feet, enjoying the attention as if she had known the woman all her life. That is the only trouble with Border collies. They will literally go home with anyone and start a new life as if nothing had ever been different. Mandy had trouble at dog parks because Lyle would never come back when she called her. She just darted from human to human, giving any toy, stick, or ball she could find, in an attempt to engage anyone in a quick game of fetch.

"This is Lyle and I'm Mandy. I guess you already knew that. May I ask your name?" Mandy inquired.

"Gillian. I'm the receptionist or assistant or whatever needs doing around here. I've been here for eight years. Heard all about you from Anna. I think we'll make a great team," said Gillian.

"Hmm, well, I…" Mandy was interrupted by Mrs. Price walking in with Suzie waddling behind her. Suzie was a rather obese golden Labrador with a smirk on her muzzle, the kind of smirk dogs have when they love life but don't have much thought process behind why they love it. Suzie had one ear up and one down and a bit of a stiff gait as if arthritis was starting to set in. She didn't look like she had missed many meals and chocolate must have been a favorite of hers.

"Here's the record Dr. Bell. I'll just weigh Suzie for you," said Gillian. Mandy looked down at Gillian's hands and forearms, noticing how well-leathered they were from some kind of hard labor. Her fingernails were short and functional with neither a wristwatch nor jewel in sight. Mandy always figured you could tell a lot from a person's hands.

Mandy's train of thought wondered to her great grandmother who had probably the most narrative hands she had ever seen. She had raised sixteen children starting at the turn of the century with the first born. In those days, you grew your own food in the garden, butchered your own chickens and cattle, kneaded your own bread, toiled over the washboard to provide clean bedclothes for your family, all with one kid on your hip, and two hanging off your feet. She hadn't known her long; Great

Grandma Priscilla had told the most wonderful stories about working hard for your piece of this earth. Mandy contemplated if settling down was something she'd been fighting all of her life and maybe Great Grandma Priscilla had a few things figured out.

Meanwhile Lyle found a well-worn chair in the reception area and had curled up with a plush toy she found in the children's toy box under one of the chairs. Ever since Mandy had taken her from the litter as a very young puppy, Lyle had fallen asleep with a plush toy under her chin. Lyle's favorite was a hippo, named Gertie, that she carried around the RV. However, it looked like she had found a bear to suffice in Gertie's absence. Mandy had sewn Gertie back together and re-stuffed it several times. It barely resembled its once adorable rotund form, with one missing eye, a crooked nose, and one leg that had lost its form, dangling like a limp stump. Despite all the repairs, Gertie held her place in Lyle and Mandy's nomadic life across the American continent.

"Sixty-three pounds. That's five more than last time she was here. Tisk, tisk Mrs. Price. You know how we talked about giving Suzie less table scraps and encouraging Suzie to get up off her corduroy bed every now and then," said Gillian. "Just go into the consult room and Dr. Bell will be right with you. Actually, maybe we better put you guys out in the dog run so we can clean up easily."

Although Lyle had been a fixture in many clinics, this was a new atmosphere. She got up out of her chair to greet the new patient.

"Lyle, mind your manners. Give Suzie some space," said Mandy. Lyle reluctantly climbed onto the chair Mandy had set up for her. The chair had to be the right size for Lyle's whole body to fit in it as well as be in the most opportune position to watch the comings and goings of the clients and patients. Lyle brought the bear she had found with her to the new chair.

As Gillian was walking over to the pharmacy cupboard, she asked Mandy "How many apomorphine tablets should we give her, Dr. Bell?"

"Um, let's start with one," Mandy said as she followed Gillian out to the dog runs.

"How long ago did she eat the chocolate, Mrs. Price?" asked Gillian.

"About twenty minutes ago."

"And how much did she eat?" said Gillian.

"Almost the whole block."

"Hold her back end still, Mrs. Price and I'll get her front end," said Gillian as they got Suzie in a headlock. "Here's the tablet, Dr. Bell."

Mandy came over and took the tablet from Gillian and placed it under the right eye lid of the wiggly Labrador. Gillian left the dog to retrieve something from the pharmacy.

"So, how do you like it so far here?" asked Mrs. Price. Since this wasn't the first time this had happened to Suzie, Mrs. Price knew the drill and could resume small talk calmly.

"I only just got here last night," said Mandy. Gillian returned with a 10 cc syringe filled with water.

They all stood back to watch the medicine do its work, all of them knowing things could get messy. Suzie's whole body started to shake as she started to pace. She circled a corner of the dog runs and started to wretch. The contents of the vomit looked suspiciously like pieces of baking chocolate.

Suzie started to wretch again and by now had vomited up about a whole block of chocolate. "That'll do the trick it looks like," said Gillian as she started to rinse the tablet from under the eyelid using the syringe of water she had brought.

"Oh, thank you so much, Dr. Bell. I really should try to be more careful when I am baking but Suzie has a way of distracting you right at the pertinent time. I was just getting the chocolate muffins ready for the Halloween bake sale when she snuck up and ate the whole bar, not leaving a single crumb," said Mrs. Price. "At first I thought I hadn't even unwrapped it and put it on the counter yet. Suzie had that guilty look on her face so I knew I better bring her up here for the experts."

"At least you caught her doing it so we could deal with her straight away. She should be fine now but I would watch her the rest of the day to make sure. Any problems, give us a call," said Gillian.

"Thanks again. I will bring some baking by when I have replenished my chocolate supplies. The boys are out late every night and up early every morning to get the crop in before the weather sets in for winter. I am keeping everyone fed and chocolate is a popular treat for the boys. I have to make a trip into the big city to get more supplies for the hungry mouths. The little general store here doesn't have everything we need. It was lovely to meet you, Dr. Bell. I do hope that you come to the Halloween Hoedown next week. I might even be able to convince the boys to come along for a few hours," said Mrs. Price as she was walking back out to reception. Suzie saw Lyle sitting on the chair and Lyle jumped down to check on the four-legged friend post treatment. Tails were wagging and noses were sniffing. "It looks like Suzie is feeling better already! She didn't even notice Lyle on the way in."

Suzie and Mrs. Price left in a much calmer fashion than they entered the clinic.

"She seems nice," said Mandy.

"She is lovely. She is one of the wives to the Price boys. They own quite a bit of land outside of town. They are grain farmers so you will only see them in town for their dogs. Mrs. Price is a regular here because all of the Price boys and their sons have Labs for hunting."

"I see. Anna wasn't fibbing when she talked about the farming families in this area," said Mandy. She thought about how important this town had been to Anna and what an honor it was to finally meet the characters of the town.

"Well, your next appointment isn't for ten minutes so let me show you around the place. This is the reception area, this is the consult room. Normally, we only have one client in here at a time; if an emergency comes in, we can use the treatment area. This is the wet table for dentals. That's the surgery room. These are the kennels, separate rooms for cats and dogs. This is the pharmacy. Out back are the dog runs which you've already seen. Your office is down this hall and there's a little break room beside it. Out the back door is where the yards are. My horse is back there today. I hope you don't mind. I have to take him to Mr. Jennings' after work. We have a muster to do this week so I thought it'd be easier to bring him today," said Gillian, hardly taking a breath between sentences. Horses, thought Mandy. I bet that explains the manly hands of Gillian's.

Mandy wasn't sure how the plan had been lost in translation. Her intention was not to take over the clinic. She had come here to sell the place. Just when she was about to explain this to her, Gillian had already gone up front to greet the next client.

Chapter Three

"Hi Walter. This must be your new litter of pups from Selby. My, how they've grown. It seems like just yesterday you were calling us to tell us she had delivered all six that we had seen in the x-ray. They're going to be worth a pretty penny since both their parents are stars at the county dog trials. Here, let me put you in the consult room and Dr. Bell will be with you," said Gillian. As she walked to the back to find Mandy, she got the six injections out of the fridge to start mixing up. "Your next appointment is here. I'll get the injections together," Gillian called out. She took six bottles of dried vaccine and six bottles of diluent. She opened one syringe and sucked out the diluent, adding it to one of the dried vaccine bottles. After giving it a good shake, she sucked the whole contents out and removed the sticker from the dried vaccine bottle to stick on the syringe.

While Gillian was preparing the vaccines like an expert, Mandy walked up to her. "I'm not sure we're both on the same page. I came here to settle up the clinic for a buyer. I'm not going to stay on as the vet here. I have my own life," Mandy said.

"Anna told me about you. She said you're not too keen on staying in one place. Look, I've thought about this already. You're a vet and this town needs a vet. Why don't you just stay and help out *until* the clinic sells. It can't hurt to make a little money for the clinic while you're here, can it? At least for Anna's legacy's sake," Gillian said.

Before Mandy could answer, Gillian had walked back into the treatment area to get six pet health records for the new pups. She returned with all of the items needed for the consult room's occupants and said to Mandy, "Righty-o, let's vaccinate some puppies!"

They entered the consult room to find six roly, poly Australian shepherds, each with different markings. Some had blue eyes, some brown, and some a mixture of each. There was a little puddle in the corner where one had peed. Walter was all smiles, proud of his new pups.

"Hi, I'm Dr. Bell," said Mandy.

"Well, hello there. I'm Walter. These are Selby's newest litter," said Walter. He had his gangly long legs crossed over one another and he was leaning over his palm. Even all folded up like a pretzel on the chair, one could see that he was a very tall, lean man. His head was crowned by a straw hat with more holes in it than would surely allow for it to do the job of keeping the sun out of his face. But, Walter looked like a guy who wasn't fond of shopping, judging by the boots as old as time and coveralls that had evidence of many a project on them.

"They're lovely. Any problems at all with any of them? Any coughing or sneezing? Everyone eating ok?" asked Mandy.

"They're fit as fiddles. No problems here. I was out tending to my crops but I don't have anyone else to bring them in and no puppies of mine miss their shots. So, here I am," said Walter.

Gillian picked them up one by one for Mandy to examine and administer the vaccination. They were wriggly but Gillian was a great puppy handler. She had a gentle touch while still managing to maintain authority over animals.

"I appreciate you taking time out from the crops to come in. And is Selby receiving enough calcium in her diet? It must be quite a feat to feed six growing puppies," said Gillian.

"Yep, I've had her on puppy food since two weeks before she whelped, just like Anna said to do. I didn't want her to get the clamps like she did last time," replied Walter.

"Ecclampsia," said Mandy with a smile. She really did love being a vet, especially in rural towns where people were so genuine. Ecclampsia can be a shocker to a pet owner; it causes seizure-like issues until the calcium level in the blood is corrected. "That's great that you are giving her calcium. And do you have plenty of dewormer for Selby and the gang?"

"Sure do. Anna, bless her heart and soul, gave me plenty when we did the x-rays to see how many pups were brewing in there," said Walter.

As Mandy was finishing up the last of the vaccinations, she instructed, "well, these will be due for another shot in three weeks. Between now and then, their immune systems are jump-starting so don't let them near any unvaccinated animals. We don't want any of these little guys to be back in here sooner."

"Thanks Dr. Bell. Will do. You have a nice day and Happy Halloween! Back to the fields I go," said Walter.

"It must be time for another cup of tea," said Gillian.

"You sure drink a lot of tea," Mandy said.

"My mother was from New Zealand and we grew up drinking cups of tea at hourly intervals throughout the day. There were always cookies, or biscuits as mom called them. It seems to help the day go by nicely so I've kept the tradition going."

"New Zealand. I have always wanted to go there. Have you been?" asked Mandy.

"No. She emigrated here before I was born. An overseas trip is a little out of my realm financially. I have seen loads of pictures so it feels like I have been there through my mother's stories and memories," said Gillian. As the kettle boiled, Gillian smiled and said, "Well, Mandy, what do you say, will you stay on until the clinic sells?"

Lyle heard the sound of a food wrapper and came over from the chair she was sleeping on. Despite Mandy's efforts to raise her without the temptations of people food, years of being in the reception area of clinics made her familiar with the characteristic sound of food being unwrapped. Most people could not resist her intense eyes so she usually got a tidbit. It was like Pavlov's response to a wrapper, not a bell. She showed off with her best sit and gave Gillian a deep stare. Gillian sneaked a little piece of vanilla wafer to the gentle mouth hiding under the desk.

Mandy pondered the prospect of staying here for a bit. She remembered a story Anna had told her of her first late night call when she opened the clinic out here, and about the kind of folks

Anna had encountered. It was to meet Mr. Kingle at the clinic because his daughter's chicken had been attacked by his best dog, Max. Out in this part of the country, a dog that attacks an animal has a short life span so it was going to be a sad call. When Mr. Kingle had brought the chicken and dog in, she had a closer look at the chicken first. She found a bit of barbed wire matted in with the blood and feathers. She told Mr. Kingle that Max may have been at the scene of the crime, but the barbed wire was definitely the source of the problem. She cleaned the chicken up and sent Mr. Kingle on his merry way with Max at foot. The next day, Anna's clinic was bustling with locals. She was a hero after she managed to save Mr. Kingle's best dog from being put down for attacking chickens.

Mandy thought about the fact that she had already paid off her student loan and she owned her RV. While she was close to her family, they were always up to come and visit her wherever she was. She had no real engagements anywhere and this seemed like a good way to pay her friend Anna some respect. After a deep breath, Mandy said, "I suppose I could just stay until we get an offer on the clinic. I have no other plans at the moment and I brought my house with me. Why not?"

Gillian grinned and dunked her vanilla wafer into her fresh cup of tea.

"I haven't given you the keys to Anna's house. Here they are. I was watering the plants and feeding her cats until you got settled in. It's yours now. I will take you over there and show you around when you are ready," Gillian said as she handed Mandy a set of old-fashioned keys.

"I can't say that I am looking forward to looking through Anna's house. Although we were close friends, it's kind of strange to finally see her home and her not be the one to show me around," Mandy said, looking down thoughtfully.

"I understand. It is all very weird and sudden. She has, er had, the most wonderful cats. One is Emma and she is a giant tabby cat with more personality than a whole room full of comedians.

And then there is Jimbo, he is a tuxedo and just likes to be around people, not touch them. He is often eerily, silently staring at nothing. Anna thought maybe he could see things, you know, that we can't see. He goes crazy for kitty treats."

"Well, perhaps after work we can make a detour to her house so I can take over looking after the cats. You do enough."

"I really don't mind. I've grown attached to the cats. In fact, I thought about just bringing them to live in the clinic. They must get lonely in the house. Now that you're here, it's totally up to you."

"That's not a bad idea. All clinics should have a cat or two, right? And Lyle loves cats."

"Let's go after work and start the relocation process. We can go together in my truck after the last appointment."

The rest of the day was filled with fairly routine small animal appointments. A few skin infections, a coughing Siamese, and limping terrier. Gillian totaled up the day's earnings and canceled out the register. She prepared the deposit for the night

drop at the bank.

"Are you ready to go meet the kids and see your house?" Gillian

asked.

"Sure. Let me go put Lyle in the RV."

"I'll meet you at my truck. I'll lock up the clinic."

Mandy smothered some peanut butter inside of a bone for Lyle

and left her snuggled up on the rug in the living room area.

"I won't be too long and you'll get to meet your new brother and

sister tomorrow." Lyle looked up as if understanding what

Mandy was saying.

Taking a few deep breaths, Mandy boarded Gillian's truck. They

silently drove the few miles to Anna's house. Mandy paid close

attention to the route so she would be able to make her way there

next time. The house was a little A-frame cottage off a long

driveway from the main road. Even in the wind-down to winter,

Mandy could tell that Anna's green thumb had infected the

whole area. There were flower beds and a veggie garden, as well as nice mature trees around the property.

Anna had never married and had no living relatives. Mandy was her closest friend in life. It wasn't that Anna wasn't marriage material, she had just chosen a life of solitude and animals. She had set up a nice life for herself in this little town and Mandy knew she had been happy here.

They entered the front door via the sweet little porch trimmed with banisters and rails cut from natural timber. It gave the house an earthy character. Emma was sitting right at the foyer entrance, meowing and rubbing their legs as they tried to walk into the living room.

"Time for supper. Emma, Jimbo, come and get it," Gillian said as she filled their bowls with crunchies.

"This place is beautiful. What a lovely spot Anna had," Mandy said as she took in the ambiance. There wasn't much art on the walls, just a few photographs of wildlife had been blown up and placed front and center on each wall. The exposed beams along the ceiling provided texture for the remainder of the walls. There was an old-fashioned pot-bellied stove in the center of the home that would provide heat to the adjoining open plan rooms. The kitchen was sweet, yet functional, with a window overlooking the woods in the back. On the kitchen table sat Jimbo, staring intensely at the chimney above the fireplace before making eye contact with Mandy and Gillian.

"Hi, my little man," Gillian said as she handed him a few treats from the treat jar on the counter. He purred in response, but made no attempt to make physical contact with his treat supplier. "I took the liberty of cleaning out the fridge of anything that wouldn't keep. I didn't know when exactly you'd be arriving."

"Wow, that was very thoughtful. Thanks."

In typical Gillian fashion, she started the grand tour of the house without taking a pause for Mandy to explore herself.

"Well, here is the kitchen, living room, and a dining area.

There's central heat. For most of the year, the stove is ample for this small house if you are home to keep it stoked. There is a bathroom off this direction under the stairs." The house was open plan, with warmly colored exposed beams as support beams and room separators. Anna had used a natural color palate. There were soft blues, calming grays, and a variety of creamy whites. It almost felt like they were in a river scene. Anna must have enjoyed nature walks because there were little trinkets from excursions, like a collection of smooth, round river pebbles arranged on one of the enlarged window sills in the dining room. A variety of feathers were displayed on the center of the dining room table inside what looked like irregularly shaped gourds. The curtains were plain, leaving the main focal point in each room the view from the windows. Someone had taken time placing the windows to highlight the property surrounding the house.

She made her way up the stairs, waiting for Mandy to follow. "Up here is the main bedroom and another bathroom. There are only two bedrooms and two bathrooms. This is kind of a second living room in the loft. Anna used this space a lot. The loft had an overstuffed leather couch and thoughtfully placed reading lamps.

"Going back downstairs, I'll show you the other bedroom and laundry area." They made their way downstairs again and veered off from the end of the kitchen to the extra bedroom. The house was cleverly built with the use of all of the nooks and crannies that an A-frame home creates. There were adorable little shelves in many of the unusable areas and closets in other crevices, providing ample storage, although Anna clearly was not a hoarder.

The laundry room was nothing fancy. The highlight of that room was an antique porcelain utility sink with ornate faucets. In the spare bedroom were stacks of boxes, some empty and some full, with piles of household items surrounding them. Anna must have been doing some cleaning. She also must not have been expecting any visitors as there was no way someone could sleep in this room the way it was. At some point, Mandy would have to do some sorting here to see what needed to be kept. For now, she was happy to leave it be. It still seemed a bit like an invasion of privacy, with Anna only just recently deceased.

"Isn't it a nice little house?" Gillian asked.

"It is indeed. I've always though A-frames had more character than the standard box house. Anna had nested very purposefully here."

"I agree. I have dreams one day of building a little house. I haven't yet settled on what type to go with. This house has many of the elements I would want. In reality, I live in a rented trailer. Well, should we pack up the cats and bring them into the clinic?"

"We shall. At least that will save us both making trips over here for now. I will have to come back and start sorting through things. I am not quite ready for that yet."

As Mandy was talking out loud, Gillian was rounding up Jimbo and Emma. She located Emma easily since she was sitting in front of the sink meowing. Jimbo, on the other hand, was playing a little hide and seek game. Although an aloof cat, he loved this game. Mandy spotted him running up the stairs and scooped him up when he tipped over belly up in defeat. With the cats safely in their cages, Mandy and Gillian loaded up the cat bowls and food. They emptied the litter pan and brought the remaining litter and liners.

"Alright, let's see how they are in the car. At least it's a short drive. I'm not sure they've ever even been in a vehicle because Anna always brought home what vaccines or medicines they needed," said Gillian.

After a noisy car ride, they all arrived safely at the clinic. Since the appointments were done for the day, they would be able to settle in at the clinic tonight before meeting any people. Mandy opened Emma's cage while Gillian opened Jimbo's. They set up some snuggle spots under the window in the office and made sure the cats knew the location of their food, water, and litter pans. They sprinkled a bit of cat nip in some choice locations to encourage the cats to explore and become accustomed to their new digs. Mandy thought about the long term plan for these cats. They could live in the clinic and be sold with the property although she never trusted just anyone to look after an animal, especially a friend's animal. She could adopt them herself and travel in the RV with them. At least for a while, she didn't need to think about it. She had a fair amount to do before she would even be able to try to sell the house and clinic. And if Gillian got her way, she would never be allowed to leave.

The cats were already sniffing around. The cats would be occupied all night trying to take in all of the scents that a vet clinic inevitably offers, regardless of how clean it is.

"Let's leave them to explore. I will come in early and check on them to make sure they are ok," said Gillian.

"I can check on them later tonight, too."

They quietly sneaked out the back door, leaving Jimbo and Emma with privacy.

"I don't suppose you'd like to go out to dinner tonight?" asked Gillian.

"Sure. I can't be bothered cooking tonight." said Mandy.

"I'll meet you at the Inn at 6:30pm after I have fed my horse and checked up on Hamish," said Gillian.

"Sounds good. Who's Hamish?" said Mandy.

"Oh, he's my son. He's 10 going on 20."

"You look pretty young to have a ten-year old."

"Well, we can't all be wise when we're young. I made a few poor decisions when I was younger. Hamish sure has made my life full. I don't regret a thing. We struggle at times to make ends meet. He helps out a few of the local farmers in exchange for some feed for our horses. We had to sell two last year because we couldn't keep up with the feed bills even being subsidized. We still have two horses and we don't want for much. He's fixin' to be quite the horseman, too."

"My life hasn't been too straightforward either. I'm no stranger to working hard which is why Anna and I were such close friends. Everybody else in vet school had life handed to them on a silver platter it seemed. It was refreshing to meet someone who had their feet firmly on the ground. I look forward to meeting Hamish."

"Right-o. Not tonight, though. He has a project he's working on with his Grandma tonight. I'll bring a few friends for you to meet instead. I'll see you in a bit. I heard you already know where it is, so I won't bother with instructions."

"Cheers," said Mandy with a smirk.

Chapter Four

Mandy opened the back door and Lyle darted up the stairs to the RV. She gave Lyle her dinner and sat back in the Lazy-boy chair. She had a book on hiking in America and pulled it out to look at where she could go for some outdoor time. There was a sizable lake not far away that sounded like it had adequate camping and a nature trail. They allowed pets, remarkably. It claimed to have good bird watching although Mandy had never been patient enough for that. Perhaps she would check it out at the weekend, if she could make some headway with Anna's possessions.

Anna had described this area of Illinois when they were in vet school as being pretty flat with not much for miles but corn, soybeans, and isolated stands of woods. Farming was a huge part of the economy here. Anna had described the frenzy in the air during planting and harvesting. Anna had always said that if Mandy could come visit, Fall would be the best time because the trees were losing their leaves, peppering the countryside with deep reds, oranges, and yellow. She warned Mandy about the dangers of driving on country-roads during harvest time because of the bustling combines and grain trucks. She had said that it was her favorite time of year because of all of the festivals. Each town seemed to have a tradition to keep up with via a charming town fair. Some of the town celebrations that Mandy could remember her mentioning were for the harvest of apples and of broom corn. Anna had vividly described the Halloween Hoedown that her town had where everyone took a break from the demands of crop harvesting to gather and celebrate the fruits of their labor. Mandy was deeply sad that she would be witnessing all of the Fall energy without Anna to be her chaperone. She would carry the torch, albeit it temporarily, in Anna's absence.

Mandy's attention wandered back to the book in her hands. Mandy had come to be an expert at seeing the brighter side of any landscape. A few rivers here and there and some trees, and she could be happy during a relief vet stint. Driving in the countryside, Mandy had seen many old wooden pole barns and stands of elder trees. She didn't know as much about the trees in this area as she would like. She could go to the library to find a book about the trees to learn something while she was stationed in the Midwest. She had also seen an old-fashioned bridge up the road that looked like a great spot from which to jump into the river. She would be long gone by the time it was swimming weather, if all went according to her plans.

Mandy put aside the book with the page earmarked for the local nature park. She pulled out the outfit she was altering for Lyle's Halloween costume. It fit nearly perfectly; she just had to perfect the wings. It wouldn't take long. Mandy always made Lyle a costume for Halloween. Mandy was a little shy and Lyle was the ice breaker everywhere she went. As such, Mandy tried to bring some holiday cheer to every clinic she worked at using Lyle as her conduit. A little snack of some cottage cheese and cucumbers on a tortilla served as a snack to get the energy she needed for sewing.

Before long it was time to walk to town. She had every intention of leaving Lyle in the RV. Lyle, on the other hand, wasn't planning to miss out on the fun. She sat by the door, ready to be harnessed for the walk.

"Fair enough, you can come," Mandy said to Lyle.

It was a nice walk through town. Halloween decorations were hung from every light post and every window. It seemed like there were additional decorations from the ones she saw yesterday. They were clearly die hard fans of the holiday here. The businesses had standard decorations including pumpkins, straw bales, witch silhouettes, gourds, and ghosts. Some had even gone a step further with motion-sensing interactive displays. They even decorated the rails around the grain silos with Fall decorations. She passed one shop window and a witch jumped out of a cauldron at her. Mandy jumped. She hated scary Halloween things. Although she encouraged holiday enthusiasm, it was a little-known fact that she was completely terrified of Halloween pranks, particularly spiders. Haunted houses were the worst for her.

She recovered from her spook with the help of Lyle's kind licking and carried on through town toward the glow of the Inn. Entering, Mandy found a quiet booth. Lyle took her spot under the table and sat quietly. Lyle had been by Mandy's side through so many relief positions that she knew the drill in a new place. If she behaved, the towns often conceded that wherever Mandy went, Lyle was sure to follow. The chief was sitting at the counter and said hello. The owner of the Inn, Merv, was about to ask Mandy about the dog when Gerry chimed in.

"Don't worry about the dog. That's Lyle but she's a girl. She's named after Lyle Lovett, so she's bound to fit in."

"If you say so, Gerry," said Merv, as he helped another customer. Merv was a tough old man, with yellowed teeth, evidence of the ever-present pipe dangling from his chapped lips. His smile, though used infrequently, was as warm as they come. For some reason, he always had a bit of stubble on his face, which showed that if he had hair on his head anymore, it would be a speckled grey and red mane.

"Nice to see you again, Mandy," said Gerry.

"Same to you," said Mandy.

"Are you dining alone?"

"No, Gillian is on her way with a few of her friends."

"I see. Hope your first day went well."

"Yes, thanks."

Gillian arrived with a few people behind her. One of them was a middle-aged woman with chubby cheeks and the sort of plumpness that made you believe that she was capable of cooking some really welcoming stews. Her convivial eyes gave the impression that she had a heart of gold. She chortled softly to herself when she sat down among friends. Beside her was Rhonda, a tall red-headed woman with a definite Southwestern fashion sense. She looked like she'd walked straight out of a Sante Fe boutique, with a squash blossom necklace, a layered denim skirt, a paisley shirt with pearlized buttons, tall brown leather cowboy boots with red detailing, and a concha belt outlining her perfectly thin waistline.

"Hi Mandy. This is Ginny," pointing at the plump woman with the rosy red cheeks, "and this is Rhonda," she said, introducing the red-head.

"Hi Gillian. Nice to meet you, Rhonda and Ginny. Have a seat," said Mandy.

"So, how are you finding it here?" said Rhonda.

"I am impressed with how friendly everyone is here," said Mandy.

"What was that?" said Rhonda. She looked down to find out

what the wet sensation was that she had just felt on her shin only to see a very happy Border collie under the table.

"Sorry, that's my dog, Lyle. She greets everyone with a lick in one place or another. Be happy you got it on your leg and not your face!" said Mandy.

"I love dogs. I breed dachshunds. I have twenty-three now. I also run a little shelter at my house for transient dogs. I help them find homes. It keeps me busy when I am not doing the accounting for the town's people. I'm sure we will cross paths soon as I have just mated one of my girls and I always come in for an early x-ray to check for numbers and overall health. I also have a few due any day now. My husband says that I only work to support my dog hording, and I can't help but think he's right! I would never admit that to him though," said Rhonda.

"Dachshunds, huh? They are one of my favorites," said Mandy.

"Me too. My favorite is a Dachshund puppy. Anna and I, bless her heart, spent many a night sharing cups of tea and waiting for one of my girls to deliver her litter." The mention of Anna brought a sudden solemnness to the group. Changing the subject, "Hey, are you coming to the Halloween Hoedown? You can come with me if you want. I always bring my famous pumpkin scones. This year I am entering in the bake-off with a new cake recipe. The whole town goes so it's the perfect setting to get acquainted with everyone," said Rhonda.

"I might have to come and check that out," said Mandy.

"So, Mandy, do you have a significant other?" asked Ginny.

Blushing, Mandy replied, "not really. I am pretty much just taking life as it comes. It's just Lyle and me in our RV." Mandy had a habit of blushing a lot. It was one of the qualities people found so endearing about her. Even though she was confident professionally, the slightest personal conversation would cause her cheeks to glow with red.

"Wow, an RV. My parents have one of those. I never thought of someone younger than them having one," said Ginny.

"I find it suits me perfectly. I can come and go as I please. I often just drive off into the sunset on a weekend to go camping or get some peace and quiet," said Mandy.

"Not a bad idea. I bet it would be nice to get away from things for a bit. My life is always crazy. I have two very active kids who seem to always be up to something. You'll meet them at the Halloween Hoedown. But don't you want to settle down?" asked Ginny.

"The thought has crossed my mind. I have just never found the right place," said Mandy. She thought of how she would stay up with Anna all hours of the night, discussing their perfect future. Anna always knew she would return to the Midwest to service the small rural community in which she had grown up. Her parents had been older when they had her. Her family unit was not very large so Anna had learned to fill any gaps by immersing herself in the town that she grew up adoring. The feeling was mutual. Nothing catches the attention of a town like a young person going away to college and returning with a profession to offer the people of the town. Mandy, on the other hand, wanted to see the country while admiring Anna's grounded attitude. Mandy imagined somewhere she could have a little piece of land and run some goats or sheep.

Merv came over to collect the orders, extracting Mandy from her thoughts. At the Inn, menus aren't offered. With hardly any tourists, the locals practically grow up knowing the dishes available. There's always a special of the day, which most people select. Merv likes to please people so if there's a special request, he's up for the challenge.

"What's the special tonight?" asked Gillian.

"Pot roast with all the fixin's," Merv beamed. He took pride in offering fresh, wholesome, home-cooked meals. The residents of Crestview could all be said to be regulars at the Inn since the food was so wonderful. Merv and his wife made it feel like going over to one's grandparents' house for dinner. Plus, it was a good spot to catch up on any local happenings.

"Yes, please," everyone chimed. Mandy was pretty hungry and some Midwestern fare sounded perfect. Once they ordered their drinks, Merv retreated to the kitchen.

"So, tell me about this Halloween tradition," said Mandy.

"Oh my, it is such fun. We have all the best parts of Halloween. Apple bobbing, a Jack-O-Lantern contest, a campfire with marshmallows, a hay-ride, a bake-off. Quite a few people dress up in a Halloween costumes. We award prizes to the best costumes at the end of the night. Basically, the whole town loves an excuse to get together and let their hair down in one of the busiest times of the year: harvest time. We do something for Thanksgiving and Christmas as well. Halloween is just a way for us all to start getting into the holiday spirit. It is also held at the end of the county fair season. Many of our town's children are members of FFA or 4H and have shown their animals at other shows. The Hoedown is the chance to show their animals here at home to anyone who couldn't travel to the other shows. It becomes a family event."

"Gillian's right," said Rhonda. "We take keeping the small town feel pretty seriously around here. Because we are off the beaten path, it's not really a tourist attraction so town events are just us having fun as a community. You are going to love it! There is a softball game, food vendors, a few rides, and dance at the end of the night."

"That sounds pretty idyllic. Anna always spoke so highly of Crestview. It's nice to finally see it in all its glory." As she spoke, Mandy was pondering whether maybe she should just stick it out here until after Christmas in honor of Anna. She really didn't have any other plans and it might take that long to get things in order at the clinic.

Merv and his wife came over to the table with what looked like a feast for far more than four people. "Here you go, ladies. Welcome aboard, Mandy. Here's a little bowl of water for

Lilly," said Merv's wife, Myrna.

"It's Lyle, but she's a girl," said Gillian.

"Lyle. I like that name even better," Myrna said.

"Thanks very much. This looks fantastic," Mandy replied.

Silence ensued as the ladies enjoyed their meals. Pot roast can be a bit of an art and Merv and Myrna certainly had it worked out. The beef came from one of the local cattle farmers and the vegetables were all grown in the garden behind the Inn. After filling up on the main course, the ladies had no room for dessert.

The conversation was mainly chit chat once they had eaten their meals. Everyone was curious about Mandy's background. It was as if they were probing for ways to keep her happy here so she couldn't possibly think of leaving.

"Do you have a special hobby or interest?" asked Ginny.

"I suppose it's similar to what I do for a living but I have always been interested in wildlife rehabilitation," said Mandy.

"What is that exactly?" asked Rhonda.

"It means that I helped injured and orphaned wildlife get better so they can be released back to the wild. I've been doing it on and off since I was a kid. My poor parents had to put up with all kinds of animals lurking in their house. I also had to raise mice to feed to some of the animals. It was a regular food chain," Mandy explained.

"That is very cool. I bet you have worked with some amazing animals. What kinds have you helped?" asked Ginny.

"Mostly mammals: raccoons, squirrels, opossums. I once got to work with a baby bat. That was neat. I can work with birds, but they often require more of a facility than I have at my disposal. I mainly triage and send them to someone who has the proper facilities."

"We can certainly make the appropriate housing for your

patients. There is plenty of room at the clinic," Gillian said without hesitation.

"We shall see. I haven't worked with some of the species you have around here. However, long-term plans are a tad up in the air for me," Mandy said.

"We can work on that," said Rhonda. "I never thought I would settle in the Midwest but here I am. Doc Tom and I met when he was at a conference out West. I was a waitress and he was such a gentleman. It was love at first sight. I followed him back here. We still go out West once a year and he claims we will retire there one day. For now, I dress like I still live there and the town has succumbed to my elaborate fashion sense."

"I just came from out West so I didn't think you were dressed oddly at all. Now that you mention it, you are a little more dressed up than others I have met," said Mandy.

"We all have our quirks," Rhonda said and smiled.

They ate and continued to exchange stories. Mandy wasn't keen to offer up too many details about her past. She liked to try to get to know the people around her before they knew too much about her. She usually thwarted questions by talking more about Lyle than herself.

"Well, I'm pretty tuckered out after all that baking I've been doing," said Rhonda, yawning. "I might head home and reserve a more lively night to welcome our new friend for another night."

"It was nice to meet you. I'll look forward to trying some of that baking. I think I might head on to the RV and catch some shut-eye myself. Gillian sure does keep my schedule full," said Mandy, darting a smile over to Gillian. The truth was: it was nice to be busy and feel needed for Mandy. She felt like she was fulfilling her friend's wish of the clinic serving a town, even if it was just temporarily.

"Gosh, you guys are boring!" Ginny said with a wink. "But, I understand. We'll live it up one of these nights. I should have you all over. I'll wait till after the Halloween festivities though."

"Do you want a ride home, Mandy?" asked Gillian.

"No thanks. Lyle and I will have a little stroll."

"Ok. Don't forget that you have that McMurphy call first thing in the morning. I put the vaccines you'll need in that portable cooler in the fridge by the back door. 8:30 am sharp. It'll take you about 25 minutes to get there. He's a bull of a guy who doesn't like starting late so I'd get a hurry on in the morning."

"Thanks, Gillian. What would I ever do without you?" said Mandy.

"Do I detect a hint of sarcasm?"

"No," Mandy said as her face blushed from ear to ear. At that, she waltzed out of the Inn with Lyle afoot.

Chapter Five

In the morning, after some oatmeal and a hot cup of coffee or two, Mandy prepared with Lyle to head off to the McMurphy Farm. They had a cow-calf operation in the hills behind the town. Mandy retrieved the vaccines Gillian had packed and wedged them in the backseat of the Jeep. Nothing could be in the front seat because Lyle had long ago established that as her seat. Luckily there weren't many cars for Lyle to lunge at on these country roads. Gillian had drawn Mandy a map to the farm. Even though there weren't many roads, it was always tricky to find a farm because you had to know which dirt track to take to get to the yards. Often the landmarks were a shrub or a tree, instead of a standard street sign. Sometimes, Mandy noticed that people called a corner by something that had long since been torn down or that didn't even resemble its namesake anymore. She remembered a farm back in Montana that was said to be on five mile corner. No one in the whole town could explain what it was five miles from or how that name came about.

She turned off at the double-trunked tree just like the map said. A red-shouldered hawk was perched on the barbed wire fence off to the right. In the distance, Mandy spotted a set of yards and an old Ford pickup. This must be the place, she thought. When she pulled up, she hopped out and started to put her overalls and gumboots on. Stan McMurphy was walking to join her at the Jeep. Towering about a foot above Mandy, Stan wore a green John Deere hat that had long since lost its trademark green color. A tuft of thick brown hair stuck out on either side of his head. He had nice big white teeth and wind-chapped red cheeks. His face was framed with crow's feet around his eyes and smile lines around his mouth.

"Hi there," Mandy said as she pulled out the lunge lead and tethered Lyle to the bull bar on the front of the Jeep. If Mandy let her off, she would be off rounding up all of the stock on the farm before Mandy even noticed she was gone. Mandy had learned that the hard way. Mandy left a bucket of water and Lyle was already positioned in the shade of the Jeep with a front row view of the upcoming show.

"Hello, you're not from around here are you?" said Stan as he walked up.

"Not exactly. I'm not really from anywhere. I fill relief vet positions around the country, helping when people want maternity leave or vacations and such. For now, I am here to keep the clinic going until we find a buyer," said Mandy.

"You look pretty young, are you still in training?" asked Stan.

"No, I'm a full veterinarian and I have been for fourteen years," said Mandy as she got the vaccinations out of the backseat of the Jeep. She started to prime the gun for the vaccinations. She was used to this discourse. She had inherited the young skin of her father's side of the family and looked about ten years younger than she was.

"Hmm, well, we've got 350 yearlings for you to vaccinate today. I hope you're ready for it," said Stan.

"I'm loaded up and ready to go," said Mandy. Each animal would receive three ccs of vaccination under the skin. She had brought plenty of needles, which was handy because Stan didn't seem like a forgiving farmer.

Stan's son, Ned, was loading up the yearlings into the race. He, too, was no short man. Unfortunately, the race was made for the height of the McMurphy boys. This was a problem she had encountered before and she had learned the knack of using her balance to reach all of the animals even if the platform was far too low. She would inch along the middle plank of the fence, clinging to the top of the yard with her arms. When she first started, she used to climb higher on the fence and hang over the fence but one time, she had lost her balance and fallen head first into the calves. This was a scene the farmer had taken great pride in explaining and often re-enacting at the town pub every

Friday night. That was one thing that Mandy had learned: farmers never forget when you have made a fool of yourself.

Mandy climbed up to the second rung of the fence and started vaccinating. She had done this a thousand times and was a pro at it. Before Stan could start up a conversation about the weather, Mandy was done with the row.

"Fifteen," she said. She had learned to always count as she went so she could compare notes with the farmer and make sure that she charged them the correct number. Vaccinations are not just a service that vets give for no reason. It is really important that every animal be vaccinated at the same time or there isn't much point. If the count at the end of the vaccination is the same as the farmer had predicted, then all is good. If not, then some stock was missed in the round up and Mandy always scheduled another visit to take care of them.

"Come on Ned, load them up," barked Stan. Their working dogs were in the yards pushing up the stock. Not collies, but instead

Blue Heeler-looking dogs. They were doing a fairly consistent job moving the cattle, but kept getting distracted.

Mandy stepped down to let the stock move by her without being startled by her presence. She had a system of working down one row and up the next so she never had to make wasted movements. She finished that row pretty quickly as well.

"Fourteen plus fifteen, we are up to twenty-nine now," Mandy said. Ned let out the row and started to load up the next row. They worked in silence. Mandy figured that Stan was watching her every move to see if she could hold her own on the farm, so she was making sure to be extra efficient. She had counted another seventeen, bringing the total to forty six. She was just finishing the next row. The front gate of the chute started to give way and the leading stock were pushing through, a few close to breaking out. She darted to the front to stop them all from stampeding through the gate. Her noble efforts were for not. The two in the lead busted right through the gate before she managed to get the rest contained. Luckily, they each had characteristic coloring and could be spotted in the already vaccinated mob.

Stan instinctively jumped aboard his trusty Ford and raced to keep the two rogue cattle separate. Mud flew as his tires spun in the mud. He got his footing and sped off after the cows. Ned took Mandy's place in front of the dodgy gate. She was using all of her weight to lean into the gate. Ned craftily began to mend the hinge mechanism. He was determined that there wouldn't be additional escape artists.

Taking the opportunity, Mandy scooted off to her Jeep, unhooking Lyle on the way, and securing her vaccination gun in the pocket of her coveralls. Between the Jeep and the Ford, they cut the two yearlings out of the mob and wedged them against the fence of the paddock. Mandy jumped out and vaccinated them before they could get away.

"Wow, those were some fast moves, Dr. Bell," said Stan, out of breath. These were the first words uttered by anyone, apart from colorful obscenities during the ordeal. Everyone was so experienced with stock that they leapt into action with no discussions necessary. Now that is was all over, they all caught their breath. Lyle had remained calm throughout, knowing that her role would only be necessary if they were unable to separate the two beasts. Even though she didn't have formal training, her instincts were spot on.

"Thanks," said Mandy. As quickly as the mishap had occurred, it was over. They drove back to the yards and resumed vaccinating. This time, Stan was chatty about the weather, the price of beef, and the growing season. Mandy felt like she must have held her own enough to win the respect of Stan.

"I might be new to the area, but these yearlings look like pretty good growers. What's the breed make-up?" asked Mandy.

"Angus and Simmental. It's an old family recipe," answered Stan. Mandy was enjoying talking with a farmer again. It had been a while since she'd worked in a true mixed practice. Dogs and cats don't have the same draw as fresh air and a paddock full of cows. She had recently done a few stints at city practices where the medicine was on a different level than calving cows and chatting about weather. She missed the ruggedness of farmcalls.

"Let's have a quick iced tea break," said Stan. He brought out a thermos and enough glasses for everyone. "You coming to the Halloween Hoedown?"

"Everyone keeps asking me that; it must be worth attending," said Mandy.

"It is. The whole town gets into it. I'm not sure whether the Halloween Hoedown or the Christmas Mingler is my favorite," said Stan, starting to warm up. He placed his empty glass down and looked in the distance. "Well, enough thinking about festivities, let's get back to work."

They got back into their rhythm of loading up stock and

vaccinating again. They went through another ten rows with no complications.

"Stan, I'm just going to go to the little girl's room, I'll be right back," said Mandy.

"Do you want me to drive you to the homestead?" asked Stan.

"No, I'll just make do out here," said Mandy.

The only problem with being a rural vet and a woman is that every once and a while you are caught in the middle of nowhere with a full bladder. Not only are the overalls an obstacle but you have to find a way to excuse yourself to go find a bush. This is the worst in the desert where there aren't any bushes. Luckily, today Mandy was surrounded by good solid Midwest shrubbery. She ducked out behind the yards and followed a little stock path until she found a nice big poplar to shelter her.

Once she was done, she used the hand sanitizer she kept in her coverall pockets. She started to make her way back to the yards when she spotted a shoe sticking out from under a shrub. It was a freshly shined black lace up with barely worn tread. She reached down to pick it up but it wasn't loose. She followed the shoe up and found it was attached to a leg. She knelt down to find the leg's owner and found a limp body. Knowing some CPR, she found the face and checked for a pulse. There was nothing. The face of the body was colorless and frigid. She shrieked and backed up cautiously. She could see a pool of blood seeping from underneath the body and knew she better seek help before there were two victims needing an ambulance. Despite being a seasoned veterinarian, the sight of human blood had made her faint before. Human injury was not her forte.

Mandy started to make her way back to the yards, but was feeling lightheaded and stumbling.

"Are you ok? You look like you've seen a ghost. Sit down," Stan said as he helped Mandy take a seat on the yard rail.

"We need to get the chief out here," stuttered Mandy.

"What?" asked Stan.

"There's a body back there. A dead one."

"What in blazes are you talking about?"

"See for yourself. Back there," she said as she pointed a shaky hand toward the bushes. Stan walked the path that Mandy had come down and traced the foot to the body. He checked the pulse just to be sure.

"Ned, call the chief." Stan bellowed. "They will need to investigate this. It's a strange place to just drop dead without being murdered," Stan continued, speaking aloud, not to anyone in particular. He examined the area for any explanations. There was no car or any other evidence of how this body appeared here. Stan recognized the body as that of Buck Dawson, not the most revered of the town's people.

Ned pulled out his cell phone and rang the chief. He had to walk toward the yards for better reception. Stan returned to Mandy's

side while Ned was calling it in. Mandy was rather shaken up.
Stan was speechless, not knowing how to console Mandy. They
sat in silence.

"You stay here, Mandy," said Ned when he hung up. "We will
let the rest of the cattle out. The vaccines can wait and the chief
will be here quicker than a cat can lick his ……"

"That'll do, Ned. Watch your language in front of a lady," Stan
interrupted.

"Thanks guys," Mandy said, still trembling. She didn't want
them to know it was the blood and not the body that had her
weak at the knees. She did her best to hide that little fact about
herself. She watched as Don and Stan moved the remaining
yearlings into another holding paddock.

Larry and Gerry arrived at the scene in their tan and brown
chief's car. Gerry jumped out to see how Mandy was. She was
starting to get the color back in her face. Stan had let Lyle out of
Mandy's Jeep. Lyle knew something traumatic had happened

and was doing her best to comfort Mandy, curling up in Mandy's lap with her head in Mandy's hands.

"I'm just glad I had already piddled in the bushes or I might have wet my pants," Mandy said as Gerry put a blanket around Mandy and Lyle. She was trying to put her bravest face on, but she was ready to go home to her RV.

Larry and Gerry went down the stock track to the dreaded bush to see for themselves what had happened. They found Buck face down. They had to section off the crime scene and get to work. Gerry got yellow crime scene tape from the chief's sedan. They called in the town doctor and coroner, Doctor Tom Brown, to examine the body and try to determine the time and cause of death. They didn't want to disturb anything until Doc Tom had a chance to see it for himself.

Stepping back from the area, they leaned against the yards to collect their thoughts.

"Man, I didn't see that coming," said Stan. "I really thought you'd jabbed yourself with a needle or something. Who would've thought you'd found a dead body. And Buck, poor guy."

"I wasn't expecting this when I woke up this morning, that's for sure," said Mandy. "Who was Buck?"

"He was a jack of all trades and a master of none. He didn't have a great rapport with the community. He was into a little bit of gambling. He did have a perfect shot, darts or a gun," clarified Stan.

"Poor guy indeed. I hope he didn't suffer. I better get back to town anyway. I have a full schedule of appointments. I can come back after that to finish up the cattle we hadn't vaccinated if you'd like."

"I think we can reschedule for another day. I'll call Gillian and see what we can do. What a welcome to Crestview for you. At least you found him before something else did. There are bobcats and coyotes around here."

Mandy was completely relieved that she had not come across that scene. A pool of blood was bad enough.

"Do you want a ride into town?" asked Gerry to Mandy.

"No, I've got my Jeep and Lyle to take home," replied Mandy. "That's kind of you, though." She unhooked Lyle from the leash and loaded her into the truck. Lyle took her place in the front seat, ready for the ride. She loved to sniff the wind as the Jeep zoomed along.

"We'll need to get a statement from you about what you found. Without a thorough examination, this tentatively looks like a murder. There will be an investigation. I can stop by the clinic later today," said Larry authoritatively as Mandy started to get into her car. Doc was just pulling up in his Buick. Dressed in a smart tweed suit, he stepped out and went to the trunk of the car to get his equipment. Mandy stayed just long enough to study Doc so she'd recognize him the next time she saw him. She wanted to know what he'd find when he checked Buck over.

Chapter Six

Mandy pulled up to the clinic to find Gillian rushing out the front door to meet her. "Are you ok?" Gillian asked. "I heard what happened. Do you want a cup of tea?"

"I'm fine. This town sure jumps on news like a duck on a junebug. I just don't really know why anyone would kill anyone in Crestview. Everything seems so welcoming. Who would do such a thing?" said Mandy.

"I guess we'll have to wait to find out. Are you ok to see appointments this afternoon? Suddenly we are getting a lot of calls. I guess people want to hear first-hand what you went through this morning. Not many things like this happen here so people are making a big deal out of it," said Gillian. "Why don't we have a nice lunch first? I brought some leftover home-made chili mac from last night and I could use some comfort food. You can tell me all about it."

"Lunch sounds like a good idea. All of a sudden I am famished.

But, what is chili mac?"

"Oh, it's chili over spaghetti with lots of cheese. I'll heat it up in the toaster oven. You'll love it."

"I'm up for trying that. I love cheese on anything. And I think seeing appointments would be fine. When is the first appointment?"

"One-thirty, so we've got forty minutes to unwind and fuel up. I'll get that cup of tea," said Gillian.

Mandy cleaned up, changing out of her coveralls before joining Gillian in the break room to feast on her first cheesy goodness meal of chili mac. Lyle had a bowl of dog chow. Except for Lyle's crunching, they ate in silence. When Lyle finished her bowl, she stretched her whole body, starting at her front legs and ending with a satisfying groan as her back legs elongated behind her. After her unwinding dog yoga, Lyle tried to curl up while the girls finished eating but she seemed unfulfilled. She left the room and came back with a length of rope for the girls to throw.

She dropped it at Gillian's feet and backed up. Gillian giggled, breaking the silence. She threw the rope which Lyle caught in the air, bringing it back to Gillian for another throw.

"So, are you really ok?" asked Gillian.

"Yep, but the more I think about it, the more I really want to know what happened. I might ask a few questions around town to see if I can figure out what happened," said Mandy. The thought of staying in town a bit longer was not ideal in some ways though it did mean she could find out what kind of murderer was on the loose, which she knew Anna would want.

"Just don't get too involved or Larry will be upset with you. He's a real stickler for formalities. I think he wanted to be a big shot detective. Instead, he is our little town's chief. He can be a tad territorial at times. And the people here may seem welcoming on the surface. However, everybody tends to keep their cards close with newcomers," said Gillian.

"Duly noted. I'll tread lightly. I have to see what I can find out," said Mandy, sipping her tea and subconsciously tapping her finger on the mug.

They cleaned up their lunch dishes and took their tea to the front to look at the schedule for the afternoon. Rhonda was coming in with one of her dachshunds to be pregnancy checked. That would be the perfect place for Mandy to start asking questions about Buck Dawson since she was married to Doc Tom, the coroner.

"Are you going to tell me more about your morning?" asked Gillian.

"Do you want the short version or the long version?" countered Mandy.

"What's the difference?"

"I have a touch of eidetic memory."

"Whoa, doc, that's quite a big word. Care to explain?"

"It means I can recall way too much information about a scene. Some people call it photographic memory. That's a bit of a misnomer. For me, I can recall visual memories with astounding detail. Sometimes, it gets in the way of my concentration because I will go off on a tangent when triggered by a cue someone has mistakenly shown me or spoken of. I manage it pretty well. Over the years I have learned to curtail it more or less. It comes in awful handy with remembering patients. I've never used it to recall a murder scene though."

"I see. I didn't know that about you. Good to know. Given our time constraints, let's go with the short version."

Mandy proceeded to give Gillian a synopsis of her morning, ending with the crime scene tape and the arrival of Doc Tom. She left out the part of her being afraid of human blood. Gillian didn't need to know all of her quirks in the first two days of meeting her.

"That was an action-packed morning for you. I can assure you that people don't find dead bodies in Crestview on a regular basis. Don't let this cloud your impressions of the town."

"From what Anna described, I know it can't be the norm. That's even more of a reason to sort out the particulars of the dead body's appearance in a random pasture," said Mandy.

"Did you end up doing all the vaccines or do I need to reschedule?"

"We had to stop once they started taping things off. We don't have that many left to do so it won't take long."

"I'll give them a call and make a date for that. Do I need to set aside some time for you to go down to the chief's office for your statement?" asked Gillian.

"Nope. Larry said he would stop by later here at the clinic," Mandy said. "I'm going to check on a few things before appointments start." With that, she retreated to the office to clear her mind before the appointments. Visual recalls could be exhausting and distracting. Lyle joined her in the office. She sat back in the chair and tried to remember as many details as she could from the moment she started walking away from the cattle yards and toward the place where she discovered the body.

She knew that if she concentrated hard now, it would be easier to check her mental images for details later. She didn't see blood anywhere except under the body. There was no sign of a struggle that she could see. There was a dilapidated section of fence near the body that she had not examined well when she was there. She might have to check that again up close. She would have to sneak out without the police getting wind of her inquisition. She had plenty of questions to answer before she needed to make that trip out.

Chapter Seven

The first patient for the afternoon was a poodle named Marge, with her owner, Fred. They had come in because Marge's ears were red and sore from her incessant itching. Fred was the hairdresser down the road. He rented a space behind the general store. He was a very fashionable hairdresser, a little out of place in this small town. Today, he was wearing a sparkly blue shirt underneath a white cardigan. His pants were tan smooth-washed, tailored, boot-leg khakis. On his feet were unusual loafers with a blue accent on the side. Fred had a very effeminate posture and spoke with a lilt. His haircut was clean and neat, with highlights and lowlights and a little gel sculpture. On his right hand was a single gold ring. His poodle had a perfect clip for a miniature poodle, complete with a pink studded collar. From the look of Marge, she wouldn't have a flea on her.

"What seems to be the problem?" asked Mandy.

"Marge here is as mad as a March hare. She keeps scratching

her ears," answered Fred.

"Have you taken Marge swimming lately?" asked Mandy.

"Oh no, not for Marge. She never touches water unless it's for a bath. We lead a very clean life, don't we, Margy?" he asked, talking to his dog.

"Have you changed her diet at all?" said Mandy.

"Nope. Nothing has changed at all," answered Fred.

Mandy grabbed the otoscope and examined Marge's inner ears. They were indeed irritated. She took a swab to have a look under the microscope. She applied a stain to the slide. She placed it on the stage of the microscope, adjusting the knobs to bring the sample into focus.

"That's a fancy little trick there. What do you see?"

"It looks like poor Marge has a bit of an infection; some yeast and bacteria have set up shop in her ears."

"What do we do to make her feel better?"

"I'm going to give you some topical drops to put in Marge's ears to help solve the local problem. I will also give you some oral antibiotics to make sure that we zap this before it gets worse. When you get home, I want you to clean Marge's ears thoroughly with this solution. Once they're cleaned out, start the drops. The drops have a steroid in them to help soothe the irritated ears straight away while the antibiotics start to take effect. Does that all sound doable?" said Mandy.

"Sure thing. Anything for Marge," said Fred. "How are you holding up anyway, dear? I heard about the tragedy."

"I'm ok," said Mandy. She was amazed that he had already heard about her morning scare.

"Welcome to the family. Poor Buck. Although you could say he had it coming. Not only did he wear brown shoes with black belts, but he wasn't exactly a favorite around town," said Fred.

"Really, what do you mean?" said Mandy.

"Well, I know you shouldn't speak ill of the dead. But, since you're new in town, I may as well give you the town noise. Buck wasn't the most gracious loser. He was a pretty competitive guy. When we were little, he used to get to the sack race before everyone else and choose the biggest sack. It wasn't much of an advantage, but he believed that he needed to have the biggest sack in order to maneuver to the finish line the fastest. I don't think that he ever outgrew that mentality," said Fred.

"Interesting. Well, it looks like my next client is here. Here is your sack of medicines for Marge. If you have any questions, please let me know."

"I think we are good."

"It was nice to meet you, Fred. I might come down to have you cut my hair sometime," said Mandy.

"Nice to meet your acquaintance, and thanks for helping Marge.

I would just love to have a chance to play with your hair. With all of that body, we have loads of styles we could play with. You know where to find me," said Fred.

Mandy always thought it was interesting that hairdressers couldn't wait to get their hands into her mane even though she had fought with it most of her life. And now the story of Buck was getting a little more complicated. She walked into the waiting room to meet her next client. There were two clients in the waiting room, though.

"Hi, I'm Dr. Bell, can I help you?" Mandy asked the toned man in the boot cut Levi's.

"Oh, he's my friend from New Mexico. He's in town visiting for the Halloween Hoedown. We went to school together. Then his Dad got a job out of state and he ended up settling out West. We get together once a year to catch up. Dennis, this is Dr. Mandy Bell," Fred said as he clutched Marge on one side of his waist.

"Pleased to meet you, ma'am. That's some handshake. Are you

going to be playing softball at the Hoedown? We could sure use all the help we can get. Fred here is our expert cheerleader," Dennis said as he looked at Fred.

"I did used to play in college, but I haven't played since. That could be really fun. I'll see if I can dig out my mitt," she said.

"I played football but these days softball is much better on my joints. I'll see you there," said Dennis.

Mandy turned to the next customer, a grey-haired gentleman in greasy overalls. "What can I do for you?" asked Mandy.

"I'm Alvin. I run the town garage. I would shake your hand but I've just been working on the gears of Jim Moore's Ferguson tractor and I'm a bit greasy. You can't leave a guy without a tractor this time of year so I need to get back lickety split. I just came in for some flea medicine for my dog, Spud," he said.

"How much does he weigh?"

"About 150 these days," said Alvin. They put him on the scale to check.

"158 today. Far out, that's a big dog. Here's the stuff you need," said Mandy, handing over a pill for fleas.

"Yeah, Spud's a Mastiff. He keeps me company at the garage. He's friendly despite his appearance. My wife loves to call him my junkyard dog. She says he's uglier than homemade sin," Alvin said. Spud was laying on the floor with his back legs behind him. Alvin reached down to give him a pat and Spud flipped over to get some petting on his belly. "I heard you got yourself into some kind of mess this morning," said Alvin.

"Indeed I did."

"Poor old Buck. A lot of people are going to be unhappy around here. He had a few debts owing to people," said Alvin as he paid for the flea medicine.

"Interesting. What kind of debts?"

"He was the kind of guy who wouldn't just play pool. He always had to put a wager on the game," said Alvin. "I'd love to stay and gab. I need to get back to the Ferguson. It looks like it's gonna clabber up an' mildew out there."

"What?" asked Mandy.

"You'll learn our sayings around here. That means it looks like it might rain and I don't want to get wet working on the tractor."

"Ah."

"I'll see you at the Halloween Hoedown."

"See you there," said Mandy. Mandy figured that the Hoedown would be the perfect place to learn more about the mysterious deceased man.

Gillian came back up front with a couple of cups of tea and some chocolate chip cookies.

"Sorry it took me a while, I had to fill the sugar container while I was back there and I made a bit of a mess. I figured that I need to keep you caffeinated and sugared up to ensure you get through

the day. Right, well it looks like Rhonda is next up to walk

through the door," she said. Mandy wasn't convinced it was her

that needed the stimulants. Gillian seemed to be hooked on tea.

She must have one of those metabolisms like a hummingbird

because she definitely didn't have the figure of someone who ate

sweet treats all day long.

Chapter Eight

Almost on cue, Rhonda and her dachshund Sugar opened the door and made the old cow bell on the door frame ring. She was wearing a camel-colored leather dress with a giant concha belt loosely around her hips. The belt had chunks of turquoise embedded in sterling silver. She made Mandy feel a tad frumpy in her jeans and fleece pullover.

"Ooh, it looks like I am early. Have your cups of tea, girls, I am in no rush. Tom won't be home for a while. He's finishing all the paperwork on Buck Dawson. I just don't know how Tom can examine a dead body and then come home for dinner. I still love him though," Rhonda said.

"I suppose you get used to it," said Gillian before she blew on her ceramic horse-themed mug and took a sip of tea.

"Do you know what happened?" asked Mandy.

"Well, I'm not supposed to say. You *were* the one to find him so

I suppose you are more entitled than most to hear the news. Apparently, Buck was definitely murdered. Somebody shot him in the chest. Ironically, it was a one-shot bulls-eye through his heart. Obviously someone other than Buck was a perfect shot. Poor old Buck," said Rhonda.

"That's awful. What do you mean it is ironic?"

"Buck was the town aims-man. Anything with a target and he was in, from darts to hunting to rifle ranging. He had quite a competitive spirit," said Rhonda.

"Does anyone know who might have done it?" said Mandy.

"Nope. He didn't have a long list of enemies or anything. He sure wasn't Mr. Popular either," said Rhonda.

"I hate to be the slave-driver. We should get a move on these x-rays," Gillian said as she took down three lead gowns for the girls to wear for radiation protection while they held Sugar on the x-ray table. Normally they anesthetized animals for radiographs.

With Sugar being pregnant, they didn't want to administer drugs for sedation that might affect the puppies. Instead they would have to hold her still for the x-ray. The radiation exposure to the puppies would be safe if they only took one x-ray.

"I've got the book right here. Let's see, the factors we used on Maple last time seemed to give a good image. Maple and Sugar are about the same size. So, we'll try our luck on those," said Gillian, changing the exposure factors on the x-ray machine. Meanwhile, Rhonda and Mandy put Sugar on the table and positioned her with her right side down on the table and her legs extended out. Mandy adjusted the x-ray beam to aim for the abdomen.

"All clear?" asked Gillian.

"Yep," said Mandy. Gillian pressed the foot pedal to expose the film. She then took the x-ray cartridge to the dark room for development. While she was gone, Mandy took the opportunity to ask a few more questions.

"So, what do you mean he wasn't Mr. Popular?"

"Buck was always the alpha of his age group. Despite his relatively small stature, he sure did stir up some trouble. Maybe it was small man syndrome. I remember one time he poured soap in the gas tank of Howie's scooter. Howie is a sweetie. I don't think you've met him yet. He delivers the mail and does odd jobs like lawn care for people in town. He's not Einstein. He's made a life for himself and never causes anyone any trouble. When he was younger, he was a great bull rider until he had a bit of an accident one year where he fell off and suffered a bad concussion. Buck was always tormenting him even though Howie would never hurt a fly."

"I see. Does Howie have any brothers or sisters?"

"No. His parents are older now and Howie lives in a little carriage house out the back of their house. He keeps to himself mostly. He always goes to the bull riding at the county fair to cheer on his comrades. His parents normally accompany him to

any town festivities to keep a close eye on him. They don't want
to see him hurt or taken advantage of."

"I sure wish the killer could be identified before he or she strikes
again," said Mandy. "The thought of someone at large is
disturbing."

"Tom always says you can wish in one hand and crap in the
other. See which one fills up faster. It's a bit crude, I know.
Just don't get yourself into trouble trying to solve this. A killer
is a killer," warned Rhonda.

Gillian returned with the x-ray and a big smile. "Well, I'm not
the vet here. It looks like we are in for a nice litter!" Rhonda
shuffled over to the x-ray viewer. She'd seen so many x-rays of
her bitches that she was getting the knack of reading them.
Mandy walked over to stand beside her while Gillian put Sugar
back on the floor.

"Nice exposure, Gillian. I avoid shooting more than one film
since the pups are so vulnerable at this time. It looks like you

nailed the factors since you can see everything clearly," said Mandy. As she ran her finger along the x-ray, pointing at a skull and then following the spine of each pup, she counted carefully to herself.

"Eight," said Mandy.

"That's what I get too. That's fabulous. What a clever girl you are, Sugar!" squealed Rhonda. "Oh, it's going to be a busy few months. Honey is due with a litter of six in the next few days."

"Well, you know the drill. Give us a shout if you run into any troubles," said Gillian.

"Sugar hasn't needed help before. Honey, on the other hand, had a c-section last time. So, you might be getting a call in the near future, Dr. Bell," said Rhonda.

"Not a problem. Cesarians are such fun. I love bringing pups into the world. Somehow in my head, it evens out the unhappy karma for all of the animals that I have had to put down as a veterinarian. Don't get me wrong, it's part of my role: to help animals pass peacefully. I just prefer to bring them into the world every now and then," said Mandy.

"Hear hear," said Gillian. "I will go file this away with our other puppy count x-rays." She left them to head to the archive room.

"I best take Sugar home to spoil her rotten and keep an eye on Miss Honey," said Rhonda. Sugar must have known what Rhonda was saying. She had stayed very relaxed through the whole appointment but was now waddling in anticipation toward the door. She was almost as round as she was long so her body had a swagger as she shuffled. For a dachshund, late pregnancy ambulation is very entertaining to watch.

"Sounds good. Can you let me know what Dr. Tom finds out about Buck. I'm pretty curious about it all," Mandy said.

"Oh, call him Doc, everyone else does. I hardly see what a few details among friends could do, though I'm not supposed to," Rhonda said with a wink.

"My lips are sealed," Mandy said.

Once Rhonda and Sugar left, Mandy went back into her office and pulled out a blank piece of paper. At the top she wrote Buck and underlined it. Underneath, she wrote Howie, friend of Howie, someone he owed some money. She stopped there, to twiddle her pencil in her hand and bite the end of it. This was a nervous habit she had developed back in grade school, when pencils were standard writing implements. She detested the newfangled mechanical pencils.

She pushed her glasses up on her nose. They always slid down when she was concentrating too hard on biting her pencil or anything else that required focus for that matter. The glasses were vintage. She'd had them for years. A few too many times of bending over for lame cows and falling asleep looking at maps and they didn't quite stay on as well anymore. She didn't have the heart to get new ones as she'd become quite attached to them.

Lyle had joined her in the office. She was whining incessantly and pawed at the chair in the corner.

"What it is girl. Is Timmy in the well?" Mandy asked Lyle. Mandy sometimes joked with Lyle about rescuing Timmy. It seemed to make Lyle even more insistent.

Mandy left her list to see what Lyle was jazzed up about. Under the chair was a ball. It must have rolled under at some point. Lyle was obsessive about which toy she would play with. Even if there were ten tennis balls at her disposal, if she started to play with one, it was the only one she wanted until the next play session. Mandy handed the ball to a thankful Lyle. Gillian popped her head in the doorway.

"Next appointment is here."

"I'll be right there." Mandy shoved the list under some files. She'd work on it again later. She grabbed her stethoscope, putting it around her neck. She cleared her mind and made her way to the consult room.

Chapter Nine

Gillian intercepted Mandy just before she went in the room.

"I would have taken vitals. It's a hamster and I'm not sure exactly how to get a heart rate or a temperature for that matter," said Gillian, holding back a chuckle.

"That's quite ok," Mandy returned a smile.

"Hi there. I'm so happy you've decided to stay. I heard from Alvin at the garage that you are coming to the Hoedown. It's so nice that you are going to be part of the community," said Mrs. Bouvier. She had a nice big bun of gray hair on top of her head and a string of pearls around her neck. Her blue cardigan looked like it had been knitted by hand and the mismatched ceramic buttons gave her an artistic flare.

"What seems to be the problem with Pumpkin here?"

"Well, he's been stuffing his cheeks with every bit of food that my son gives him."

"Let's have a look." Mandy picked Pumpkin up and started with his tail. He was a particularly rotund animal, unable to even turn around to sniff her as she lifted his stubby little tail. "Well, for starters, Pumpkin is a she Mrs. Bouvier."

Mrs. Bouvier gasped and held her hand up to her mouth.

"How much do you feed her and what do you offer?"

"Lettuce, hamster food from the feedstore, and pinecones. We read that they wear down teeth. I think he, I mean she, always has food in her bowl. She shares the cage with Marvin, our other hamster."

"Have you noticed Pumpkin gaining weight recently?"

"Well I suppose so. We thought she was just getting fluffy for winter. She isn't even a year old and we thought she was pretty clever to know that winter in Illinois is worth getting extra fluff for."

Mandy grabbed a tongue depressor, a pair of hemostats, and an otoscope to visualize the mouth. She gently pried the mouth open with the tongue depressor and used the light on the otoscope to look inside Pumpkin's left cheek pouch. She inserted the hemostats with her steady hands to feel the cavernous pocket. They are pretty far in there so Mandy couldn't see much even with all of her tools. Instead, she palpated along the outside.

"Yep, it feels like there is definitely some food squirreled away in there. How old is Marvin?"

"Oh, they're the same age. We got them at the same time from one of my son's friends. It must have been around Valentine's Day."

"How do you know Marvin is a Marvin and not a Marvina?"

"Well, we had a look at both of them together and decided they were both boys."

"Hmm, well, I think perhaps you are right with Marvin but it seems as though Marvin and Pumpkin might be expecting a family."

"Oh dear. Can they do that? They are related and all."

"It doesn't seem to stop hamsters. I'd say Pumpkin is due pretty soon by the looks of it. I'd get another cage and separate them for now. Not only do you not want Pumpkin pregnant again but sometimes male hamsters get a little aggressive with the babies. You'll be needing to look around for some good hamster owners because they don't often have one or two. You'll be run out of the house if you keep them all."

"I'll start right on that. I know loads of people."

"And make sure you bring them all in once they are born so we can determine who's what from the start."

"Sounds like a great plan to me. Now that we've solved that mystery, how are you holding up after, well, discovering Buck?"

"I'm ok. I'm sure interested to know who would have done such a thing."

"We may never know. Larry and Gerry don't have the best track record with solving this sort of thing. The last time we had a problem in our community, it wasn't solved until the culprit got sloppy and went to the next town over. That was just serial burglaries but it sure was frustrating. Around here, cattle are gold. The thief would wait till dark and then steal a few cattle at a time from this farmer or that farmer. They never left any clues. Finally, somebody hooked up a camera outside the paddock their cows were in and they caught the guy."

"Do you have any ideas as to who could have done this to Buck?"

"My best guess would be somebody he owed money to. That's a pretty long list though. I'd say they're going to be talking about it at the Inn tonight: it's pool night. I better take Pumpkin home and get back to baking for the Hoedown Bake-off."

"There must be some yummy treats at the Bake-off. Everyone

seems to be busily baking," said Mandy.

"I can't enter. I help run it. I still bake because the proceeds from the bake sale go to a different worthy cause each year. Plus there is never any shortage of people to sample baking at my house. I seem to run a day camp for many of the kids in town. During harvest time, lots of parents are busy. Around here, the saying 'it takes a village' is completely true," said Mrs. Bouvier.

"Yummy baking and a good cause. Ooh la la. Keep in touch on those babies. I'll keep my ear out for someone who might want a little hamster of their own."

Mandy returned to her office and pulled out the piece of paper. More of a visual learner, she needed to write things out to think. With the pencil in her mouth, she stared at the list so far. The only way to make more headway would be to go to the Inn tonight. She hated pool. She didn't like the feeling of the wood in her fingers. She never knew where that came from. Any kind of wood near her skin or anyone else's drove her mad. The worst are popsicles and corndogs. Several times over the years she had asked clients to remove the toothpicks from their mouths just so she could make eye contact.

"Reggie is here," said Gillian, poking her head in the door.

"Righty-o." Mandy left the office to find Gerry in the consult room with a big fluffy ginger cat on the table, purring away.

"I didn't expect to see you here. You must be awful busy with this case," said Mandy.

"Well, while I was waiting for Doc to give us the verdict on what he reckons, I figured I better take care of Reggie here. He's been, well," he took off his hat and blushed a little. "He's been pissing on my good boots. I can't work out why. He's always been such a good cat."

"Hmm. How long has this been going on?"

"About a week."

"Any changes in diet?"

"No."

"Has he been drinking more than normal?"

"Hard to say. He has a big bowl that he shares with my Coon Hound."

"Does he strain when he pees?"

"I'm not too sure, it seems like he does it at night when I'm asleep."

Meanwhile, Mandy was doing a quick physical on Reggie. She started at his head, checking his teeth, tongue, ears, and eyes. She palpated his abdomen and examined his back end for any irritation. She had a listen to Reggie's heart and lungs. Gillian had already taken the temperature and it was normal.

"Well, it could be a couple of things. Is Reggie indoor only?"

"Yep."

"What type of litter do you use?"

"I had been using clay but there was a deal on some of that modern clumping stuff so we are onto that now. Man, it's so much easier!"

"Does it have an odor to it?"

"Well, I keep it clean but I guess it does smell like a litter box."

Laughing, Mandy said "No, I mean is it scented?"

"Oh, I see. Yep, it smells like a rainforest, so the packet says."

"That could be the culprit. Sometimes cats stop using the litter pan or use it intermittently if something changes that they don't like. It might be that he misses his clay litter. Since you took it away, he might be telling you he's not impressed by marking something of yours."

"That makes sense. It did start about the time I changed litter."

"I'd go back to the old stuff pretty quick smart. Just to be sure that we don't have a urinary tract infection which can also cause inappropriate urination, I'll take a urine sample and check it out for you."

"Best to be safe. I'm pretty attached to the old guy."

Mandy left to get Gillian and together they obtained a urine sample. Gillian held Reggie on his side and Mandy palpated and isolated the bladder in one hand, pressing it against Reggie's backbone. She then took the needle and syringe and penetrated the abdomen where she was holding the bladder. The syringe filled with yellow as she sucked it back.

"That's a neat trick," said Gerry.

"Let me check this in the lab for you," Gillian left the room with the sample. She put Reggie back in his cage. Gillian returned with the results a few minutes later and handed them to Mandy.

"Looks like a mild infection which may have been brought on by the stress of changing litter or the litter could be unrelated.

Either way, we'll put him on some antibiotics to help sort him out. I would get rid of the scented litter too."

"Whatever you say, Doc. You're a pretty good sleuth if you could figure out all that just from the questions you asked. Maybe we should put you on the force to help us with Buck's murder."

"To be honest, I wouldn't mind helping. I find it so disturbing that someone would do that in such a sweet little town."

"I'll tell you what. Let's meet tonight and talk it over. We can't let Larry catch wind of it. I figure you might give us an angle we haven't thought of. Do you want to meet at the Inn at seven? Besides, I think you've earned a drink after this morning. Just don't tell Larry I'm giving you information. He would never let anybody in on any details from the case. You can't tell anybody else either."

"I think I can keep a few secrets. Although that doesn't seem to be one of this town's strengths. Everyone who has come in today seems to know what happened. Tonight would be a smart choice to go to the Inn because I hear they have a pool match. From what I understand, Buck was in on that circle so we might overhear something helpful. "

"You're not wrong there. Anything competitive, he was all over it: darts, pool, archery, target shooting. I shall see you at seven then." Gerry put his hat back on and collected Reggie in his cage.

"One more case and then we can rest for a bit," said Gillian as she came in and wiped the counters off in the consult room. "Larry should be in after that to get your statement."

"This is Babe Ruth." Gillian ushered in the next client and handed Mandy the file. A young man carried in a small shoe box. He had mousy brown hair and wore white overalls covered in spatters of paint. He placed the box on the counter and pulled out a turtle about the size of the palm of his hand.

"Nick, how do you do?" he said as he extended his hand to

Mandy. "I named her that because she's only about that size and I found her when I was on a break from painting. I was eating a Baby Ruth and looked down and there she was, all alone. I didn't know too much about them. I thought she would be a low maintenance pet. Boy, was I wrong. It takes a fair bit of effort to keep a turtle here in Illinois."

"It sure does. What's the trouble?"

"She's started swimming in circles. It's the weirdest thing."

"I see. Let's have a look." Mandy picked Babe Ruth up and examined her shell. That's about all she could look at because Babe had hidden in her shell. Mandy pulled out her stethoscope and tried to listen to her chest. Turtles are a bit tricky to examine altogether but Mandy had a good idea as to what was wrong. She placed Babe back on the table. "Have you got a heat lamp for her?"

"I do, but the bulb went out over the weekend and I haven't had a chance to fix it. I've been so busy with painting at the rifle range."

Babe stuck her head out to explore the counter and Mandy could see that there was a bit of discharge around her nose and eyes.

"I'd say that Babe here caught a chill and has a bit of pneumonia. We can take x-rays to confirm. That'd cost a bit and I'm not sure it would change the treatment I'd recommend. She has some crustiness around her face so it's in her upper and lower respiratory tract."

"So why is she swimming in circles?" inquired Nick.

"Well, she's probably got more crud in one side of her lungs than the other and they use the air in their lungs to help swim. She's not balanced so she favors the bad side when she's swimming."

"That's interesting. What can we do for her?"

"The best bet would be to put her on a good course of antibiotics. I'll go get them for you."

Mandy returned with a bottle and a dropper. "We can do oral antibiotics and see how she gets on. If she's not improving, we'll have to switch to injectable. I can teach you how to do it. The main thing is that you stick to the instructions and finish the whole course I give you. No cutting corners. And make sure you get that lamp going. I'd keep her out of full submersion water until she's better. She can get wet under supervision to keep her shell healthy. We just don't want her to catch cold."

"I can handle that. Thanks."

"So you've been painting at the rifle range?"

"Yep, they sure did run it down over the years. It's a busy place. We like our hunting around here and it's key to keep your shot up to speed. It's a bit of a social place too. Old Buck was always out there."

"I guess they'll miss him then."

"I guess so. Although there's going to be a scramble for the top shooter now."

"What do you mean?"

"Well, Buck was always the top which is a big deal around here. Looks like it'll be between Jim and Barney now."

"Who are they?"

"Jim Moore is a local farmer and Barney Saunders owns the general store in town. I'm sure you'll meet them both soon enough."

"I look forward to it."

Nick left with his shoe box and antibiotics and Mandy went back to the office. She pulled out the list and added Jim Moore and Barney Saunders, only because they had motive and knowledge. She'd work on meeting them soon.

Gillian popped her head in. "Phone's for you. It's Rhonda."

"Thanks Gillian."

"Hello," said Mandy.

"I've got some news for you. The one shot through the heart was it and he was dead instantly. It looks like he was shot from the front so he probably knew it was coming. There was no sign of a struggle and nothing missing from his person. He had some cash in his wallet so it wasn't theft. Buck didn't look to have a weapon on him."

"I see. Any idea when it happened?"

"Probably sometime last night between midnight and two a.m."

"And did it happen there or was he brought there from somewhere else?"

"Tom says there was no blood trail so he wasn't dragged. It seems like it must've happened right there. Weird place to be meeting someone in the middle of the night."

"Indeed. Well, thanks so much for that. How is Sugar?"

"Oh, she's good. See you soon, darling."

"Will do, Rhonda."

Larry had arrived to take Mandy's statement for the investigation. Gillian showed him into the office so they could have some privacy.

"It's not typical protocol to take a statement here and not at the station. I understand you might be a tad shaken up so I opted to bring the necessary equipment here to make it legitimate. I will be recording our conversation on this recorder. You are not under arrest so I do not need to read you any rights. However, you may have a lawyer present if you feel more comfortable."

"I don't think that will be necessary. Let's get started," said Mandy.

Larry proceeded to ask her standard questions. Mandy relayed the scene she had found in extraordinary detail, though she only answered the questions that Larry asked. She did not offer any more information than was required. Otherwise, the statement could take a rather long time due to her memory caliber.

"I think that will be all that we need. Thank you for your cooperation. Should you think of anything else that might be of assistance, please call me. I take this matter seriously as I am the protector of this community. As such, giving your statement is the only involvement you will be required to provide. That means you are not to investigate this on your own. I am the authority. I do hope I will not need to remind you of that," said Larry.

"No problem, chief. I respect your position," said Mandy. She escorted Larry out of the clinic. Gillian had been cleaning and squaring everything away in the clinic.

Chapter Ten

Mandy and Gillian closed up the clinic together. Lyle was pretty

excited to be let out for a run in the yards. She was still looking

for those sheep. Instead, she found a piece of two by four and

dragged it over to Mandy and Gillian.

"That's a bit big love. Let's get you a ball. It's a bit safer for me

and you."

"I'll see you tomorrow," said Gillian.

"Okey dokey."

Mandy grabbed a ball from the cupboard above the stairs of the

RV and played fetch with Lyle. No matter how long Lyle played

fetch, she never got tired of the game. One of her favorite things

was to watch sports on TV. Her beloved game was basketball

since the ball moved quickly on the screen. She was also

intrigued by golf, tennis, and football. She would bark at the

screen and follow the ball with her whole body. If the ball went off the screen, she would look for it behind the TV. Fetch in real life was far more fulfilling, though. Finally, Mandy succeeded in slightly wearing her out, as indicated by the tongue hanging completely out of her mouth. She brought her in for some supper. She fixed herself a cup of coffee and sipped it while looking at her list of suspects. She decided she would focus on the gambling angle tonight since she would be at the Inn. She could track down Howie and his parents on a separate occasion. She really needed a good lead.

"Well Lyle, it's about time to go to the Inn. You wanna come?" Lyle catapulted herself from the couch to the landing at the top of the stairs and sat with very keen eyes. That was her signal that she was indeed interested, even if it meant wearing a harness.

Walking down, she noticed a few more decorations in the windows. As a child, she had been frustrated by small changes like decorations. It took a few years before her parents worked out that she had eidetic memory. Their first clue was when she would point out minute changes in her surroundings that most people didn't even notice. Over the years, she had learned to not let it bother her but instead use it to her advantage. In some ways, it made her a better vet because she could remember exactly what a tumor looked like from one visit to the next. She had learned to try not to take in every part of her environment at all times. Sensory overload prevention, she had learned to call it.

Entering the Inn, she saw Gerry sitting at a small booth. She sat down and Lyle took her place under the table. Myrna arrived shortly thereafter and they each ordered the night's special: meatloaf with mashed potatoes and corn.

"So, what do you know so far?" asked Mandy.

"Buck wasn't popular, but everyone knows that. The question is, why now. Why not years ago? What changed recently that made someone so angry with him?"

"Has anyone new moved to town, other than me?"

"Not that I can think of."

Larry came in the back door of the Inn and made his way over to their table.

"What do we have here? We aren't discussing the case, are we?"

"No, just unwinding after an unsettling day," Gerry sighed.

"Well, you leave the sleuthing to me," he said and turned to go put his name down for the dart competition.

The food arrived with more generous helpings. Mandy realized she'd need to do a lot more walking around town if she wanted to eat like this every night. They each started to enjoy the steaming plate of comfort food.

"I think it's weird that the killer didn't take the money that Buck had on him," said Mandy.

"How do you know that?" asked Gerry.

Blushing, Mandy tried to think of a non-incriminating

explanation. "Um, well..."

"Rhonda told you, eh?"

"Well…"

"Oh, who are we kidding? Nothing stays a secret in this town. As long as you know, we may as well work together to narrow down the search, but keep it quiet with you know who," he said, pointing to Larry.

"Sounds good to me. I don't want a killer on the loose. We know he was a competitive person. What else?"

"We know that there are a few debt collectors after him from this town. He had struck deals that led nowhere with people so he owes them money. Plus there were a few people around who never got paid from bets that he had made, that sort of thing."

"I see," said Mandy.

"I am still interviewing people to see if anything seems

suspicious."

"I am hoping to find out more information at the Hoedown. The pool competition should also yield a few clues, with any luck, as long as I avoid Larry. Of course every client who comes to the clinic seems to offer more information."

"That's handy for you. People aren't as willing to talk to the law. Larry doesn't exactly bring out the conversation in people either. He's very by the books."

"Anything else of note on the autopsy?"

"It was a small caliber that got him. Whoever did it was close enough to get a perfect shot. He probably didn't get to put up a fight so it caught him off guard, which means he probably knew the murderer. Another question is why on the farm? Why were they out there?"

"Hard to say. Something we need to look into."

"So far, it's a bunch of dead ends. Let's talk about you. Have you been to every state in the union in your travels as a vet?" asked Gerry.

"Almost. I haven't been to Hawaii," said Mandy. "Have you traveled much yourself?"

"I have a thing for national parks. I take one trip a year and aim to see the national parks in the area. Last year, I went to the Badlands. That is a very strange landscape if you haven't seen it. It is almost hard to get a perspective as to whether you are a giant in a martian landscape or an ant in a runoff. The geology out there is astounding."

"You are into geology?" asked Mandy.

"It's a little of a hobby of mine. Geology tells a story if you are just open to the language it speaks," said Gerry.

Myrna made her way over to their table.

"There's a call for you at the counter."

"Me," Mandy said, completely surprised.

"Yep, it's Rhonda and she sounds a little panicked."

Mandy walked to the counter and picked up the phone.

"Hello?"

"Hi, it looks like we are having a little trouble with Honey. I have tried to assist her but I think a puppy is stuck. I hate to bother you afterhours. But this is an emergency. Shall I meet you at the clinic?" Rhonda said.

"I'll be there in a jiffy." Mandy hung up the phone and headed back to the booth. "That was strange. I wonder how Rhonda knew to call here."

"Get used to it. We are such a small community that we tend to know a little too much about everyone's business. I'll take care of the check. We can meet again to discuss the case," Gerry said picking up the check.

"Next time dinner is on me," Mandy said.

Gerry just winked in reply.

Mandy set off down the main street of town back to the clinic. Lyle was bouncing along beside her. Lyle must know their abrupt departure from the Inn indicated an adventure on the horizon. Gillian was already at the clinic and was starting to prepare for a possible cesarean. She had a heating pad in a laundry basket, towels in the drier, and was putting out the necessary instruments for the surgery. Hamish, her son, was with her.

"Hope you don't mind, I brought Hamish along. He is great with puppies and I thought you'd want to meet him." Hamish was every bit as rugged as his mother. He had on worn-down Redwing work boots, carpenter's pants, and a plaid flannel shirt tucked in to reveal a big oval pewter belt buckle with a horseshoe on it. His cap was literally held together with shreds of material around the edges. He clearly never took it off.

"Pleased to meet you, Dr. Bell," Hamish said as he tipped his hat.

"Nice to meet you as well. Ready to get your hands dirty?" Mandy smiled.

"Yes ma'am."

"Excellent."

Rhonda was pulling up as Mandy was introducing Lyle to Hamish. Lyle had always had a fascination with kids since they typically will play fetch for hours longer than adults. Lyle and Hamish hit it off famously as they played up and down the hallway.

As the door opened to the clinic, Dr. Bell could see Honey was swaddled in a baby blanket and panting. Rhonda placed her on the exam table and Mandy got to work. Using a rubber glove and lube, she carefully examined to see what was exposed. A little dapple tail was visible and she couldn't quite get her hands around the pelvis of the puppy to reposition it. It was quite a large puppy for a little mama dachshund.

"Looks like we will need to take an x-ray to give us a better idea," Mandy said and Gillian was already on her way to the x-ray room.

"I thought she was pushing so hard and nothing was changing."

"It's ok. We will see pretty quickly here but it feels like we have a breech puppy that's too big to turn around."

Gillian whisked Honey to x-ray room and positioned her for the correct view. Rhonda and Mandy waited patiently as Gillian went to the developer. Hamish was still playing with Lyle in the hall, safely away from the x-ray radiation.

"So, did you find out anything from Gerry?"

"I suppose I shouldn't be surprised that you knew I was at the Inn and you knew I was with Gerry. We were trying to put our heads together to see what direction to take with this Buck

Dawson murder. So far, we both are perplexed."

"Just don't let Larry know you are helping. He likes to keep it all by the rules. Even though you are a doctor, veterinarians are not part of the police force."

"Duly noted. I can keep a secret." Gillian reappeared with the developed x-ray and placed it on the viewer.

"Well, it certainly doesn't look like that will come out naturally. Who wants to help bring some puppies into the world?" Mandy said this is as she did this little shimmy with her shoulders and hands. Obviously, this sort of surgery got her excited as a veterinarian. Gillian and Rhonda exchanged a glance and they all got to work. They made their way to the surgery room and Mandy was humming as she put the catheter in Honey's front leg.

They hooked Honey up to IV fluids as a precaution and as Mandy calculated the dose of anesthesia, Gillian shaved and prepped Honey's abdomen. Gillian unwrapped all of the instruments while Mandy scrubbed and gloved up. Mandy

placed a large sterile drape that covered Honey's entire body.

She made her incision through the skin, muscle, and peritoneum.

She instantly found the enlarged uterus, making a careful

incision through the body of it. She located the first puppy,

removed it from the uterus and embryonic sac, and handed it

over to Gillian with a hemostat around its umbilical cord. After

the first one, her surgical speed increased until she had safely

removed all of the puppies and given them to Rhonda, Gillian,

and Hamish so they could stimulate them to breathe. Everyone

worked quietly at the task at hand so all that could be heard was

the beeping of the pulse oximeter on Honey's tongue and the tiny

little whines of the puppies as they started to take their first

breaths. Only once did Gillian have to push Mandy's glasses

back up on her nose. They tended to slip during surgeries since

she was concentrating and had her head down. With sterile

gloves on, she couldn't push them up herself. Any normal

person would get a new pair of glasses, but not Mandy.

The surgery went very smoothly, with Honey's vitals staying within normal throughout. All six puppies were whining and writhing in their warm blankets. Mandy closed the incision expertly. Honey was just starting to come out of the anesthesia when Mandy was cleaning around the incision. The litter was split evenly between males and females. Mandy would leave the fluids hooked up until just before Honey was going home to allow the fluids to support her cardiovascular system as long as possible.

"Oh thank you, Dr. Bell," Rhonda said happily as she inspected her new brood.

Mandy carefully checked each puppy for any obvious abnormalities like a cleft palate or inadequate size. Mandy worked quickly to remove the hemostats from the cords and tie each one off with a small knot of suture. The puppy that had been stuck in the birth canal was definitely the biggest and was a beautiful little dapple girl.

"It's superstitious to name them when they are this young but that little girl will be named Candy, after you, Mandy. I can't name her just Mandy because all of my dogs have names in the sweets category."

"That is very kind of you! I'm touched," Mandy said as she put a hand on Rhonda's shoulder.

"I just love new puppies," said Hamish, as he reached under the blanket to watch them. Although he clearly had a masculine fashion statement and demeanor, his sensitive side came out with the puppies. Gillian looked on with pride. Although hard to raise a son on her own, Gillian had encouraged Hamish to find male role models in the community to fill in the blanks.

"I don't normally send mothers home on antibiotics unless there is a problem. Everything went well so let's allow Honey to recover first. Any signs of redness at the incision or mastitis, let me know and we can put her on something. I hate exposing the babies to drugs via the milk if we don't need to. I will send her home on more pain medication though. This pain medication will not affect the babies negatively. No matter what, pain is unacceptable for my patients."

"That's the smallest incision I have ever seen for a cesarean. I'm impressed. Anna always said that you were her idol for surgery and now I have been able to witness it firsthand. I'd be honored to be your surgical assistant from here on out, Dr. Bell!" Gillian gushed.

"Why thank you. I just get in the mode and off I go. I have always loved surgery, big animals or small animals," said Mandy. "I think that we can settle up the bill tomorrow. You get those puppies home."

Gillian and Hamish carried the basket of puppies while Rhonda carried Honey out to the car. Lyle, of course, followed everyone. She never missed anything, particularly puppies. She had kept her distance during the surgery but she was very inquisitive now. Honey was still groggy from anesthesia and didn't mind Lyle's curiosity. Lyle had actually helped Mandy through the years with the wildlife she had raised. Mandy was careful not to let the wildlife become complacent with dogs. When they required bottle feeding every few hours through the night, Lyle was a great nurse to help Mandy wake up. She also always alerted Mandy if anything started to make unusual noises, indicating distress. She had once saved a squirrel's life by retrieving Mandy when the squirrel was choking on a piece of acorn.

Once the new litter was safely in the vehicle, Gillian and Hamish hopped in their truck. As Mandy watched them drive off, she felt a huge sense of accomplishment for the night. It wasn't until she did surgery at a clinic that she started to feel at home. Some people say that they don't feel bonded to new home until they have cooked their first meal in it. For Mandy, it was doing her first non-routine surgery. This town was definitely starting to grow on her. If only she could figure out that murder.

Chapter Eleven

The morning began with a thin layer of fog enveloping the town. An early riser, Mandy enjoyed seeing the evidence of the cool mornings. The automatic coffee maker went off and she poured herself the first cup of the day. She poured Lyle some kibble in her bowl and started preparing oatmeal for herself.

"I wonder what's in store for today," she said as she poured a second cup of coffee. Lyle dropped a ball at her feet and backed up. "You never get tired of it, do you?" The RV is a bit small to play fetch so she opened the door and let Lyle out for some exercise. She made a beeline straight to the sheep yards and proceeded to roll in some dried sheep dung.

"Nice. You know what that will earn you!" Laughing, she opened the door to the clinic and Lyle pranced in, so proud of her accomplishment. Luckily, there was a nice big stainless steel tub for bathing so Mandy started warming some water for the bath ahead. Lyle was always good for her baths, having been bathed regularly since she was tiny due to her love of getting dirty.

While Mandy was lathering up Lyle, Gillian came in whistling a chipper tune. "Good morning, Doc. How are we? And what is that smell?"

"Lyle thought she would have a roll in the sheep dung out the back. It'll smell better shortly."

"She may have to stay in the clinic this morning to dry off. It's getting colder out there and you have to go out to Jim Moore's to pregnancy test some his cows. If Lyle is in the rolling mood, there's no telling what she'll find out there. Jim doesn't run the tightest ship, shall we say."

"Good idea. Two baths in one day would break a record. She can curl up with you here. How many are we testing?"

"It'll be about 10, but Jim tends to underestimate so you might want to double that."

"Gotcha." She had finished rinsing Lyle and was drying the

excess moisture when Lyle shook and water went everywhere. Then Lyle hopped out of the tub herself and made her way up to the front desk where she curled up on the dog bed behind the counter. She started to lick between each paw with such purpose, evidently attempting to erase all evidence of the bath as quickly as possible.

"Guess she's done with that!" Mandy said, laughing. "I'll grab some supplies for the farm call if you want to draw me a map for how to get there."

"Done and done," Gillian said. Mandy smiled. Gillian was an indispensable right hand. "Must be time for a cuppa before you go," Gillian said.

"Cuppa? Is that short for cup of tea?" asked Mandy.

"Sure is," replied Gillian.

"That'd be great. I didn't quite get that second cup of coffee and I just can't do much without my morning fix of caffeine." They settled down to steaming hot cups of tea and a few biscuits. "So what can you tell me about Jim Moore?"

"Well, he's pretty old school. He had a wife who smoothed his rough edges a bit but she died tragically in an automobile accident. He keeps to himself more or less now. He's very devout, so don't curse in front of him. His herd is his life now so he tends to do a very good job with them. He doesn't keep things non-cow-related very clean though. I think his wife did more of that and with her gone, he just focuses on the cattle."

"I see. A bit of a loner then." Mandy thought that at least he would likely be crossed off her list of suspects. Since she was new to town, basically everyone was on the list until they could be removed by either an alibi or no motive or both. It was a tricky and potentially dangerous way to learn all of the people of the community. She embraced the challenge.

Lyle was nudging Gillian, almost spilling the hot tea all over Gillian.

"Lyle. Off," said Mandy. "She can smell the milk and sugar in your tea and she wants some."

"I see. How did she become your sidekick anyway?" asked Gillian.

"I was vetting in the great Northwest and way up in the steeper country, I went on a farm visit. They had the most wonderful line of collies for herding their sheep. They are slightly taller and more agile than most that you will see. Plus, they have less fluffy coats. I fell in love with one of the six week old puppies when she broke loose from the pen, dropped a stone by my shoe, and started backing up while staring at me. She came home with me that day and literally has not left my side since then."

"That is truly love at first sight," said Gillian.

"Truthfully, Lyle would likely go home with anyone. She's not terribly loyal. If you can throw, she's yours," said Mandy.

"That is not true. I can see that she is extremely devoted to you.

She always maintains a sight-line of you, no matter what she is doing," said Gillian.

As they both finished their cups of tea, Mandy commented "I best be getting on the road then."

"Indeed because we have a full afternoon of appointments too."

Lyle tried to rush out the door with Mandy but Gillian held her back, refocusing her attention on a nice new tennis ball. Mandy got in the Jeep and checked to see what supplies Gillian had prepared. There was a full bottle of lube, large animal gloves, gumboots, a gown, a towel, and a clipboard. Some vets use ultrasound to check for pregnancy. Mandy and Anna had been trained before that technology became popular and neither had picked up the new skill. Mandy could see how if you were doing hundreds of cows per day that the ultrasound would come in handy. For ten to twenty here and there, she preferred manually checking them. It is slightly more accurate in some cases anyway. It had been a few months since she had last pregnancy tested. Once you know how though, you never forget.

As she drove out to the farm, she saw Fred walking Marge. She pulled over and rolled down her window.

"How is she doing, Fred?"

"Oh, much better already, Dr. Bell. Thanks again. I just hate it when she is upset."

"No problem. I was thinking of coming over for a haircut sometime this week. Are you open late any night? Gillian is keeping me pretty busy at the clinic."

"You are in luck. Tonight I can see you after the clinic is closed. Say, 5:30. Does that work?"

"Perfect. With all of this wind, my hair is getting unruly and I want to be ready for the Halloween Hoedown."

"Leave it to me. I can make you the belle of the ball."

"Oh, I don't know about that!"

"Trust me! It's nice to see a vet who likes to keep up her appearance. Don't get me wrong, I liked Anna. She wasn't much for spending a lot of time in front of the mirror," Fred said.

"I hear you. She was a rugged gal," said Mandy.

"I'll take you under my wing, honey," Fred said and winked at Mandy. He then started his walk with Marge again.

Mandy resumed driving, following Gillian's perfect instructions. The farm was down a long gravel road at the front of which stood an old western style gate with a wooden plank across the top that read "Moore & Sons." Mandy didn't remember Gillian mentioning anything about a son. Perhaps the plot would thicken after all.

As she opened the back of her Jeep and started donning the pregnancy testing apparel, Jim himself appeared from within the cow shed. "You must be Dr. Bell. I am Jim Moore and these are a few of my girls," he said pointing to the mooing ladies circling the round yard beside the shed. They appeared to be Jerseys though she couldn't tell since they were standing in the shade of the barn.

"Yes, nice to meet you. How many do we have today?"

"Eighteen."

"And do we want to know yes or no or do we need to know approximate age as well?"

"Just yes or no will do. I know when they were bred. I have all of my records here," he said, pulling out a very well-worn pocket notebook from the breast pocket of his overalls. "I have them listed by name but they also have numbers that correspond to their left ear tags. I can load up one at a time in the chute and we'll just take it slow and easy. I don't want any of them getting stressed."

"Righty-o. Let's get started."

Jim moved a few cows into the race toward the chute with the head stanchion. He locked them in the race and coaxed the first one into the stanchion, closing the neck brace. He closed the gate so the others couldn't move up while Mandy was checking the lead cow. Mandy climbed up on the platform, placing some lube in the cup she had attached with a belt at her hips. Her waterproof jacket helped keep her long glove up above her elbow so she could keep mostly clean through the morning.

She reached into the cow and felt for the uterus. She could feel a calf easily. "This one's pregnant," she said as she removed her arm.

"Excellent," said Jim as he recorded it in his book. He sprayed pink tail paint on her back and released her into the pen to the right of the chute using the swing gate he had rigged up. It was quite clever really. Standing in one spot, he could pull a rope to let a cow go straight, left or right. He had obviously spent a lot of time working on the shed and races. She could tell he was used to working by himself, just him and his cows. He let the next one through, locking her neck in the stanchion. "This one is, too," Mandy said as she got down from the platform.

"Wonderful." The process continued for the remaining 16 cows. Jim didn't really say much, obviously concentrating hard on the hope that all were pregnant. All but two were in calf. The two not in calf were marked with blue paint on their tails and they were released to the left paddock. Typically, farmers would cull the non-pregnant cows once they stopped lactating, but Mandy had a feeling Jim wasn't the culling type.

"What will happen to the barren cows?"

"Well, they are both still young so they will wait for the next mating season, only a few months away."

Mandy's eyebrows raised. A few months wasn't very long to wait to breed them again. Normally, cows are only bred to have calves in the Spring.

"Only a few months. Do you know something I don't?"

"I have split calving here so we calve twice a year. I supply

Crestview and a few neighboring towns with milk all year round."

"Ah. Of course. That system is quite clever for this area. You have grass almost all year round so it works. I had a few farmers that did that over on the East coast."

Mandy thought about the genius of this system for Jim. With one hundred percent devotion to his herd, he was the perfect farmer to have year round milking and twice a year calving. He was likely one of the only farmers in the area that had a split calving scheme. She wondered how many were in his Spring calving versus his Fall calving herd. Though it made the feeding a little trickier in harder years, it meant that any cow not in calf could have another chance with the other portion of the herd. Most people had enough trouble keeping track of calving once a year. Jim, on the other hand, had all the time in the world to watch over his girls. He had a herd of only 150 which made it a manageable number for one person.

All in all, Mandy could see that he was a very devoted farmer. The cows were in very good condition and they were very well-mannered, obviously being treated gently from birth. You can always tell a herd that has been subjected to rough handling. They tend to be a lot less trusting of being examined. Mandy had encountered all kinds of herds in her travels as a vet.

Jim was setting up the gates to release the tested cows into a larger paddock to graze. It makes a huge difference for cattle not to feel like they are locked up before, during, and after being handled. The next time they need to be yarded, they won't associate it with long periods of waiting and stress which will keep them easy to handle.

When Jim returned, Mandy asked, "How long have you been farming?"

"Oh, I inherited the Moore and Sons farm from my father. My brothers didn't want to carry on the torch and I have loved this land ever since I was knee high to a grasshopper. I have never known anything other than dairy farming."

"It shows that this is in your blood. You are a very gentle handler."

"I started the split calving system with this farm. I don't have much else in the world. I put everything into making this farm the best that I can make it."

"Who will take over when you retire? Do you have children?"

"No. My wife, may she rest in peace, couldn't have children. We put all of our parental love into raising calves. We enjoyed it so much. I'm not sure what will happen to the farm when I retire, though I can't imagine doing anything else. Retirement would be hard for me."

"I can understand that."

Jim stared off in the distance, looking as if he was worlds away. Mandy took off her gear and started cleaning up using the buckets of warm soapy water Jim had placed at the foothold of the shed. She didn't have too much to clean since it was a small number of cows today. They were so calm that not one had pooped when they were being examined.

"Do you have a bathroom? All this running water…"

"Around the corner. We had set up this portion of the dairy shed to be for our kids," Jim said and went silent. It was clear that he missed his wife and maybe wished that things had gone quite differently.

While Mandy was heading to the toilet, she noticed a very fancy dartboard cabinet, scoreboard, and supplies. She took the opportunity to be nosey. In the shelf next to the board were very high quality darts with steel tips and a scorpion on the flights at the other end. They were accompanied by a matching carry case. Obviously Jim was a pretty avid dart player so Mandy made a mental note to check into his whereabouts on the evening of the murder so she could rule him out.

After using the facilities, Mandy came around the corner to find

Jim doing some paperwork at a desk. He was concentrating hard

and she could see that he was updating his records after the

results of today's testing.

"That seems like a nice dart board in there," Mandy said,

pointing behind her.

"Yep, it's my one vice. Since my days are pretty much devoid of

people, I made myself start going to the dart club once a week

for a little human interaction. I started getting really into it. It's

a nice stress relief. Shame about old Buck. Man could he throw

a mean dart. I never have managed to beat him."

"I have heard that he was the champion around here. I suppose

now you might be next in line."

"To me, it's the thrill of the game, not really the results. I'm not

very competitive."

"Don't take this the wrong way, but I am trying to investigate the

murder. I feel somehow like I owe it to Anna to clear this town of the bad vibe the murder has brought. Do you have any ideas as to who may have wanted him dead? You guys must have all gotten pretty close playing darts together."

"I understand your question. I really liked Anna so in her honor I will answer. I can't really say that I noticed any major strife, at least not about darts. We all played within the rules and respect for a good game. The one thing that I noticed about him was his interest in the ladies. There was always someone different waiting for him."

"I see. Thanks. And just for the record, can anyone vouch for your whereabouts the night of the murder?"

"Nope, just the cows. I really don't get out much at all. You'll have to take my word for it that I didn't have anything to do with it."

"Ok, thanks. I apologize but I am just being thorough. I will see you next time."

"Sure thing ma'am," he said as he kept working on his records.

Chapter Twelve

Mandy returned back to the clinic to have some lunch with Lyle
and Gillian. It looked like the afternoon appointments had filled
up. Mandy found that whenever the seasons changed, she would
be busier in the clinic no matter where she was in the country.
She had a theory that changes in weather brought out issues with
pets.

"Dr. Bell, the lawyer came by from Anna's estate and said that
we need to find the deed for the house. They have a copy of the
clinic deed on file. The house deed must be somewhere in the
house. I have looked everywhere here," Gillian said.

"I see. I will go out there and have a look around to see what I
can find. How soon did he say he needed it?"

"*She*, actually. She said it wasn't urgent but she's trying to get
all the ducks in a row so you can choose to do whatever you
would like with the properties."

"I will have a look when I get a chance."

"Do you want me to go with you?"

"Nah. I think I remember how to get there. I should be fine."

"Let me know if you change your mind."

"Ok. What do we have on this afternoon?"

"A little of this and a little of that. It should go by fairly quickly. Must be time for a cuppa tea."

Mandy and Gillian settled in for a quick cup of tea and a few biscuits. Lyle took her spot on the floor under the table. She kept sighing as if she was losing her patience waiting for some biscuit samples. Mandy sneaked a piece to her.

"How did it go at Jim's?" asked Gillian.

"Fine. Sad about his wife."

"She died so young. The whole town rallied to help him through that. He has put all of his grief into those cows."

"It shows because his cows are so well behaved. You know, they are his alibi for the night of the murder."

"What? You don't suspect him?"

"I noticed he had some darts and asked him about it. Apparently he competed with Buck at the competitions and never could beat him. I was just being thorough to make sure he wasn't involved in the murder," said Mandy.

"Fair enough. I didn't know that he was a dart player. He keeps to himself so I don't know that much about him," said Gillian.

"Even though the cows can't truly give him an alibi, I think I believe that he wasn't involved. I need to keep looking."

Lyle was bored by all of this talking. The bells tied to the front door rang to indicate someone had entered. Lyle was excited to have something else to check out. She raced up the front to find Sonya, the local librarian, coming in with her Boston terrier. The dogs sniffed each other's bottoms. Both their tails were wagging so the greeting was non-threatening.

"What seems to be the issue with," Mandy said as she looked down at the file Gillian had given her, "Bubba?"

"He just keeps scooting his bottom on the carpet. I think it's those glands again," said Sonya, rubbing Bubba's little squashed face as he grunted in ecstasy.

"That's an easy fix. Let's put him up on the table and have a look," Mandy said. "Lyle, go to your matt."

Lyle left them as she was instructed to. As Sonya reached down to pick up her little black and white Boston, a loud click came from her knee.

"Oh my, what was that?" Mandy exclaimed.

"Aw, that's just my peg leg. I was in a massive car accident a few years back and they weren't that advanced with the prosthetics yet. This one works well enough for me so I haven't replaced it. It does click when I bend it. It can be kind of noisy sometimes in the library. Luckily, all of my patrons are used to it." Bubba gave her a big juicy kiss on her face as if to say she was perfect for him just the way she was.

"I see. Forgive me for not being more sensitive, I didn't know. I am so trained to worry about joint issues in an animal when I hear clicking during a physical exam. I don't often hear it coming from their owners."

"No problem," said Sonya.

"So, you operate the library. I have been meaning to come in and set up a membership. I mostly read on my Kindle. It's so portable and convenient. Sometimes, though, I just need to read a good old fashioned book and feel the pages in my fingers as I turn them. Plus some of the books are not available as an ebook."

"I completely understand. What type of books do you read? Can I help you find something?"

"I seem to be on a history kick at the moment. I have been trying to read one book about every president of the USA. I've been working on it on and off for a few years."

As Mandy and Sonya conversed, Mandy made a quick task of emptying Bubba's anal glands which were indeed full. Bubba received a few treats as a reward for being so good. He was standing proudly at Sonya's feet.

"I, too, enjoy history. If you give me a list of which presidents you have read, I can start finding some books to fill in your gaps. What a noble effort. I have read tons of history. Focusing on presidents only is a smart way to get a sense of American history."

"It's been a fun way to fill in the gaps of knowledge I had of our nation's past. Plus, the perspective of history can change if you are reading it with one main character in mind."

Bubba let out a huge burp. It was so loud, he shocked himself into sitting down and letting out a little toot.

"Don't you just love Bostons?" asked Sonya.

"They do have their charm," giggled Mandy.

"Anna always thought Bubba was such a manly little guy," she said as she petted Bubba's head. He responded by puffing his chest out. "Such a shame about her. I will surely miss her at the library. She and I were in high school together and we've always had a special bond."

"She was a special gal. I miss her, too. And it's kind of weird to be living her life so to speak."

"I can see that. Oh, the trouble we would get in to. She would be shocked to hear of Buck's murder. He had a bit of a thing for her in high school, and I'm not sure he ever got over it. Though, she was the apple of a few boy's eyes. She had kind of a raw beauty. Around the Midwest, you don't just want a pretty-faced wife, you also want one who can throw a calf and drive a tractor. We always thought she would marry. Instead, she remained a spinster like me. That kind of made us peas in a pod. Of course, the closest person who came to getting her to settle was Dennis. I don't know whatever came of him."

"Dennis? I think he is in town visiting with Fred."

"That could be. I don't know. Neither one would be the type to come to the library and I don't get out much so…"

"If it's the same Dennis, you'll see him at the Hoedown. He is playing softball I believe."

"Perhaps I will. You are doing a very good job learning the small town rule of knowing a little bit about everyone's activities." They looked down to see Bubba taking the opportunity to pee on the trashcan. "If only I could stop this little guy from marking," said Sonya.

"When was he neutered?" asked Mandy.

"I don't know. When I adopted him, he was already neutered and they weren't sure how old he was."

"Let me have a quick look under his hood."

Mandy popped Bubba back up on the table for Sonya, so her knee wouldn't pop again. She held Bubba up to look for a neuter incision and couldn't quite find one. She felt around and thought she could feel a retained testicle in the groin area.

"I think this may be the problem. He may not have been neutered at all. Some dogs have what's called cryptorchidism which is where the testicles do not descend to where they should but stay somewhere between where they develop embryologically and where they are supposed to end up. I think I can feel one right here. Most vets won't remove the descended one if they can't locate the other. So, he may have both nestled in his abdomen area somewhere. They would still produce enough testosterone to cause marking, but not enough to allow mating. And, if we leave them in there, they will certainly cause him trouble sooner or later, like cancer."

"Wow. You figured all of that out just now. What do we do?"

asked Sonya.

"If my theory is correct, we can fix it with surgery. It would be handy to run an ultrasound on him but we don't have one here. We can start with the suspicious lump I can feel, and if it is a testicle, then I will go searching for the other. I've seen this once before in an adopted animal so I always check now."

"Sounds like a plan. Do you think it will help with his marking?"

"It may help some. He is old enough where the behavior may outlast the hormones, if you know what I mean. More importantly, we can prevent cancer."

"Ok, I'll coordinate with Gillian for an appointment. You know, you should be a sleuth. That was some pretty impressive intuition."

"Well, I am sort of looking into this murder. Having a murderer on the loose wrecks the idyllic setting of this town."

Sonya gave her a wink and said, "I will keep that a secret for your own protection. If I can help in anyway, let me know."

"Thanks. I will."

Chapter Thirteen

After finishing up the appointments for the afternoon, Mandy grabbed a quick snack and a cup of coffee at the RV. Lyle took the opportunity to point out that perhaps she should have an early supper. She laid down in front of her food bowl and placed her head on the rim, looking up with big brown eyes. Mandy placed a scoop of kibble in the dog bone-shaped bowl. Mandy sat at the dinette in the RV and looked over her list of suspects. Since learning of Jim's passion for darts, she added him. He seemed like a very hard-working, honest man yet he had to be considered since he did not have an alibi. The competitive nature of humans could be unpredictable. She also wondered if the death of his wife in the automobile accident was important. She would look that up in the archives at the library with Sonya.

She put her pencil down and turned on the shower to warm up the water. She figured she would grab a short shower because no matter how much gear you wear when you work around cattle, the smell of cow pats penetrates one's skin. She knew Fred would not appreciate her eau de beast. Tonight was the night to go over to Fred's for her much needed haircut. After working hard this morning pregnancy testing, she was ready to sit back and have someone look after her. The search at Anna's house for the deed would have to wait until another day.

She stepped out of the RV once she had dried her hair with a towel. The sun was just starting to make its way down in the sky to rest for the night and she couldn't help relating to the need to wind down. Tonight might be an early night.

Arriving at the salon, she was greeted by a happy little Marge. Despite the fact that Fred kept the heat rather warm in the shop, Marge was wearing a little pink polka dot dress. Fred must be cold-blooded because within seconds she was too warm for her jacket and her sweater. She stripped down to just her turtleneck to avoid sweating.

Dennis came from out the back. He was only wearing a T-shirt.

"Hi Mandy. I'll just go get Fred for you. He is just pulling some scones out of the oven. He is on a real baking kick right now, preparing for the bake-off at the Halloween Hoedown."

"Thanks. Good to see you again. That must be the heavenly smell."

"I sure can't complain about the smells. He's been baking a new batch every chance he gets and I get to sample them for critiquing purposes. It's a hard life!"

"It sure is warm in here."

"Fred keeps it warm all year round in here. He has a passion for rare cacti and they don't do well unless it's above 70 degrees. I can never wear more than a short-sleeved shirt in here. His clients learn to layer so they can dress down upon arrival."

"Ah, that explains it."

Dennis disappeared out the back. Fred had a little apartment attached to the salon which had a kitchenette, a bathroom, a living room, and a bedroom. Living at the salon meant he could see appointments throughout the day while still tending to his cacti and cooking feats. It also gave the salon a very welcoming feel, as if people were invited into Fred's home.

"Try these," Fred said, handing Mandy a freshly cooked scone. "These are cranberry and pistachio. Here is some butter. The butter is the real deal. I get it from Ben King's dairy farm here in Crestview. It's one of the secrets to perfect scones - real, old-fashioned butter. All these health nuts these days use whipped butter substitutes and wonder why nothing seems to satiate their taste buds. Anyway, enough about butter. I could go on forever about that. I have to stop myself. Let's talk about my other passion, hair. What are you looking for?"

As they all sat around, tasting the scones, Fred produced some style books. He was neatly dressed in a pair of plaid slacks and some Sperry shoes. His shirt was a pressed short-sleeved button up shirt that matched a stripe in the plaid in his pants. He sat in a chair next to Mandy with his legs crossed at the ankles like a charm school graduate. One of the books he handed her was specifically for curly hair, like Mandy's. While they were sitting on Fred's pink corduroy overstuffed chairs, Marge was doing her best to try to convince someone, anyone to give her a morsel of a scone. Dennis reached down with a Marge-sized bit. Mandy noticed that there was a tan line on his left wrist where a watch or bracelet must normally be.

"Have you lost your watch?" Mandy asked.

"Hmmm?" Dennis replied, focused on sneaking morsels to Marge.

"Your watch, have you lost it?"

"Oh, um." He retracted his left arm and covered his wrist with his right hand, rubbing it as if to make the tan line go away. "I took it off yesterday to wash someone's hair for Fred. I must have forgotten to put it back on."

"Oh. Ok. Well just don't feed Marge too much. I wouldn't want to see her for a tummy ache tomorrow," Mandy replied.

"I think I'm going to go to the house side and watch the game," Dennis said. "Nice to see you again."

"You, too," Mandy said.

"Well, let's look at some of these pictures," said Fred. "So what are you imagining?"

"I hadn't given it much thought. I trust you. If you have something in mind, just go for it. I just can't have anything too high maintenance. I don't own a straightener or blow dryer. In fact, I don't even use a brush. I just shower, add a little product, run my fingers through it, and let my hair air dry. I used to fight my hair and now I just let it go."

"I see. Come and sit in the chair here and let me run my hands through your hair while I ponder."

"Sounds good. I just washed it. You may need to wet it again since it dried a little on the way here."

"As the greatest artists say I'll just remove what shouldn't be here and what will be left is the perfect haircut," Fred said, already in deep concentration. He pursed his lips as his fingers moved through her hair. His forehead wrinkled as his thought process unfolded. All of the tension in his face finally subsided and he started to spray her hair down, to tame the parts that had started to dry. Mandy's thick hair hadn't dried underneath at all yet.

Mandy looked around at Fred's domain while he worked. The salon was decorated with a rich flare of Victorian colors and textures. The window treatments were thick drapes of lace and taupe damask. Candelabras were mounted on the walls between the silver fleur-de-lis patterned, embossed mirrors. Mandy could see that hair was not his only outlet for his creativity. It was like being in an artist's studio, seeing what kinds of ambiance gave them inspiration.

A selection of scissors and combs rested on the antique vanity below the mirror in front of Mandy. Fred selected the gold handled pair of scissors and an ivory comb and started to trim the backside of Mandy's head. Since she couldn't see what he was doing, all she could measure his progress by was the clumps of hair piling up on the floor. It had been a while since she got a trim, so she knew a fair amount would have to come off. Mandy reached her hand into her leather satchel on her lap and pulled out a red gummy bear, slipping it into her mouth.

"And what was that?" Fred asked.

"A little slice of heaven," Mandy replied with a smile. "Want one?" She opened her palm to reveal several little gummy treats.

"Oh, a woman after my own heart. Some people think adults are a little too old to eat gummy bears. They happen to still be one of my favorites. Don't mind if I do. I like the green ones."

"Perfect, I'll save you all of the green ones. I always leave them for last."

"Deal. As I am shaping the back, I wonder how you prefer the length. Do you often wear it up?"

"Sometimes, but if it is short and I need to have it out of my face, I can just wear a hat."

"Tisk, tisk. I suppose you are a working girl, though. Hats leave hat hair and no one looks good in that. Uglier than homemade sin, some might say."

"Well, when I am calving a cow, I don't really care about the style."

"Fair enough. We are getting somewhere here. It's all about feeling how the curls will want to sit."

"It feels lighter already. Thank you. So, do you see most of the town through the salon?"

"More or less. Some people do their own grooming at home. You know the type. The number 40 blade with a guard, shave the whole family on the back porch. All the boys with matching haircuts."

"Yep, I think I know the style."

"Did you know Buck Dawson?" Mandy inquired

"I think it's heart breaking. I never saw that coming. He'd come in here from time to time for a trim. He kept himself pretty manicured. I think he thought of himself as a bit of a ladies man, though I don't think he was serious about anyone," Fred said while spraying Mandy's hair to keep it wet.

"Hmmm, a ladies man. Any particular recent relationships you can remember? You seem to have a finger on the pulse."

"Not that I am aware of. He was pretty private. Came in, got his hair cut the same way and didn't say a whole lot to me. He was a member of the dart club and they seemed to meet over a few friendly beers. They might know something. Why do you ask? Are you investigating the murder?"

"Sort of. I can't help but wonder what would inspire someone in this little town to murder someone and since I saw it for myself, I can't seem to let it go until it is solved."

"I can understand that. Just don't step on the toes of the law."

Fred had been busily trimming Mandy's mane to remove the rest of the hair that didn't go with his vision. The layers nicely framed her face but were short in the back to take away from some of the density of her curls.

"Ok, I'd like to let it dry a little naturally and then we will have the final touches. In the meantime, would you like a coffee, tea, or pop? I have a cappuccino machine."

"Oh, a cappuccino would be fantastic."

"I'll make you one. These new one cup brew machines are simply divine. Do you have one?"

"No, I have an old school coffee maker. It does have a timer so I'm not a total dinosaur."

"Here is the cup of joe. Enjoy."

"Oh, this is delicious. I may have to invest in one of those machines. You have some interesting gear here. Why the cacti and growlights?"

"I became a little obsessed with the Southwest a few years back. The Midwest can be so plain Jane. I decided to start my own desert oasis."

"It's very neat. You're place is gorgeous. Have you thought about doing interior design?"

"It's not exactly a hot market here for that," said Fred. "My grandmother always encouraged my sense of fashion. My parents not so much."

"You were close to your grandmother?"

"She practically raised me. My parents were salt of the earth people and didn't like my flamboyance. I spent most of my time with my grandmother instead of fighting it. She was an artist and a pillar in this community. You probably haven't heard of her. She is Crestview's little claim to fame, though. She painted landscapes of the Midwest and scenes of our town. Kind of like Norman Rockwell. She was the first artist to capture this area of the country and make it cool to have a tractor painting in your house."

"That is very neat. What was her name?"

"LouAnne Devor."

"I haven't heard of her. What a legacy. You must be very proud."

"I am. She had a way of seeing the world like no one else could. Everybody loved her," said Fred.

"I could see that," said Mandy.

"How about you? Are you enjoying yourself here? With the exception of finding a body?"

"It's nice. People seem friendly."

"It's a welcoming little town. All this talking has allowed your hair to dry quickly. Let me just take a few little pieces of from this side and you are officially re-styled."

Once Fred had finished, he held a mirror up so Mandy could see the back.

"Wow, that is really fabulous. Even I can manage this style."

"Next time we might want to think of a few lowlights and highlights. They always look so lovely with curly hair. But this is a very good start."

"Indeed. I've never done color. In your hands, I could trust trying it out. Thanks so much. I will definitely be saving all of my green gummy bears just for you."

"Lovely. It's a deal."

Fred saw Mandy to the door. "Thanks again and say goodbye to

Dennis for me."

"Sure thing, dear," Fred replied as he swept up the tendrils of

curly hair on the floor.

Chapter Fourteen

The next day, Mandy decided to get up early and make a trip to Anna's house to start sorting through some things before the Hoedown. Mandy would shower when she returned to the RV. She grabbed a breakfast sandwich for herself and gave Lyle some kibble. Lyle was excited for a break in the usual routine. Mandy and Lyle loaded up in the Jeep before the sun had even risen.

Arriving at the house, she saw that someone had been carefully putting Anna's mail on the landing in the front screen porch instead of in the mailbox. How thoughtful, Mandy thought. See, it just doesn't add up. Why would someone murder anyone in this town where people are concerned about mail piling up? I guess it only takes one to ruin it for everyone else, she thought.

She brought the mail in and put it on the table. Not seeing anything pressing in the stack, she decided to start sorting through stuff in the living room first. It was quiet in the house without Jimbo and Emma there anymore. She was pleased with the decision to move them to the clinic. They would be so lonely here. Plus, it was getting quite entertaining that anytime anyone turned a sink on to wash their hands, Emma came thundering into the room to jump in the sink. She had quite the obsession with running water. She would sit in the sink and alternately take sips and paw at the stream of water. Clients enjoyed watching her.

In the living room, Mandy decided to sort items into two piles: those which she could donate and those that were too personal and should be dealt with individually. Her overall goal was to find the deed so she would start in locations she thought that might be. First, she came across a number of books which she decided would be best donate to the library. She would call Sonya about the arrangements. She needed to get up there to look into the death of Jim Moore's wife anyway so she might stop in sometime in the next few days. A few of the titles looked interesting to her so she put those near her keys to read before sending them to the library. She made a mental note to start

saving boxes from the clinic deliveries to help with transporting

and sorting.

Next, Mandy came across some photo albums. She went to the

kitchen and decided to make a cup of instant coffee to help

inspire a few hours of sorting. As she settled on the couch with

Lyle at her feet, Mandy picked up the first album. Before she

even started looking at the photos, a stack of letters fell onto her

lap. She opened them up.

Each letter was to Anna from Dennis. It was clear that Dennis

had a particular obsession with Anna and she must not have

reciprocated. The letters spanned over several years. Clearly

Dennis continued sending them, despite the fact that not a single

one indicated that Anna had shown any interest. The strange

thing is: why would Anna keep them if she didn't entertain some

sort of possibility?

Mandy pulled out the albums to see if she could find some

answers. She found one album that seemed to feature Dennis in quite a few photos. It must have meant that at some point they were an item. She thought back to what Sonya had said about Dennis being the only one who might have convinced Anna to marry. She wondered what the real story was here. Was it a bad break up, a case of unrequited love, a high school romance revisited? She would have to check into it further by asking Sonya and maybe trying to talk to Dennis.

Mandy then went to the next shelf which had yearbooks from college and high school. To reminisce for a while and give her brain a break, she pulled out the college yearbooks. In it, she found pictures of her and Anna. Since they were nearly always together in vet school, every time one was pictured, the other was too. What a time they had. They were both overachievers and always signing up to help with research studies for a little extra rent money. They had both come from humble beginnings and needed to find as many ways as possible to make money through vet school.

One time, they took part in a study where they had to take shifts through the night to watch cows calve. The study was trying to test the effect of ad lib feeding in the last trimester of pregnancy on the ease of calving for the cow. They had to sit in a little portable trailer with flashlights and keep checking on the cows through the night. Poor Anna slipped on a cow pie and landed in the mud. It was a cold night for her since they had no power in the trailer and she got quite wet in that mud puddle. They sure had a blast, drinking coffee and chatting quietly through the night. It was exciting to be part of a research project even if it wasn't a very lucrative post. They oversaw the most calvings out of anyone in the research study. They also signed up for more shifts than anyone else so it may have been an unfair competition. They both found it was a great time to study and test each other so it only enhanced their overachieving tendencies.

Smiling, Mandy returned to the task at hand. She pulled down some of Anna's high school yearbooks. She was hoping to get some insight into the Dennis and Anna dilemma. She found that both of them served on the high school newspaper staff. Mandy wondered whether late nights editing the paper started a bond between them. Even though she was trying to find the deed, she couldn't resist looking into angles that might help with the murder investigation. And what if somehow the Dennis and Anna connection added to the murder?

She found a picture in their senior year where Dennis and Anna were standing proudly outside the school with the rest of the staff of the newspaper. Mandy studied the photo closely. In the byline, she noticed a familiar name, Buck Dawson. He too was on the staff of the newspaper. This meant they all knew each other. She would have to look into that as well. Her list of leads was growing, even though this was supposed to be her day off from the case to sort Anna's house.

She sat back on the couch to have her sandwich. Lyle obediently sat at her feet with her intense eyes staring at Mandy and her sandwich. The sandwich had cheese in it and Lyle's fetch obsession was only matched by her affinity for anything made of milk. Mandy tore a little piece of cheese off and put it on the bridge of Lyle's nose. Lyle stared, cross-eyed, waiting for her cue.

"Wait, wait," pause, "Ok." Lyle took her command and tossed her head up to throw the piece of cheese in the air before catching it. As a Border collie, Lyle could learn tricks easily and enjoyed the challenge of any form of training.

"Well, maybe we should put these in piles and go on home. We have some investigating to do." Mandy said to Lyle who stood up and stretched her full body as if she knew exactly what Mandy had just said and was preparing to leave.

Mandy gathered her things together and locked the front door with Lyle right beside her. Lyle hopped into her side of the Jeep and started panting with excitement. Even though they did a fair amount of traveling, Lyle never tired of the anticipation of a ride in the truck. One time, they had been driving through a busy city in traffic and Lyle couldn't curtail her enthusiasm. She was bouncing and barking with each truck that went by in the oncoming traffic lane. Their lane wasn't moving at all which made the trucks going past seem so much faster. This continued with no break in the action until Mandy smelled a foul smell and opted to get off the highway to investigate. They pulled over to a gas station and Mandy determined that the source of the smell was that Lyle had expressed her anal glands all over the seat of the Jeep. It took Mandy months to get rid of that smell. The upshot was that by getting off the highway, they found an alternate route to avoid the traffic.

With the few items that she might peruse at home all loaded in the jeep, Mandy and Lyle made their way back to the clinic to get ready for the Halloween Hoedown. The sun had risen, shining warm rays over the sleeping town. These warm days would soon be replaced by cold, dark winter mornings. Mandy absolutely loved winter and couldn't help getting excited about the wind-down to winter.

Chapter Fifteen

They arrived back to the RV and Mandy took a nice hot shower to get ready for the day ahead at the Hoedown while Lyle snoozed on the bed. Lyle was a highly intelligent, active Border collie who knew the morning routine of Mandy so well that she had figured out how long she could nap without missing anything. Being a small area, her spot on the bed was a perfect vantage point to monitor any activities inside or outside the RV.

Taking significantly less time in the shower with her new haircut, Mandy shocked Lyle when Mandy reappeared so soon after entering the bathroom. Lyle leapt out of bed and trotted toward the kitchen dinette, trying to score a second breakfast since the first had been so early.

"I see. You want another helping?" Mandy asked Lyle. Lyle nudged her bowl with her freckled snout. She had a perfect beauty mark on her face that made her look like a model dog. Mandy consented by giving Lyle a snack of kibble. Happy with her second breakfast, Lyle curled up under the dinette table while Mandy sipped her coffee. She was pleased with her new hairdo and excited to showcase it at the Halloween Hoedown.

She pulled out the list of possible suspects compiled so far. She added Dennis. The way he hid his wrist after she pointed out that the watch was missing concerned her. He couldn't have known that she was investigating the murder. Being a visitor to town, he had no reason to hide anything from her. She was still perplexed by his secrecy. She still needed to look into Howie, the injured bull rider. There was also any unpaid debts of Buck's. After talking to Fred, she also needed to explore the females of the community. Perhaps there was a love interest or a jealous husband even. Then there was the dart club to investigate. Her glasses slid clear to the end of her nose as she chewed on the pencil.

She had her work cut out for her today at the Hoedown.

To re-fuel for the festivities after waking up so early, Mandy ate an extra-large bowl of oatmeal. Although she knew there would be food there, she was also prepared to hit the ground running, trying to focus on the investigation. Once she finished her breakfast, she went outside with Lyle to check on the weather situation and let Lyle go potty.

"Sunny with a breeze," Mandy said to herself. Almost understanding, Lyle flopped over with her belly up to catch some sun rays. With Fall upon Crestview, soon there would not be many sunny days. Lyle wanted to enjoy them.

While Lyle soaked up some vitamin D, Mandy went back inside to gather her belongings for the day. She would need her softball mitt, a hat, a light jacket, and some emergency gummy bears for energy. Planning to take Lyle along, she would need a way to tie her up somewhere during the softball game. She didn't want any team to have an unfair advantage as Lyle was definitely the world's best short stop. Though not perfect at getting the ball to a base to stop a runner, no ball would ever get past her. Lyle would go through any extreme to catch a thrown object. One time, someone had thrown a tire onto a silage stack while Lyle was watching. She saw the tire and ran after it, catching it in her mouth. Unfortunately, Lyle fractured a tooth in her upper jaw catching the tire. Mandy removed the tooth since the root had become exposed and painful. Despite one less tooth, there was nothing she wouldn't try to catch. Mandy felt bad sometimes because she knew Lyle would much rather be herding sheep than playing fetch. Having never settled down, Mandy had yet to be able to provide sheep for her herding dog. Maybe that would change someday, if she could only solve this murder.

Since costumes were encouraged at the Hoedown, Mandy pulled out the special outfit she had made for Lyle. Mandy didn't want to be in costume so she figured she could still show town spirit if Lyle took one for the team. Mandy fitted her little wings that were held on with a harness. The wings were an iridescent lace that mimicked an insect wing perfectly. The harness had black and gold stripes and the antennae completed the bee suit. Lyle's extreme energy and attention to all things moving made a bee costume a suitable choice.

Mandy went into the clinic to make sure everything was squared away. Though Gillian would have done a thorough job last night and Mandy knew there were no animals in the hospital, she wanted to just do a walk through. Although Emma and Jimbo were current live-in residents, clinics were like living beings, even with no animals in it. There was any number of things that could go wrong or stop working, more than just a house. Over the years of working in so many different kinds of clinics, she had seen all kinds of mishaps. One time, she had known of a clinic that lost thousands of dollars because the fridge stopped working and all of the vaccines went off. All looked well here, though. She gave Emma a drink at the sink and freshened up their bowl of crunchies.

As she was checking the front desk, she saw the message light blinking. Everybody from town would be at the Hoedown today.

Still, she thought she'd better check to see what the message was. She hit play and heard Dennis asking if he could meet with her sometime to discuss a few personal items of Anna's that he'd like to take off her hands. She wrote down his number and put it on her desk of things to do when she returned to work the next day.

With the clinic, Jimbo, and Emma all squared away, Mandy and Lyle started their short walk to the town fairgrounds. Lyle was starting to learn the layout of town and she pranced along, curious about where they were going today. They had never turned down this road before. The trust between Lyle and Mandy was so intense that Lyle never showed fear of anything new. Mandy had led her all over the country, always making sure Lyle was comfortable and happy. In exchange, Mandy never had to feel like the new kid on the block anywhere she moved because her constant companion would always make her feel welcome on her first day at a new job.

Mandy pondered how people could live without an animal. They provide such unconditional love that rivals no other. In her whole adult life, she had been without an animal for a total period of six months. It was during a portion of her veterinary training and she had just lost a cat due to old age and hadn't yet found a suitable new pet. Other than that, she had always had at least one pet, if not several. Sometimes they were not even pets. The hobby of wildlife rehabilitation had provided many transient animals in her life. Usually they came in groups during the breeding season. At one point, she had seven baby squirrels she was bottle feeding. It was almost easier to raise multiple animals of the same species because the likelihood of imprinting decreased, compared to a single orphaned animal. Only once had Mandy inadvertently imprinted an infant animal. The raccoon had come in late in the season and she had no others his age to raise the little guy with. She tried everything to teach the raccoon to be normal. She even wore a mask so he never saw her face. He ended up being released at a conservation area where he could be looked after by the rangers. He needed supplement feeding for a few years until he caught on to what kinds of food he could eat in the wild. The rangers let her know some years later that he had finally had raccoons of his own and was integrated into the population. His only vestige of the earlier imprinting was that he had a strange admiration with fuzzy slippers. He would take them if someone mistakenly left their slippers within reach of his mischievous little hands. It made sense that he had bonded with slippers since Mandy had worn a version of plush footwear during the rehab process. When he was starting to explore, he would follow her feet since that was all he could see he was little.

As they strolled down the street, Mandy was smiling thinking of that little raccoon. It was evident the whole town had come out for the festivities. People were milling about talking, while others were busily preparing booths and stands for the events. Everybody seemed so relaxed and happy. Taking a break from harvesting was a big deal for the townspeople. They had been working 17 hour days to try to bring in as much as possible before the weather turned. Many of the men she saw looked like they were holding back a yawn from the exhaustion they carried. It was nice to see that, despite the pressing farming responsibilities, people were able to take time out for community morale.

Mandy smiled as Lyle sniffed along the road. Not typically reliant on sense of smell, Border collies more often used their keen eyesight and hearing to explore their surroundings. However, Mandy knew that there would be livestock at this event and she suspected that Lyle had picked up on that and was trying to find their whereabouts. Mandy, on the other hand, could smell lots of yummy food. The oatmeal was not as filling in the presence of street food.

As a treat for being such a good dog, Mandy decided the livestock tent was the first place they would go. She checked the little map tacked up at the center of the main yard to the fairgrounds.

Chapter Sixteen

"Hey Mandy. Hi Lyle. Pleasure to see you two. How's the hair style feeling this morning?" asked Fred.

"I like that it is less maintenance. Thanks so much." replied Mandy.

"Love the bee costume. Glad to see you are getting into the spirit. You guys look like you are on a mission. What do you want to go look at?"

"Well, I think Lyle would like to check out the sheep in the livestock area." Lyle sat and perked her ears up in agreement.

"I certainly won't be accompanying you for that. I have on my new cashmere sweater today and it is simply not compatible with livestock." He preened his sweater by brushing off non-existent lint from his shoulder. The salmon color of the sweater matched his socks perfectly. Mandy figured it was important for a hair stylist to have fashion under control at all times. It was like a veterinarian having a stunningly healthy animal. Public image is free advertising.

"We understand. We will see you at the softball game. I hope you brought a change of clothes."

"Sure did. I wouldn't want to get any blemishes on this outfit. I have a cheer-leading outfit ready for later."

Mandy laughed and they bid farewell for now. Lyle happily stayed close to Mandy as they made their way to the animals. The tent wasn't huge but there were pigs, sheep, cattle, and a few goats. Mandy saw Jim by a few of his cattle. Though there were 4H kids here with their show cattle, adults were also there with some stock, networking and comparing farming tales. Some of the grain farms in the area ran a herd of cattle as well to diversify their assets. Most of the grain produced in Crestview was eventually fed to cattle somewhere in the country or used for human-grade products like corn syrup. The climate in the area and rich, black soil provided acres of land suitable for crops to feed the whole nation most years. Spirits were high this year because there had been no major droughts or flooding so the harvest was turning out to be bountiful.

Lyle and Mandy arrived at the sheep pens. There were neatly trimmed rams and ewes of a few different breeds, including Dorsets, Leicesters, and Romneys. Lyle's eyes were focused intensely on a group of three sheep in a pen. She hunkered down and watched them through the lowest rung of the gates.

"That's a good looking dog you have there. Does she work?" asked a man in a plaid flannel shirt with wool pants and a pair of well-worn gumboots. He was leaning over the fence behind the group of sheep and picking at his nails with a pocket knife.

"I've never had the time to work her. She has the instincts for sure. She is from a long line of tested sheep herders. She was just a pup when I got her from a big sheep station out west. She was raised on milk and sheep livers. She's a definite throw back to the old school sheep dog."

"She is a beauty, even with a bee costume on. I would love to work her some time with my sheep and see what she's made of."

"Well, I'm Dr. ..." Mandy started.

"Bell, I know. I'm Luke. I run a few hundred sheep on the west side of town. I'm sure you'll come out there sometime. I don't tend to need a vet often. I know who to call if I do."

They shook hands and Mandy thought perhaps that would make a great extra-curricular activity for Lyle. Mandy never thought about putting roots down anywhere before. However, this town certainly had a lot of pluses that were making her reconsider her steadfast rule of moving right along. She had always secretly imagined a place where Lyle could have just as much to get out of life as she could. Running her with sheep would be just another reason to settle down here. If only she could tie up the murder investigation. That was definitely a point in the negative column.

"I keep forgetting that I need not introduce myself in this town.

Everybody already knows who I am. I would like to see your place sometime and also run Lyle with your sheep. She would enjoy that."

"Sounds like a plan. No costumes allowed when we do that. I better get to my rounds. I am checking up on a few flocks here while the farmers have a look around. We all take turns since we are not really competing for anything here. It's just a fun day for everyone."

"Nice to meet you. We are doing our own rounds. Lyle gets first pick on what we check out and she chose livestock, of course."

Mandy made her way through the rest of the pens with Lyle by her side. They ended up through the other end of the tent and almost bumped into Larry and Gerry.

"Hi Mandy. And how are you, little Lyle?" Gerry asked, leaning down to fix the antennae into position. They had fallen down and were pointing down under her chin instead of up on her head.

"Hi officers. Everything ok?"

"Yes, we are just here as a precautionary measure. Without the murder wrapped up, we need to be on our toes. Since the whole town attends today, we are looking for any suspicious activity, antennae out of place not included," Larry said as he shifted his gun belt. "We've heard that you are sticking your nose into the investigation. I ask you for your own protection and for the interest of not impeding justice, to stop all efforts on finding the murderer."

"I understand. I just keep happening upon people who tell me things. I don't seek information," Mandy said as she crossed her fingers behind her back. "I would like to know the ending though because this little town shouldn't have a murderer at large."

"We agree and we are working to tie the pieces together. Trust us," said Larry, matter-of-factly.

"You have my word," Mandy said with her fingers crossed in her pocket.

"Thanks. Now, are the citizens of Crestview showing you adequate hospitality?" asked Gerry.

"So far, so good. I am thinking about a snack. Any recommendations?" asked Mandy.

"Well, the apple fritters are pretty stand up. If you want something savory, the kebabs are filling. They are made from local beef marinated in a special recipe," Gerry said.

"Hmm, I think I will start with the fritter and save the kebab for later."

"We will see you around," Gerry said, nodding his hat as they departed.

"Look forward to it," Mandy said, making eye contact with Gerry.

Chapter Seventeen

"Ok, Lyle let's get a snack," Mandy said to a very attentive Border collie. They made their way back to the snack stall area of the park. The smell of a variety of fair foods was wafting in the air, making it easy to find their way to the selection. The apple fritters must be a popular item because there was a bit of a line forming. Mandy took a spot and didn't realize who was standing in front of her.

"Hi Mandy. How is the day treating you?" asked Rhonda.

"I'm having a blast. How are the puppies doing?" inquired Mandy.

"Oh, they are doing quite well. She is such a great mom. I just love puppies. I am already getting great applications for forever homes for them. I have to make sure they go where they will be loved or I would just keep them all."

"I bet it is hard to let them go."

"I know we'll always have another litter in the future and that makes it easier. Love the bee suit."

"Thanks. Oh, we are next. What are you having?"

"An apple fritter, please."

"Make that two. Put that away," Rhonda said, pushing Mandy's hand with a five dollar bill in it out of the radar of the cashier. "This is just a small thank you for helping deliver those puppies, darling."

"Why, thank you. That is very sweet."

They retrieved their steaming hot, sugar-dusted fritters at the next window in the stall. Together they sat at a picnic table surrounded by the rest of the food stalls. Mandy's glasses slid down her nose and she couldn't push them up with a free hand until they sat down. Lyle received a few bites of fritter in exchange for sitting nicely under the table.

"Any more news on the murder?" asked Mandy.

"Well, they were able to find some shoeprints that were a rather large shoe. Apparently, they believe it was a man's boot, size 13 narrow. Although Tom is a doctor, they had him help out with the crime scene analysis as well. Small towns breed multi-taskers."

"I see. So we are looking for a man with large, narrow feet who had a motive," thought Mandy out loud.

"Indeed, though I wouldn't say we. I am happy to lend tidbits of information. I am not getting caught looking into anything. You are on your own there, honey."

"Fair enough. But thanks for your input."

As they finished their fritters, Mandy contemplated what to look at next when a whole crowd of people went by all dressed in costumes. There was a clown, a witch, a devil, a Bo peep, a fairy godmother, and a few other costumes which were a little hard to discern through all of the creativity.

"And there's the die-hard costumers. Every year they have a bit of a costume party of their own. One year I joined the fray and dressed up as a hot dog to honor my dachshunds. It was fun but a fair amount of work to make that costume," said Rhonda as they watched the procession.

"What a great idea. I love when it's perfectly normal to be different."

"There's room in this town for all kinds of eccentricities, except murder."

"Preach that, sister," said Mandy. "Speaking of the town, I think I might explore some more of the Hoedown before the softball game."

"Enjoy, dearie. I'll see you later on."

"Thanks, will do."

Chapter Eighteen

Mandy stood at the map again, she was approached by Mrs. Bouvier.

"Oh, I'm so glad I found you," Mrs. Bouvier breathed out.

"Why is that?" asked Mandy.

Catching her breath, Mrs. Bouvier clearly had a mouthful to get out. "One tradition in the Halloween Hoedown is the annual bake-off, where everyone presents their best cakes, cookies, muffins, and breads. Normally, the judging is done by Merv and his wife Myrna, since they are well-versed in tasty fare and it would be an unfair advantage if they entered. However, Myrna's migraines are acting up and she just could not fathom being in all the noise and lights of the town festivities. The only unbiased person that the town agreed could stand in for Myrna was none other than the new veterinarian in town, you," exclaimed Mrs. Bouvier.

"Me, well, it would be an honor. I wish I hadn't just eaten that apple fritter. When is the event?" Mandy asked.

"That's the thing. It is just about to begin. So I found you just in time."

"I see. I guess there's no time like the present. Show me the way."

"Excellent. You will not be disappointed. It sure is a hoot. And there's no hard feelings."

"I'm all over this. I love sampling delectables."

"You are in luck. We have had a phenomenal turnout this year."

They walked together in a line like ducklings, Mrs. Bouvier in front, Mandy in the middle, and Lyle last. They couldn't walk side by side due to the crowds of people. The tent with the food smelled fantastic. Mandy took her spot at the front next to Merv.

"Sorry to hear about Myrna. I hope she can make it later on."

"She took some medicine and should hopefully be down here this afternoon. Are you ready to feast? The key is to pace yourself. Tiny bites," advised Merv.

"Sounds logical. What are the parameters we judge on?" asked Mandy.

"Listen to you, sounding professional."

"I have watched a few cooking shows in my time," Mandy laughingly replied.

"Basically, there are fifteen points total. Five for presentation, five for taste, and five for originality. No half points allowed. There are a few categories: cakes, pies, cookies, and there's one savory round, open to anything non-sweet. The entries are anonymous to us so there is no favoritism and we will be on our own in this room until we have made a decision, so as not to be swayed by anyone. We are allowed to take breaks, but the sooner we get this done, the sooner we can join the festivities again."

"Ok. Here we go, then," Mandy said with a little hesitation.

They diligently went through every entry, sampling with very small bites. It felt like they had been working for hours but it was really only forty-five minutes. They declared a winner in each category as well as an overall winner. Lyle was thoroughly disgusted with all of the sweets at their disposal and yet she had not received a single bite.

"When we are all done with the competition, I will get you some," Mandy said to Lyle who had puffed her lips and sighed deeply, as if not believing her human's words.

"We can bring everyone back in now. The good news is that we haven't had an overall winner from this category in a while so it will be a nice change," said Merv.

Everyone started filing back in the area for the declaration of winners. A few friendly competitive jibes could be heard in the crowd. Obviously, this town takes cooking and competition seriously, Mandy pondered.

"Ok, everyone," Mrs. Bouvier firmly said, in an attempt to quiet the room. "Ahem. We are pleased to thank Merv and our guest judge, Dr. Mandy Bell. Let's give them a round of applause for their efforts." The room boomed with applause and whistles. "And now I will turn it over to Merv."

"Well, as usual, this was a hard decision. There were some wonderful entries. Thanks to everyone who entered. The leftovers will be cut up and ready for purchase at the end of the awards ceremony. Please dig deep and be generous. This year, the proceeds go toward improving school playground. And now, without further ado, let's hand out the awards. Mandy, if you'd like to hand them out as I call the names, please."

Mandy gave a smiling nod to Merv as she perused the awards, to make sure she handed out the appropriate one to each recipient.

"Ok, in first place in the cake round, was Rhonda with her raspberry white chocolate cake." Mandy handed Rhonda the blue ribbon with the cake pictured on it. "In first place for the pie category is Beverly with her lemon meringue toasted coconut. In the cookie category, it was the ginger snaps made by Heidi. The savory was a clear winner with the cheesy cranberry pistachio scone made by Fred. And the overall winner of the bake-off today was the ginger snap cookie. Heidi will be keeper of the silver-gilded rolling pin until next year." Mandy handed out each award with a big congratulatory handshake. "Congratulations to all of the winners and thanks to everyone who entered."

Mrs. Bouvier chimed in before the crowd dissipated, "Another successful bake-off. Thanks everyone. Enjoy the rest of the day. The softball game will begin in two hours so peruse the booths for apple bobbing, cotton candy, pony rides, and all out family fun until then. The evening will conclude with the square dancing in the main hall. We have a real treat this year. The town has assembled a band, The Shindiggers, to play for the square dancing. They have been practicing diligently and are excited to make this the best dance ever."

Merv reached out his hand to give Mandy a sturdy handshake. "Thanks for an effortless judging session. That was a real treat, no pun intended," he said.

"The pleasure was all ours," Mandy said, looking at Lyle who was happy to receive some treats too. "I think I better do some walking before I have to try to run a base in the softball game. Even with tiny bites, that was a lot of tasting."

"I'm going to go check on Myrna. See you later," said Merv.

Mandy purchased some rice crispy treats to give to Lyle as a reward for her patience. Lyle was drooling at the prospect of the treat. She devoured the morsels and sat staring at Mandy as if more might appear.

"That's enough, little Lyle. Let's do some mingling now," Mandy said. Lyle was satisfied with the thought of a walk and trotted behind Mandy.

Chapter Nineteen

Mandy and Lyle explored the rest of the booths at the Hoedown.
Both of them were in need of a little break when Gillian and
Hamish spotted them.

"Hi Dr. Bell, are you enjoying your day? Looks like Lyle is
buzzzzzing with enthusiasm," Gillian said, fixing Lyle's
antennae that were hanging under her chin instead of standing up
on her head.

"Yes, so far, this is like the small town event I have only read
about in books and wondered whether it happens in the real
world."

"It is a little slice of heaven."

"I just can't get those antennae to stay up. I'll have to alter them
for the next time she wears this costume," said Mandy.

"You can make a different costume for her every year," Gillian
said, nudging Mandy's elbow. "Hey, not to burst the bubble, but

I overheard Jim talking to some of his buddies about the dart championships coming up. He was not shy about announcing that he was glad he would finally get his rightful place in this town as the dart champion. It seemed a tad out of character for him to gloat like that. I thought you might be interested in that little scoop."

"Indeed I am. I feel like I have been so busy lately, I haven't had time to go over my list of suspects and link up the clues I have uncovered. Tonight I will sit down and see what I can piece together. It doesn't sound like Larry and Gerry are any further than I am."

"That's not a huge shock. I will see if I hear anything else through the grapevine today and let you know," said Gillian.

"Thanks. I appreciate it. I feel like if I just had one more piece of information, I could get there."

"Mom, can we go apple bobbing?" asked Hamish, who had been waiting patiently through the grown-up talk.

"Sure. Want to join us?" Gillian asked Mandy.

"That sounds good, as long as we don't have to eat anything. I am still stuffed."

They joined the other kids who were trying desperately to retrieve an apple from the tub of water. So far, everyone was splashing and getting their faces wet, but no one was able to grab one in their teeth.

Lyle's ears perked up and she watched intently at the children. If there was one thing she enjoyed more than fetch, it was children. And this almost looked like a combination of the two. Gillian and Mandy were standing at the sidelines, giggling at the jubilation of the kids, not paying attention to Lyle. No one saw her creep along the ground toward the tub to make a graceful leap into the water after one of the apples. She emerged from the tub gleefully, with an apple in her mouth. As she shook the water off of her, anyone that hadn't been splashed by her entry into the tub received a good dousing of water. Her antennae had officially fallen off and her wings were hanging like a drowned bug.

"Lyle!" Mandy screamed.

With everyone dripping in cold water, someone couldn't help but start laughing and it became infectious. Soon everyone was laughing and Lyle was standing in the middle, apple still in her mouth.

"It's just water. We will all live. What a hoot. At least someone finally got an apple out of that tub. The kids have been trying all morning," one of the parents said.

"I'm so sorry, everyone. She just can't resist being involved, especially if she thinks fetch is part of the game," Mandy said.

Someone had run to the meeting hall in the meantime and retrieved towels to help dry off some of the kids. Although the sun was shining, the wind was picking up and the last thing they needed was for all of the kids to catch a chill.

Lyle dropped the apple at Mandy's feet and backed up, oblivious to what had just happened. She was waiting for Mandy to throw the new fetch object she had worked so hard to obtain.

"Not now Lyle. I think we've done enough. Let's head on. You finally succeeded in ruining the costume, though," Mandy said. She took off the remainder of the costume and stashed it in her satchel.

Ginny was there with her two kids. They were drying themselves off after the unsolicited bath Lyle had given them.

"Ginny, I'm sorry. Lyle gets carried away sometimes," Mandy said.

"Not a problem. We were all getting a little bored anyway. It's so hard to retrieve apples from water. You haven't met my kids yet. This is Jay and Harry," said Ginny.

Ginny's kids were a miniature version of her. They were all dressed in a pirate-themed costume. Ginny must have spent oodles of time hand-crafting these costumes. She had even aged the material somehow to make it seem that these pirates had truly been on boats, roughing it through the weather.

"Arggh, hi, Dr. Bell," said Jay, handing her hook to Mandy to shake.

"Hi there, Jay."

"Ahoy matey. Polly here may need a vet later on. Will you see parrots?" asked Harry.

"Sure thing, Harry. You know where to find me," said Mandy.

"It's nice to meet your kids. I love the costumes. How did you decide on pirates?"

"We take turns choosing a theme every year. This year it was Harry's turn. He has been enjoying the classic pirate tales like Treasure Island so we honored his current interests. We home school so the kids get to explore their surroundings while we learn. Technically, it's unschooling, where there is no set curriculum. We end up learning a lot more in every subject than if we did follow a lesson plan. For example, it's impossible to make costumes without using math, and lots of it," said Ginny.

"That is certainly true. I have only ever read about unschooling, never met it face to face. It's very neat to find people living it. Let me know if you ever need help with biology. I love alternative education and would be happy to assist if I can," said Mandy.

"Thanks. We will keep you in mind," said Ginny. "We need to get these kids a snack. We've been so busy with activities, we forgot to eat lunch!"

"We don't want the pirates of Crestview to be malnourished. Go forth and feast!" said Mandy.

Chapter Twenty

With all of the excitement, time flew by and it was now time for the softball game. The teams were selected by a random drawing of those wanting to play. Nearly the entire town was in attendance or playing. Mandy made sure to tie Lyle up under a tree to prevent her from intervening in the game.

The two teams were the Woodchucks and the Quail. Everyone was in good cheer as the teams figured out their lineup. Both teams had more than enough players so everyone would be taking turns being in the field. Mandy would start off in right field. The rules were explained so as to educate anyone unfamiliar with the Crestview softball etiquette. The only rule that was novel to Mandy was that sliding into a base was not allowed. The reasoning was to prevent injury since there was such a wide range of ages and skill levels playing. It was really more of a social event than a competitive sport. The teams were supplied with sashes to wear to be able to tell the difference between the players on the field. The Woodchucks were green and the Quail, blue. Mandy thought it was very clever to use sashes, instead of full uniforms, since it saved everyone having to get changed.

The game kicked off with the first pitch. Instead of fast-pitch, like Mandy was accustomed, the pitches would be an underarm lob of a slow pitch. This made it a little easier to hit and for anyone to have a try at pitching. It also kept the action moving to keep the crowd engaged.

Mandy's team was in the field first and since the ball hadn't been hit toward right field yet, she took the opportunity to peruse the crowd for clues on the murder. She hadn't had time lately to even sit down to put her clues on paper next to her suspect list. Tonight she would have to work on it or she might not figure out the murderer before Larry and Gerry. This had become a little competition in her head.

Standing with her glove on her left hand, she could feel the sun beating down on her. She hadn't thought it would get this warm today and Mandy regretted not putting sunscreen on. There wasn't any shade in the field. Finally, a ball came toward her. It was a grounder and she effortlessly scooped it up and threw it in to second base. That was the third out of the inning. Playing softball came right back to her, even though she hadn't played in a while. That made it time to head into the dugout to see who was going to bat first on their team.

Before checking the lineup, Mandy decided to check on Lyle. With the break in the action, she was laying down. Her eyes were focused on the ball that had been left on the pitcher's mound. Mandy supplied her with fresh, cold water and then returned to her team.

"That was a nice play out there, Doc," said Dennis. They were on the same team and Dennis hadn't been on the field in the first inning.

"Thanks. It's like riding a bike; you can't forget the instincts, even if you haven't played in years," said Mandy.

"Too right. It looks like they are trying to rotate everybody through the game. Since I didn't field, I'll be batting. Don't hold your breath, I was never a good hitter," said Dennis.

"Not my strength either," said Mandy.

"Did you have a chance to go through Anna's things? Or shall I come and collect them so you don't have to dig through anything?"

"I am slowly getting through things. I don't really know what it is that you want or where it is. Can you tell me more about what you want?"

"It's personal. Can I just come over and help look through her things with you?"

"I'd rather be able to sort through it first."

"Well, I am leaving town in the next few days and would really like to have those items before I go. Kind of like to close a chapter, you know?"

"I understand, but I have been fairly busy and I don't really want to start breaking up Anna's personal items until I am sure that I have accounted for all of her wishes. I keep thinking I will find a diary or something that clues me in on who she wanted her belongings given to."

"I don't think this is a big deal. I can just come and get what I need and be out of your hair."

Mandy felt a bit of a pushy tone from Dennis and she didn't appreciate it. "I will be in touch when I am ready for you. Until then, respect her space."

With that said, she departed his company before he could say another word. She grabbed some Gatorade for herself. That sun was really getting to her. Or maybe it was the mountain of baked goods she had eaten on top of an apple fritter.

Mandy couldn't quite figure out Dennis. He was relatively friendly, but also fairly mysterious. She would definitely have to look into the relationship between him and Anna better once she had figured out this murder. For now, that didn't have a spot on her agenda.

The softball game continued, with neither team gaining any ground against the other on the scoreboard. Mandy managed to have a pretty nice hit to center field, which enabled her to get to second base. However, the third out of the inning occurred before she could make it to home plate. The sun was becoming less intense, but it had already had its effect on Mandy so she decided to join the onlookers and sit with Lyle. That way she would see if any gossip was flowing through the crowd with regard to the murder.

Gillian and Hamish were sitting with Lyle so Mandy made herself a spot with them. Also in the stands was Fred, decked out in his cheer leading outfit. It was not clear which team he was actually cheering for as he had a costume featuring both team mascots. Apparently, he was spreading cheer equally. The rest of the crowd was following his lead, providing ample encouragement to the players, regardless of their team.

"Nice moves, Dr. Bell," said Gillian.

"Thanks, but I think I am going to sit the rest out. Any more news on the murder?"

"I've been listening around. So far, nothing," said Gillian.

"Me neither. This is one tricky little town," Mandy said.

"It grows on you," Gillian said.

"Well, the murderer is making no mistakes, whoever it is."

The game concluded with a tie. The point of playing was to bring the town together, not really for a winner so everyone seemed content with the ending.

Mrs. Bouvier stood on the pitcher's mound to address the crowd,

"Great game, everybody. You'll be able to catch the highlight photos in the paper tomorrow. And now, it's time for everyone to clean up, dust off, and head to the finale of the evening, the dance. Don't forget, it is the live music that will make this year really shine. So put your dancing shoes on and be there or be square, pun intended!"

"Are you guys going to go to the dance?" Mandy asked Gillian and Hamish.

"We always go. We don't necessarily dance. It's fun whether you sit on the sidelines or not," Gillian replied.

"Well, I suppose I will see you there then," Mandy said.

Chapter Twenty-One

Mandy and Lyle wandered down the street with the rest of the crowd. Anyone who didn't live within walking distance to their house hopped in their car. It seemed like the whole town was on the move so as not to miss out on the dancing. Mandy took a quick opportunity to peruse her list of suspects and motives in the quiet of her RV.

One fact she knew was that whoever did it was not a stranger to Buck, given that there was no real struggle at the scene and he was shot from the front at close range. Also, the murderer was most likely a man based on the size shoe print found at the scene. There may have been a debt involved in the motive. A love quarrel may have been a motive since he had been known to be a ladies man.

For suspects, first there was Jim Moore. He was a bit of a loner with no alibi. His passion for darts may have fueled a need to be the reigning champion in the community. He definitely seemed interested in the recognition associated with that title.

Then there was Dennis. He had only been in town for a short time, visiting Fred. He had some kind of secret Mandy could not figure out. He really wanted the personal items of Anna's and was getting a bit pushy about getting them. She wasn't sure if there was a link between the obsessive crush he seemed to have on Anna and the murder. He also acted a tad cagey around her. Then she couldn't forget the strange tan line on his wrist and his clammy response when she pointed it out to him.

Mandy recalled the story of Howie who had been humiliated by Buck. She wrote down his name and then any relative of Howie's who might want revenge for what Buck had done to Howie. It wasn't a strong clue, but it was worth writing down in case it connected to something else later on.

Barney Saunders, owner of the general store, had to be considered. Even though Mandy hadn't met him yet, she knew that there was a competition in the community between him,

Buck, and Jim for the title of best shot. In a masculine world, maybe Barney had wanted to oust his opponent. Or maybe there was more to the dart league than she knew. She never did get a chance to talk to the boys in the Inn that night.

A love quarrel may have been at the center of the motive. She hadn't come across anyone who claimed to be in a relationship with Buck, though several people had mentioned that he was a ladies man. Even a jealous husband or boyfriend would need to be considered.

She also put an entry entitled unknown on the list. So new to the town, she could have missed an important thread that she still needed to keep her eyes and ears open for. Mandy figured she shouldn't zero in on anyone, yet.

Now that she had made a little time to work on the murder, she also made a list of things that she still needed to do. First, she needed to bump into Barney Saunders and find out a little more about him. She also needed to head over to the rifle range to see if she could find any more clues there. She needed to know more about the death of Jim Moore's wife and the relationship between Buck and Dennis and Anna. She also had to check more into Howie's tormentors and protectors. And finally, she hoped she could have a dinner meeting with Gerry to try to inadvertently discover some clues from him, this time without an emergency interruption.

With a plan in mind, Mandy decided she'd better get ready for the dance. If she wasn't there, she wouldn't hear the end of it from the community. She took a quick shower and put on her favorite long denim skirt, moccasins, and a snap button down shirt. Since the sun had really gotten the better of her during the game, she still felt warm but knew that she would get cold later so she tucked a wool jersey in her things she'd be taking. Mandy poured herself a large glass of water to chug down since she was feeling a little dehydrated after such a busy day. Lyle was curled up in her favorite chair in a tight little ball with her tail over her head. Her ears were twitching and legs paddling. A soft whimper could be heard from her as she slept.

"Puppy dreams," Mandy said. "I bet you are chasing that softball from today that I wouldn't let you have, little girl."

One eye opened and stared at Mandy, as if making contact in agreement.

"You don't have to come to the dance if you want to take a nap," Mandy said to Lyle.

On cue, Lyle leapt up from her deep slumber and sat by the door.

"I guess that's a no to napping, huh girl?" Mandy asked Lyle.

Lyle's bushy tail wagged in response.

"Well, let's get going then. Do you need a snack before we go?"

Lyle went and sat in front of her bowl. "Another clear response from the smartest Border collie ever. Here you go, sweetheart," Mandy said as she poured some crunchies into Lyle's bowl. Crunch, crunch, crunch. Lyle always ate her kibbles in three bites each. Mandy found it to be a soothing part of her life's routine.

Finished with the snack, Lyle followed Mandy down the three steps of the RV and into the crisp Fall air. They wandered on down the road, Mandy still deep in thought about the murder.

Chapter Twenty-Two

The music could be heard before Mandy even approached the building. She knew this was going to be high-paced jubilation since the town had been mentioning the Hoedown in every conversation since she arrived. Hopefully she could find a few quiet moments to collect some more clues for the murder of Buck Dawson. As she entered, there was joy in the air. People were dancing in unison while the band filled the room with traditional country music. The caller had the whole crowd jiving to the talented fiddler.

Rhonda waved her over to where she was standing on the sidelines. Mandy approached her, "Hi, Dr. Bell. How are you at dancing?" asked Rhonda.

"Oh, I'm not too shabby. I would rather gain some more clues on the murder although I might accidentally dance in the process," replied Mandy.

"I didn't hear that."

"I didn't say it," said Mandy.

The dance was coming to a close and everyone was making a line in the refreshment area before the next dance began.

"Who is that young man over there?" asked Mandy.

"That's Howie. He's the retired bull rider."

"I've heard of him. I'd like to talk to him. But first I want to watch who is close to him. I heard that Buck played a few pranks on him. I want to see who takes a protective role for him here."

"His parents are the people standing behind him in line. They are probably his closest onlookers. Although I think the whole town keeps an eye on him. He makes a living doing yard chores for people around town and delivering mail sometimes. He does a very good job because he is strong as an ox. Very trustworthy," Rhonda explained.

"I think I might go introduce myself. Do they have any pets?"

asked Mandy.

"Howie has a little Chihuahua named Rosie. She follows him everywhere but she must have stayed home tonight. Not all dogs are like Lyle and can come to the dance. The town seems to have taken a real shining to the new vet and her sidekick," Rhonda smiled as she spoke and her cheery dimples showed in her cheeks. Mandy thought in some ways Rhonda reminded her of a happy little gnome.

"Thanks for that. I think I will head over there now. I'll catch up with you before the night ends," Mandy said, with genuine warmth in her voice.

Howie was standing with his parents, sipping punch from a plastic wine glass. "Excuse me, I'd like to introduce myself. We haven't met yet but I am......" Mandy started.

"Dr. Bell," Howie finished her sentence. "I have seen you when I am collecting leaves. I wondered about your dog. What is her name?"

"Lyle. And yes, she is a girl. You are very observant. How did you know she is a girl?"

"I heard someone say that she was," said Howie.

Howie's parents appeared, one each side of Howie. "Hi Dr. Bell. How are you this evening?" asked his mom.

"Good. I'm a little full, to be honest, after lots of baked goods but happy to be here. I was just introducing myself to Howie. I understand he has a Chihuahua named Rosie," said Mandy.

"Well, yes he does. I am Pat and this is my husband, Howie's father, Aaron. We are pleased to meet you. I hope you are settling in well to the town," said Pat.

Pat was dressed in a stylish lilac sweater set with pearls and a long, flowing skirt. Aaron and Howie were both wearing freshly ironed khakis and plaid button-up shirts. The family looked very tidy and clearly watched out for each other. While Aaron wore penny leathers, Howie did not hide his love for the rodeo, wearing a large belt buckle and some fancy cowboy boots.

"I'm pleased to meet you three as well. I heard that Howie does a bit of yard work and I was wondering if I could hire him to help me clean up Anna's place. The leaves have been piling up and I don't want a fire out there," Mandy said.

Howie's eyes lit up.

"Dr. Bell, can I speak to you for a moment?" Aaron asked. Meanwhile, Pat led Howie to the line to get another cup of punch.

"Sure," Mandy said.

"I don't know if anyone has told you. Howie was in an accident in the bull ring some years ago. He lacks a little cognitive function as a result of a brain injury. He leads a very normal life, though he can be very innocent and therefore taken advantage of. I am not suggesting that you will do that to Howie. I just want to be sure you understand that he has the mental capacity of a child," Aaron said.

"First, I am sorry for his injury. I had heard about it and I think it is horrible that anyone would take advantage of him in any way. I have no intention of doing that. I would, however, like to treat him like an adult and allow him to work in exchange for money," Mandy said, with as much restraint as possible. She knew Aaron had Howie's best interest at heart but she found it difficult not to feel a tad on the spot.

"Thank you. That is all that we ask. We treat him like the wonderful son that he is while trying to prevent unnecessary exposure to the cruelties of life."

"I understand entirely. I can't believe anyone would hurt him," Mandy said. She saw Aaron make eye contact with Pat and give her a nod. She figured this indicated that she was passing their preliminary test.

"You'd be surprised. That nasty Buck Dawson was always playing pranks on Howie. I can't say that we will see Buck in heaven on the other side. He was a bad seed," said Aaron.

"I see. What sorts of things happened, if you don't mind my being nosy?" asked Mandy.

"He would sneak up and sabotage the gear Howie uses to do his yard work. We got to the point where we had to lock everything up at night and check it all before Howie used it. Not only was it not funny but it could have resulted in an injury for poor Howie."

"That is very cruel. I guess you guys are safe now from that torment."

"We are," Aaron said as he signaled that Pat and Howie could join them.

Mandy wondered if Aaron could vouch for his whereabouts on the night Buck was murdered. Before she could get a chance to inquire, Howie was back.

"Can I help her Dad?" asked Howie.

"I don't see why not," Aaron said, placing a loving arm around Howie.

"You will be able to meet Rosie, Dr. Bell," said Howie, trying to contain his excitement.

"Indeed I will. I look forward to it. We can arrange a day that works for you," replied Mandy.

"We are both retired so we will help coordinate with you. We help by driving Howie and coordinating the bookings. I will give you a call at the office."

"Sounds wonderful," said Mandy. The music started again and the caller asked that everyone who wanted to participate in the next dance take their places.

"Are you going to dance, Dr. Bell?" Howie asked.

"Sure. I will try this one. You'll have to help me. I'm a bit rusty," said Mandy.

"We can all look after each other," Aaron said as they started over to the stage.

Mandy could see that this family was very close. She wondered what lengths Aaron would take to make sure Howie was safe. She would have to find out if he had any experience with a gun.

The night carried on with many dances and breaks for refreshments. The punch was non-alcoholic so there was no display of disorderly conduct. This made Mandy happy because all too often, she had seen a fun evening end in a brawl. This town was so different, except one person in the town did murder someone in cold blood.

She was enjoying the dancing so much that she didn't manage to interview anyone else. Even Larry and Gerry were letting their hair down. Gerry managed to dance his way over the Mandy several times throughout the night. Mandy had to admit that it was nice to have someone quietly interested in her, though it was too soon for her to even go there.

At the last pause of the evening, Rhonda zoomed over to Mandy. "How did it go with Howie and his family?"

"Good, Howie is going to help clear the leaves from around Anna's house," Mandy said.

"What a great idea. Any luck with the answers you needed? I don't want details," Rhonda said.

"I have some more sleuthing to do, but thanks for your help."

"The night is dwindling. I need to get home to check on the puppies. I will see you later this week," Rhonda said, showing her dimples again.

"Sure thing," said Mandy. As the crowd was dissipating, Lyle stuck right by Mandy, clearly ready to go to bed after a very full day. "Alright, little girl, let's get home to bed," Mandy said to Lyle.

Chapter Twenty-Three

Sunday morning Mandy and Lyle slept in to recover from the activities of the previous day. Even though they got a late start, they had a few things they wanted to accomplish. Mandy started by nourishing her body with fresh pancakes. The RV smelled delightful. Lyle could not resist the temptation of the sweet syrup aromas. When Mandy was getting a second cup of coffee, Lyle made a beeline for the last few bites of Mandy's breakfast.

"Lyle, get down," Mandy said sternly. "You know you always get some but you have to wait for me to finish." Mandy had some extra batter so she whipped up a few more pancakes. She could only eat one more so the rest were for Lyle. When they finished, Mandy cleaned up the kitchen and set the dishwasher to run. Then she hopped in the shower and dressed for the chilly day ahead. Meanwhile Lyle stretched out on the dashboard to soak up the sunshine peaking through.

"Ok, Lyle. We need to get some maintenance done around here.

We have a lot to consider with the murder investigation. However, if we don't get some laundry and shopping done, we won't be much use this coming week, will we?" Lyle lifted her head but made no attempt to move from her warm spot in the sun. "Guess I am on my own then?" As Mandy put a jacket on and grabbed the laundry, Lyle rose from her nap and met Mandy at the door. "Alright, come on then."

They stepped out of the RV and walked to the clinic. Closed Sundays, it would be nice and quiet to accomplish a few tasks. Mandy first fed Emma and Jimbo, who were circling her feet maniacally, as if they may starve to death if they didn't receive crunchies immediately. Neither cat was thin by any means. Anna had clearly become trained by their hunger demands just as Mandy was now reinforcing their obsession. Once they inhaled their breakfast, Emma curled up on the cat cozy on the counter and Jimbo took his position in the window to monitor the birds outside. Lyle snuggled up on the office chair at the front desk. For a long, tall dog, she could curl up in the smallest little ball.

Mandy moved the clinic laundry over so she could start some of her own laundry. Lyle came bouncing in to the laundry room to check on Mandy. She dropped a ball in the pile of laundry for Mandy to throw should she be so inclined.

"Not right now, Lyle. I still have a few more things to catch up on," Mandy said. Lyle huffed and puffed her cheeks before retreating from the laundry room back to her chair at the front of the clinic.

Mandy went to her office and pulled all of the files from the week. She updated all of the medical notes. It was a task she detested so she tried to do it through the week as the cases came in. She never managed to achieve her goal of not having a stack of files at the end of the week. Luckily, her memory recall abilities enabled her to write thorough notes even weeks after she had seen a pet. She tried to purge all of that from her head by writing it down. Her head started to feel heavy with information if she didn't relocate it to medical files.

Even though the murder investigation and going through Anna's house were important, she needed to keep the clinic financially viable. Her desire to honor Anna's legacy was of great concern. It is not an everyday occurrence that a dear friend leaves their home, livelihood, and dreams to another in their will. She took this responsibility seriously. She had saved some money from previous jobs and had few bills. However, earning money was still a requirement of living in a society where bartering was no longer the norm. She was also concerned about Gillian and Hamish. They needed a steady income since Gillian was the sole bread winner. There was so much to consider in this equation.

She needed some caffeine to keep going. She went to the kitchenette to fix some coffee. As she was deep in thought, Gillian appeared in the doorway.

"Whatcha doing?" asked Gillian.

"Catching up on a few things. It's pretty boring but I have gotten a little behind," said Mandy. "You?"

"Hamish and I were out running a few errands so we can go home and snuggle in for the day to rest after a fun weekend. I thought I'd stop in and see if you needed anything."

"Thanks for that. I think we are good. I am going to treat Lyle to some fetch and then we will probably snuggle in too," said Anna.

"While we are here, Hamish would love to play with Lyle, if that's ok," said Gillian.

"Perfect. I need some fresh air. Let's go play. Most people can't have a Border collie as a pet. If they don't get adequate exercise, a predictable routine, and stimulation, they are terrible dogs. Lyle is finally starting to calm down at five years old. She still needs to play like a puppy on a daily basis, particularly if it involves kids."

They all headed outside to give Lyle undivided attention. Lyle was in her element. She herded them all over to the yards and proceeded to bring her the toy of her choosing to each person in a sequence. If someone tried to throw the incorrect toy out of turn, Lyle would not even fetch it. Instead, she sat with her eyes staring at the correct next person in line with the toy she had picked. Her lips puffed up in disgust at the audacity of someone throwing out of turn.

"Wow. I have never played with a dog that takes playing fetch so seriously. This is not a game for her. She has turned it into work," Gillian said.

"Yep. She does nothing that she hasn't thought out beforehand. It is entirely possible that she is smarter than me. I just happen to have thumbs," said Mandy.

Hamish was giggling because Lyle had found a log behind the yards. She was trying to bring it over to Hamish to throw.

"I think that's a little big, Lyle. How about this one?" Hamish said, holding a small stick.

"Ok, so she has some limitations to her brilliance," Mandy

admitted, giggling as well.

The ground was littered with all sorts of toys: balls, sticks, plush animals, frisbies, and her favorite hippo. Near the back door, there was a large water pan for her. She leaped in the water bowl and curled up. Even though her whole body was sticking out, she had made herself as small as she could to fit down in it as best she could.

"You silly girl," said Mandy. "That generally means she needs a break. She will literally keep playing until she gets hypoglycemic. We better stop before that happens." Mandy went inside the RV to retrieve a snack for Lyle. "Here you go. We can play some more tomorrow."

Lyle scarfed down the snack and proceeded to drink what was left in the water pan. Mandy let her into the clinic to warm up. The Fall air was a tad chilly for a sopping wet, exhausted dog.

"Thanks so much for stopping by. We needed that. She will be able to take a nice long nap this afternoon," said Mandy.

"Our pleasure. She is a wonderful dog. Sure you don't need anything?" asked Gillian.

"Yep. I'm good. I am going to bake some cookies and do some nesting today. Sundays I always try to take some time to reboot my system, so to speak. The world keeps going even if you take a break," Mandy said.

"Well said. See you tomorrow," said Gillian.

Chapter Twenty-Four

"That sure was an action-packed weekend. You guys know how to throw a hoedown," said Mandy to Gillian as they prepared the clinic for a day of appointments.

"Indeed we do. It gets better every year. The Christmas Mingler is a good time too. Of course, you'll see for yourself," Gillian said as she gave Mandy a wink. "I hope you got some relaxing done as well. This week might be full on."

"We'll see. Now what's on today's agenda?" asked Mandy. As Gillian looked at the schedule, Mandy gave Emma and Jimbo some breakfast and turned the sink faucet on for Emma to get her drink. If they didn't turn the faucet on, Emma meowed repeatedly and with increased urgency the longer it took someone to answer to her water obsession.

"Hmm, it looks like we have a few surgeries this morning and appointments this afternoon. We have the surgery on the missing testicles in the Boston terrier and an eye exam under sedation on one of Myrna and Merv's setters. I'll go get the cages ready for our surgeries," said Gillian.

"Sounds good to me. I don't remember seeing Myrna and Merv's dog. What are we exploring the eye for?"

"It seems once a year their prize setter goes with them into the woods and comes back with one eye closed. It always seems to be a grass seed that we can't get out from under her third eyelid without sedation. So, now they just cut straight to the chase and book her in for surgery without even trying with her awake," said Gillian.

"Ah, got it. Hunting dogs always seem to get into trouble like that."

"You oughta be here for the Coon Dog trials. People drive in from all over for that event and this clinic gets rather busy with hunting casualties."

"Actual deaths?"

"No, just lacerations, eye scratches, limping, worn out. The usual."

"Sounds like a busy time. When is that?"

"The next main one is next summer."

"Interesting. These surgeries don't look too taxing. We should finish in good time. I think I will try to meet Gerry for lunch to compare notes," said Mandy.

"I didn't hear that," Gillian said as she left with the cage cards to go set up cages in the surgery area for their incoming patients.

When Mandy unlocked the front door for opening time, Myrna was already walking the parking lot with her beautiful setter. When they saw the doors open, they approached the door, the setter stopping to sniff everything along the way.

"Good to see you. Are you feeling better?" asked Mandy.

"Yes, my headache is finally gone. Thanks so much for sitting in on the bake-off for me. I understand it went quite well," Myrna said.

"It was fun. Although I still feel full," Mandy said.

"Yep, we get lots of entries so it is a mouthful of a day. This is Llewellyn," pointing at the setter, "she's done something to her eye again. We took her out for a run to prepare for the hunting season coming up."

"I see. We'll have a look-see today and get her back on track for you. Let's just see what she weighs this morning. And she didn't have breakfast, right?" Mandy asked.

"No ma'am. No breakfast."

"Fifty-eight pounds. Alright, let's put her in the cage back here and we will see you back here around three."

"Thanks, Dr. Bell."

Myrna left just as Sonya was arriving with Bubba.

"The moment of truth has come for you, little Bubba," Sonya was explaining to Bubba as he sat, snorting and wiggling his stumpy crooked tail. "We are going to find out if you have a legitimate reason for some of your unbecoming behaviors." Bubba's lip was caught on his tooth, making him look like he was an Elvis impersonator.

"We sure will find out for you. Bubba didn't get any breakfast, right?"

"He did not. And he is rather mad about that. What is the reason for that anyway, Dr. Bell?"

"Particularly in our little squash-faced friend, it helps to ensure that as they are going under anesthesia or coming out of it, they do not have any food in their stomachs to throw up. You can imagine how with such a small snout, there isn't a whole lot of room in their mouths for their airway opening when they are awake. When they are asleep, everything is relaxed and floppy which means that they are even more at risk of airway blockage and aspiration issues. We take all of the proper precautions to avoid anesthetic risks."

"That makes sense. No one ever explained that to me. Thanks. What time shall I come back?"

"Why don't we give you a call. Sometimes we keep patients overnight, depending on how invasive the surgery is. It may be that we have to do an abdominal exploration if there are indeed retained testicles."

"Ok, just take good care of my little Bubba," said Sonya.

"We sure will," said Mandy as Gillian appeared from the back to take Bubba to his suite for the day.

As Sonya left, Mandy pulled the phonebook out to see about calling Gerry to arrange for lunch today. Unfortunately, she didn't know his last name and didn't want to call the chief's office to speak with him as this would raise suspicion.

"Do you happen to know Gerry's number, Gillian?" Mandy

asked when Gillian came back up the front.

"Yep, I'll get it for you. Do I want to know why you need it?"

"Probably not," Mandy said.

"Here you go. That's his cell phone number."

"Thanks," said Mandy and began to dial it. "Hi Gerry, it's me, Dr. Bell. Can you chat? Ok, good. I was wondering if you wanted to meet for lunch today to discuss, um, you know. Would one work for you? Ok, I will see you at the Inn."

Mandy was pleased that she could take a little time out for lunch today and try to put some more pieces of the murder puzzle together. For now, she better get focused on these surgeries. She had worked at clinics where she did thirty to forty surgeries back to back in one day before. Granted, they were high-volume, low-cost spay neuter clinics where she only had to scrub, glove, do the surgery, and then re-scrub, glove and do the next. Those were the most amazing places to work because if you had a good team, it was like a ballet. Everyone was perfectly in rhythm and knew their positions. Two little surgeries this morning would be a cinch and then she could spend some more time on her clues.

Dr. Bell calculated out the pre-medications for her patients while Gillian took their pulse, respirations, and temperatures pre-surgery. Mandy liked to give them a little pain medication before surgery and this also acted as a slight sedative to make the anesthesia smooth.

They injected both of the dogs and Mandy drew up the induction anesthesia for both dogs. She would likely only need a low dose for the Setter, enough to have a good look in her eye for a possible grass seed. Bubba would be fully anesthetized under the anesthesia machine that delivered isoflurane.

Even though Gillian and Mandy had only worked together a few weeks, it was as if they had worked together much longer. This was due, in part, to the fact that Anna had trained Gillian to the standards that both Mandy and Anna had been taught in vet school. Their training was more application-based than theoretical. Mandy had worked with some of the new graduates from schools around the country and they were a completely different breed. Some of them didn't even know how to spay a cat when they graduated. They could, however, recite loads of useless jargon that would scare clients away. Mandy was definitely a practical veterinarian, never discussing what she considered to be a little over the top with clients like kidney transplants.

Llewellyn, the setter, was groggy first so they started with her. They gave her the induction drugs via her front leg vein. She immediately laid her head down in the drug-induced stupor. Gillian opened the eye surgery kit while Mandy put sterile gloves on. The surgery light shined nicely into the inflamed eye and Mandy used forceps to gently pull the third eyelid up. Behind it, she took a sterile Q-tip to explore for a foreign object. Sure enough, there was a nice big grass seed wedged in the corner of her eye which Mandy removed. Gillian then poured sterile eye rinse into the eye.

To be thorough, Mandy also stained the eye with fluorescein and checked with a UV light for any scratches on the cornea. It looked like Llewellyn had sustained no injury to the cornea. She was also just starting to wake up from anesthesia so Mandy and Gillian transferred her back to her cage for recovery. Mandy went to the pharmacy and selected some take-home pain medication as well as eye drops to prevent infection and treat the inflammation.

By this time, Bubba was sleepy enough to receive his intravenous induction. He was laid out with his legs sprawled behind him, snoring peacefully. Gillian transferred him to the surgery table and selected an appropriately sized endotracheal tube which would go down his trachea to deliver oxygen and anesthesia. Gillian used her hand to make a tourniquet on one of Bubba's front legs so that Mandy could deliver the intravenous drugs. Once heavily sedated, Mandy placed the tube into the trachea and secured it around the back of Bubba's head with ties. Gillian puffed the cuff that would take up any dead space between the diameter of the trachea and the tube. This would ensure that all gases were staying contained within the anesthesia circuit so that Mandy and Gillian wouldn't breathe any in.

Gillian started Bubba off low on the anesthesia while she hooked him up to their monitoring equipment. Meanwhile, Mandy tied Bubba's feet to the surgery table and positioned him just how she wanted him. They shaved his abdomen and inguinal areas and scrubbed for surgery. His vitals were nice and strong so Mandy scrubbed and gloved up.

Mandy made her incision first over the suspicious mass that she had felt in the exam room. She bluntly dissected down through the skin, muscle, and connective tissues. Low and behold, there was a very small, malformed testicle hiding in the tissue. Since there had been one retained testicle, that confirmed her suspicion that Bubba had never been neutered. She also could not find any scar on his lower regions. Therefore, she needed to find the other missing testicle.

Unfortunately, it was not in the inguinal tissues like the first one had been. This meant that she needed to go into the abdomen to search for it. She sutured the first incision and started making a second. Gillian was adjusting the anesthesia to keep Bubba's vitals right where she wanted them.

"How was pajama afternoon yesterday?" asked Mandy.

"It was lovely. We even had our first hot chocolates of the season. I use a recipe from my mom. She used real blocks of chocolate melted in milk. It's so rich and creamy. Of course she used chocolates in New Zealand that we can't buy here so it's not exactly the same. We manage to thoroughly enjoy it anyway."

"That sounds delightful," Mandy said, concentrating on her patient's incision.

"I'll make you some one of these days."

"Yummers," said Mandy.

Mandy used a spay hook, which looks like a shepherd's hook, but very small, to start pulling up bits of tissue from deep down in the abdomen. The theory was, if you were lucky, that you could snare the ligament that suspended the testicle and use that to find your missing organ. Otherwise, it was like looking for a needle in a haystack. The object she was looking for would likely be about the size of a gumball, or smaller, and could be tucked anywhere through the abdomen. Luckily, her hook technique paid off after a number of tries. She was able to tie off the appropriate tissue and blood vessels and remove the culprit of Bubba's unbecoming behavior.

Normally, Mandy recommended sending of the tissue if she was not confident that she removed it all during surgery. However, in some cases, she could feel quite confident that the entire male tissues were removed because they so closely resembled what they should. This was one of those cases. She sutured the incision and Gillian began the process of waking Bubba up and recovering him.

Once transferred to the surgery recovery cages, Gillian clipped Bubba's nails. She checked his temperature, pulse, and respiration every five minutes until it was back to normal. Since Bubba was a brachycephalic, or short-nosed dog, she wanted to be completely sure he was ready to breathe on his own before pulling the tube from his trachea.

Mandy was confident with Gillian's ability to watch Bubba and Llewellyn so she went up to the front to call both owners and give them the good news. Both animals would be able to go home this afternoon with their medications and instructions. Two successes, Mandy thought. "This is what makes being a vet fulfilling. I love solving problems. Now if I could just find that murderer," Mandy said to Lyle, who was sleeping on the cool tile in the reception area.

Chapter Twenty-Five

Having finished surgeries in a timely manner and already written medical notes, Mandy was in good standing to meet Gerry for lunch. She gave Lyle a few kibbles for a snack and let Emma drink at the faucet. Although she hadn't gotten dirty in surgery, she decided to change clothes, particularly her shoes which she only wore in the clinic.

She gathered her notes on the murder and headed toward the Inn. It would be very useful to be able to compare notes with Gerry so she was looking forward to it. Gerry was already sitting at a quiet table in the back when Mandy arrived.

They each ordered the special which was chicken pot pie and a slice of cherry pie.

"So, who's at the top of your list?"

"I'll tell you if you tell me," Mandy replied.

"You know I can't do that," said Gerry.

"Consider my lips sealed then," said Mandy, smirking. "What *can* you tell me?"

"We are not hot on anyone's trails."

"That's not very reassuring. I have to say, this is a tough one," Mandy said. "One thing that I find intriguing is who his heirs were. His will isn't yet public record and I have been unable to link him to anyone in the community. Plus there's the fact that everyone seems to have a loan that he never paid back."

"I can tell you the will is not exciting. Anyone who would be an heir would mainly inherit debt because he seemed to be the village swindler. I do agree that money may be behind the motive. We haven't been able to isolate who would be at the top of the list," said Gerry.

Merv delivered their steaming hot pot pies. The crust was golden brown with perfect little steam holes decoratively placed on the individual pot pie servings. As Mandy cut into hers, rich, creamy gravy poured out with chunks of vegetables and cubes of white meat chicken.

"This is fantastic. There's nothing like a good pot pie," said Mandy as she started to gather her next mouthful on her fork.

"Wait till you try the cherry pie," said Gerry. "They sure can do a crust here."

"What a great addition to the community," said Mandy.

"You aren't so bad yourself. Word on the street is that the Crestviewans are taking a shining to the new vet in town. I hope you don't have plans to skedaddle."

"I'm still undecided on that front. I have never been one to lay roots anywhere. I like to keep my options open."

"Options are good. Why have one foot out the door all the time?"

"It's just the way I live."

"You can't leave in the middle of the night here. Anna left a bit for you to sort out. Maybe she did that on purpose. Maybe she

thought it was time you not have a back up plan?"

"True, there are quite a few loose ends here. Among which is the

murder. Then, there's also Anna's house and the clinic. My

departure is not a deadline. If that was Anna's plan, we'll just

have to see how things play out."

"Why don't you just move into the house? That would solve one

problem," Gerry said with a definitive tone. "You would have a

home instead of a house on wheels."

"I love my RV. Besides, I have yet to sort through everything,

so it is very much still Anna's. Also, I am making every effort to

make sure that she had no heirs. I didn't know her family history

well and I would feel awful if someone out there deserves to

have something that I didn't give them. I have been through that

in my life and it is a horrible feeling. My best advice to anyone

is to make sure that you have a very well-delineated will. I have

seen so many families irreparably damaged from fighting over money. Greed really does bring out the worst in people," said Mandy.

"I agree with that. Luckily I don't own much for people to fight over. So, what are you doing this weekend? I think it's about time I show you around. We've been so busy with investigating that I haven't taken you on a proper tour of Crestview and surrounds. Maybe I can show you what Crestview has to offer so you can at least make an educated decision as to whether you stay or go."

"Can we raincheck it? Sorting Anna's belongings is on my list of priorities. Dennis needs something of hers and I'm hoping to follow up on more of the clues I have for the murder. This weekend seems so far away since it's only Monday. Anyway, would that be a date, Gerry?" Mandy asked.

"Let's reserve calling it anything that might scare you away. Right now, I just want to spend time getting to know you while you get to know Crestview," Gerry answered.

"Points for being a perfect gentleman. You're a clever one."

"We can postpone it to another time."

"Deal. Now, back to Buck. I know the murderer was wearing rather large, narrow shoes. Is there anything else you can tell me about the murder scene?"

"Not really. Whoever did it was most likely a planning type. There were no other clues left at the site. They covered their tracks very well, except for the footprints. They also meant to kill him based on the aim they took. We think he must have had some shooting experience. But that doesn't really narrow it down since that's everyone in Crestview. And since we think it was close range, they didn't need to be the most talented shot."

"What do you think about the location? The yards out there are not exactly a place people frequent. Why there?"

"We don't really know the answer to that. Personally," Gerry continued, "I think they had pre-arranged to meet out there to settle some sort of business. It's just a hunch but I think they meant to be out in the boondocks. I don't think Buck anticipated being in danger or he would never have gone. So I think it's someone fairly unassuming."

"That makes sense."

Myrna delivered their cherry pie. Despite the fact that the pot pie was so filling, Mandy suddenly had room to try just a few bites of the cherry pie. It was served warm with ice cream, just like Mandy preferred. Not intending to eat more than a few bites, Mandy was finishing off the last bite when Gerry said, "I've lost you. Are you in pie land?"

"Oh, sorry. That is so delicious. They should have a warning on that. I swear I was full before she even brought that little treat to the table. Now I am super full."

"That's why a lot of us around here have lost our perfect figures. Myrna and Merv make it pretty hard to stick to a diet. But I work out a lot so I am not as affected as some."

"Note to self. Either eat less here or start an exercise regime."

"Oh, I wouldn't worry. Curves are very becoming."

Mandy started to blush, "I better be heading back to the clinic. I have some appointments straight after lunch." She hated that blushing was an uncontrolled reaction to flattery.

"No problem. We didn't really make much headway. This is a tricky case."

"Indeed it is. Here's my half of the bill," said Mandy.

"A curvy gal who likes to go Dutch, my cup of tea," said Gerry.

"Watch it. What happened to being a gentleman?" asked Mandy.

"I can't help it. I love making people blush."

"Lovely," said Mandy as she got up from the table and made her way to the door. It had been a while since anyone pushed her buttons. She couldn't decide if she liked it or was thoroughly annoyed by it.

Chapter Twenty-Six

"Well, how did it go? Are you going to be a famous detective?" asked Gillian when Mandy returned from lunch.

"Hardly. I can say that this is not a straight-forward case. They are pretty stumped and keep following leads to nowhere. I don't know how they haven't gotten further than me and they do this full time."

"I could book some time out for you if you want to follow up on some clues," Gillian suggested.

"I may take you up on that. This is not wasted time here because I also find that I can learn bits and pieces from appointments that come in."

"Just say the word. For now, your afternoon is fairly light. First up is a limping Yorkie," said Gillian.

Mandy got the file out of the ones pulled for the afternoon. She looked at the record. The dog's name was Ginger and she was about six years old. She was up to date on everything and the owner seemed to be in every few months for various reasons. Mandy figured that the owner must be very attentive.

Gillian brought Ginger and her owner into the room for Mandy.

"So, we are limping?" she said. It wasn't apparent which leg was the problem since the elderly owner had the dog tucked under her arm. It didn't seem like the dog really spent much time walking from the looks of her long nails.

"Yes. She started yesterday. We don't lead very active lives so I'm not sure how she could have hurt herself," Ginger's owner said. She was a well-dressed woman with a short bob of gray, permed hair. Her shoes matched her handbag of genuine, soft leather. She had the smell of someone who had time and money to invest in high-end cosmetics. Mandy smiled because she brought back memories of her classy grandmother who dressed to the nines until the day she passed.

"Let's have a look and see what we find. Can we put her on the ground so I can see which leg?"

Ginger's owner placed her gently on the ground and Ginger promptly hid between the woman's legs, taking cover under her tailored pantsuit legs.

"It's ok, Ginger. You need to show Dr. Bell," the owner said as she walked away from Ginger. "I think it's the back left leg," she said to Mandy.

Ginger took a tentative step and really wasn't keen to show anything but petrification. Mandy scooped Ginger up and started checking her back legs one by one.

"I think this might be the problem," Mandy said as she pointed to Ginger's left knee. "Ginger has a very common problem in small dogs. Her knee cap moves out of its groove and then sometimes does not pop back into place. It's called patellar luxation."

"Is it painful?"

"It can be, especially when the knee cap or patella is not in the correct place. I have popped it back into place for now. The problem is that it will likely continue to pop in and out and will lead to arthritis in the knee which will be painful. She actually has it in both knees, but her left is worse."

"What do we do about it?"

"At this stage, I would do nothing. We can give anti-inflammatories for when it flares up. I will teach you how to pop it back in place if it comes out. If she spends more time with it popping out than staying in, then we may need to do a simple surgery to correct it. I never like to intervene in joints unless we really have to because there is always a risk of making things worse. So, I want to make sure the benefits of surgery outweigh the risks. Make sense?"

"Yes. Is there anything else I can do?"

"Since Ginger is not terribly active, you do not need to limit her activity. There are some dog-friendly joint supplements available now which can help slow the progression of arthritis. I will go grab the anti-inflammatories for you which you can use on days when you think she might be in pain. Do not use it every day though because over time, high doses of these drugs can cause liver and kidney issues. We can monitor that with bloodwork every six months and intervene if necessary."

"Ok, I think I understand. Only use the drugs when she is having a rough day. No surgery yet unless we have more bad days than good. And we can start supplements. Do you have those here?"

"Sure do. I will grab some of those too. Let me know if you have any other questions or concerns."

"Thanks so much, Dr. Bell. She is my baby."

"I understand completely. I have one of my own."

"No kids though?"

"Nope. Just my dog."

"Me too. I have a few nieces and nephews. Fred, the

hairdresser, is my grand-nephew. I think you've met him."

"Yes indeed. I didn't know you were related to him."

"Of course. His grandmother was my sister. She was so artistic. That's where he gets his flair for fashion, I'm sure."

"You are pretty styling yourself."

"Well thanks."

As Ginger's owner was checking out with the Gillian at the front, a gentleman hurriedly burst in with a dog dripping blood from its hind quarters. He was anything but calm.

Dr. Bell rushed to find out what the emergency was.

"Darn dog. He has a tendency to chase cars and I didn't see him dart out from our bushes. Please tell me he's going to make it. This is our family dog and my kids would be devastated."

"Let me have a look. In the meantime, have a seat out here. It looks like I may need an x-ray. What's his name?" asked

Mandy.

"Ronnie," replied the man. "And I am Doug Reed. I run the rifle range out of town."

"Nice to meet you, though I am sorry to meet you like this. I am going to get started on Ronnie."

Mandy carried Ronnie to the x-ray room and turned the light on. She checked over his vitals and took a look for signs of injuries. She wanted to make sure he was stable enough before she proceeded with pain medication and diagnostics. It seemed that the majority of his injury was sustained on the left hind leg.

Gillian appeared with her lead apron on and pulled her book out to find the right values to put the x-ray machine on. "Are we doing a lateral and a VD?" asked Gillian.

"You got it. I want to really check his hips and back legs. Something doesn't feel stable," said Mandy.

Once the x-ray was developed, they had a look together on the viewer. Luckily the hips were completely intact. The femur, however, was shattered. There would be no way to repair this fracture. Mandy walked out to meet Mr. Reed in the waiting room to explain her findings.

"Doug, I have some bad news. Ronnie has a very nasty fracture on his left back leg. Apart from some bruising, the rest of him seems to be ok. Unfortunately the only treatment for his fracture is to remove his leg," Mandy started to explain.

"Oh no, we couldn't do that. His entire life is about running and playing. He can't be a cripple."

"Bear with me for a moment. I have amputated a lot of dog's legs in my career. Everyone has the initial reaction you are having because we tend to assume animals will have the same response we would have. However, they do incredibly well with three legs. They can still run and jump and play. Please trust me on this," Mandy said.

"I would have to discuss this with the family. I also need to know how much it would cost. We are pretty tight right now. Buck owed us a considerable amount of money and it doesn't look like we will ever see a cent," Doug said. "He had a hair-brained scheme to make fast money but it turned out to be one of those pyramid schemes. The word about the estate is not only is there a long line of people who want debts paid off, but there is not really any money in the estate. He wasn't blessed with a sense for money."

"Hmmm. Well, under the circumstances, I would first keep him overnight to ensure that he is stable enough to even go through a surgery. So, we have some time to think before we have to make a decision."

"Okay. I will leave him in your capable hands and we can touch base tomorrow. I am embarrassed about the money situation. I have to say, if Buck wasn't already dead, I think I'd kill him. I hate swindlers, the whole town does."

"Fair enough. Do you have any theories on who might have

done the deed?" asked Mandy.

"It has to be someone who lost more money than I did. I'm not sure who that would be, but I am going to his funeral to see for myself that he is dead and buried. I'm a nice guy. It's not a good idea to cross me. My family doesn't have much and he led us to believe he would help us, not hurt us."

"I hadn't heard that they had set a date for the funeral yet. When is it?"

"It's this Tuesday. They had to wait until the feds were done with their autopsy. I bet whoever did it will be at the funeral for the same reason I will be," Doug said.

"Good point. I will see you there."

"Why would you want to waste your time going to a deadbeat's funeral? Did he owe you money too?"

"No. Although, I have taken a bit of an interest in the murder and I'd like to see someone arrested for it."

"So, you're a vet and a detective. Interesting. You'll fit right into Crestview. We all have our hands in more pots than one. I'll talk to you tomorrow," Doug said as he left the room.

Chapter Twenty-Seven

"You're next appointment is here, Dr. Bell," Gillian said, poking her head in the office doorway. In the background, Emma was lapping up water from the faucet. "It's a sweet little poodle with a major eye issue."

"I'll be right there," replied Mandy. She was checking the Internet for more information on the funeral. She found it very strange that she had managed to miss the announcement of the funeral. "I guess there's no harm done. I haven't missed the funeral and it looks like it was a last minute decision," she said to Jimbo, who was curled up in the sunshine giving himself a thorough bath. He was the cleanest cat she had ever seen. Largely white, with black spots along his back and head, he never had a speck of dust or dirt on him.

Mandy entered the exam room to find a woman clutching a geriatric poodle with one bulging eye. "Oh my, what a dreadful eye. What has happened here?" asked Mandy of the woman.

"Trixie woke up this morning like this. I don't know what happened. She was inside all night sleeping so I don't think it's an injury," said the woman.

"Well, let me grab a few instruments to help figure this out," said Mandy. As she was opening the exam room door to head back to the surgery, Gillian was approaching with a metal suitcase.

"I think you'll find everything you need in here. And I'll stay to give you a hand," Gillian said.

"Wow, thanks," said Mandy. She set the case on the counter and started preparing the instruments. There was a tonometer to assess the pressure in the eye, an ophthalmoscope to visualize the eye and it's supporting structures, a large lens to magnify the eye, and two types of drops, one to numb the eye and one to dilate the pupil.

As Mandy prepared, Gillian asked the woman, "I haven't seen you in a while, how have you been?"

"Not bad. With school starting, I've been busy with that. I had a great summer, though. How about you and Hamish?"

"We are good. Thanks for asking. Mandy, this is Trudy Jean. She is one of the teachers at the school."

"So nice to meet you. What grade do you teach?" asked Mandy.

"I am a high school English teacher. I've been there for so long, I feel like I have helped raise half of this town. I was Anna's teacher, you know."

"I had no idea. Was she a good student?" asked Mandy.

"Actually, no. She was definitely into the sciences by then. English was not her passion. Anna and Dennis were such an item. They used to sneak notes back and forth at the back of class stealthily, as if I didn't see all. I always thought that they would marry. They lost touch when Anna went to vet school. When she came back, I figured they would carry on where they left off. They were such a good looking couple."

As Ms. Jean's face lit up with the memories of Anna and Dennis, Mandy and Gillian were applying the numbing and dilating drops to Trixie's eyes. So far, they hadn't found a scratch on the cornea with the fluroscein stain. It appeared that the first reading of the tonometer was elevated. This meant that the pressure in Trixie's eyes was too high.

"I'm sure that Dennis was devastated when he heard about Anna. I know he's in town. I haven't managed to catch up with him since Anna's funeral. Have you guys seen him?" asked Ms. Jean.

"He was over at Fred's when I got my hair cut. He seemed to keep in the back room. I don't really know him so I don't know if he was acting different or not," Mandy said.

"I've been a bit preoccupied with convincing Mandy to stay that I haven't really seen him," said Gillian.

Mandy was checking the structures in the back of Trixie's eye with her ophthalmoscope and lens. Unfortunately, it looked like the intro-ocular pressure was high due to acute glaucoma. Mandy opened a drawer in the exam room and pulled out her glucometer.

"We are going to check Trixie's blood glucose. It'll just be a little drop of blood that we need," said Mandy. The number on the machine read 359, too high for a dog's glucose. "Trixie here is diabetic, Ms. Jean. She has suffered an acute episode of glaucoma, or high pressure in the eyes. We need to get the diabetes under control with insulin and also treat the high pressure in the eye with special drops. You can have surgery on her eyes to help with the eye pressure. You would have to drive pretty far for that kind of specialized surgery, though. If we can't get her comfortable with drops, I can remove her eye."

"What? She would only have one eye?" asked Ms. Jean.

"It's a possibility. There are a lot of things to try before that stage. I should say at this point that dogs do very well with only one eye. The reason I really want to avoid surgery is that she could develop the same thing in the remaining eye and we don't want to leave her with no vision. So, first, we will run a full blood panel on her to rule out any other issues. Then we will keep her here for a few days to get her glucose regulated. Meanwhile, we will be trying to decrease the eye pressure. Then, once we have her stabilized, we will give you a lesson on how to give insulin and manage a diabetic dog. Lastly, we will wait and see if her eye pressures return to normal. If they don't, we will consider the surgery. Any questions?"

"Wow, no wonder you and Anna were such good friends. You are both thorough and yet understanding. I don't have any questions, except is Trixie in pain?" said Ms. Jean.

"We think that there is a headache-like pain associated with glaucoma. I will be treating her with pain medication. We just have to be careful not to compromise her kidneys with pain medications since they are most certainly affected by her diabetes. It can all get a little complicated."

"I can see that. I will leave her in your good hands then. Please keep me updated on what you find. Are there visiting hours here?" asked Ms. Jean.

"Of course. We will keep you posted on her status and you are most welcome to come and visit her," said Gillian.

"I will go home and bake her some goodies to bring her as she is recovering."

"I'm afraid she will be on a strict diet now with her diabetes. While insulin manages glucose, diet is a pivotal part of diabetes treatment," said Mandy.

"That's going to be quite a change for her. Is there something I can bake her that would be safe?' asked Ms. Jean. "She loves to help me bake."

"I will give you some diabetic-friendly dog treat recipes. I will have to dig them out. I assure you that I will find them for you," said Mandy. "We best get to work on her so we can get her home to you as soon as possible."

"Thanks so much, Dr. Bell. Is it ok to bake for the two of you – as long as you don't share with Trixie?" asked Ms. Jean.

"I have never refused home baking," Mandy said with a smile.

Gillian and Mandy worked together to get Trixie on IV fluids and get blood sent off to the lab. They had some insulin in stock and started Trixie on a modest dose. The worst thing for her would be to receive too much insulin and crash. It was always a fine line with a newly diagnosed diabetic.

Once they got Trixie sorted, Gillian headed on home to start dinner for Hamish. Mandy finished up some medical notes for the cases from the past few days. As she was just heading out the door, the phone rang. She stayed to hear the message to determine if it was an emergency that needed attention.

"Hi Mandy, it's Dennis. I'm going to be heading out of town soon and wondered if I could meet with you. I don't know if you've had a chance to clean out Anna's house. I'd really like to get those few items before I head out."

Mandy let the message end without picking it up. She knew Dennis had been trying to get something from Anna's house though she wasn't sure what. She was reluctant to divvy anything up until she was certain there would be no conflicts later on. She had already explained this to him and was annoyed with his persistence. With the funeral the next day, Mandy was focused on getting her head in the game of murder sleuthing.

Chapter Twenty-Eight

They closed the clinic for the day of the funeral out of respect. The patients were all comfortably tucked in for the few hours they would be gone. It would be a slow day anyway since the entire town would be in attendance. Mandy scurried around her RV trying to find something to wear. Unfortunately, she could find nothing suitable. She remembered that Anna's closet was well stocked and perhaps she could find something at her house that fit her. It was only a short drive to her house but she didn't have long before the funeral began.

Lyle hopped in the Jeep and Mandy grabbed a few gummy bears from the glove compartment as a little pick me up. They drove up to the front of Anna's house and Lyle trotted up the front porch stairs like she was home.

"Sweety, we don't live here, even though the whole town thinks we will," Mandy said to Lyle.

Mandy searched the closet in Anna's room for something black and classy. Luckily, Anna had a very sensible yet fashionable collection. She tried on a few items and found the right combination, black slacks and a sharp sweater. Mandy was searching in the top of the closet for shoes that might match and came across a metal filing box. She lugged it down onto the bed.

The clasp opened without much of a struggle and Mandy started pulling out documents. She found the deed to the property which listed Anna as the only holder. In the same file as the deed was another deed dated ten years prior. It listed Anna and Dennis as the deed holders.

"That's very strange Lyle. I didn't think Anna and Dennis ever shared a life out of high school. They must have bought this together and then Anna bought him out for some reason. He is not listed anywhere in the will or Anna's wishes. I wonder what happened," Mandy said to Lyle who was sprawled out on the bed with her head on a pillow, watching Mandy intently. "This must be what the lawyer and Dennis are after."

Mandy searched the rest of the files in the box. There were a number of important documents such as her transcripts from school, insurance documents, health records, and various family documents. Mandy went through each one to see if it shed any light on either Anna's wishes with her belongings or with the connection between Dennis and possibly Buck. She found nothing else of interest. She decided she would focus on going through this closet when she had more time.

Mandy took the file with the deed and went back to the front of the house to get back to the Jeep. She almost forgot Anna's clothes that she had set aside. She went back inside to grab them, making sure to keep them clean so she wouldn't have to lint roll them back at the RV. Starting the ignition, Mandy wondered which lead to look into next. She now had to figure out more about Aaron and his protective nature for Howie, Dennis's connection to Anna's house deed, Jim's need to win the dart competition suddenly, and any loose ends regarding the money Buck owed to people.

Mandy returned to the clinic and checked on Trixie who was resting comfortably. Her glucose had come down slightly. The insulin was working and she had a lot more energy. Bloodwork had come back by fax and showed mild kidney changes. That meant that they had caught the diabetes before it had caused significant organ damage. For now, she was able to have a little snack followed by an insulin injection. Trixie was so happy to eat, even if the food was not her usual home-baked splendor. This was a good sign that her appetite was coming back.

Ronnie was looking a little brighter too. His fractured leg was at least stabilized with the bandage she had put on earlier. He was making no attempt to walk. He did, however, wag his tail at the sight of company. She gave him a little breakfast to have something on his stomach and administered another pain injection to last him until after the funeral. As long as he continued to improve after the initial shock, he would be able to undergo surgery. She locked the door to the clinic, leaving Emma and Jimbo to run around free in the clinic until she got back to check on Trixie and Ronnie.

Now ready for the funeral, Mandy put Lyle up in the RV so she wouldn't try to hop in the Jeep to attend the funeral. Although the town had become accustomed to the vet always having her four-legged partner, a funeral was hardly the place. Besides, Mandy would be busy trying to garner any new information from the attendees.

Lyle put up a bit of a fight about not joining in the activities, but Mandy bribed her with a little milk. Even though the kibble Mandy gave her was well-balanced, Lyle had a long-standing obsession with anything made of milk. Her weakness was cheese, but yogurt, milk, ice cream, even cheese curds would do in a pinch. Mandy never let clients know of the rule she broke with her own dog. She was always telling clients not to give their pets people food for fear of digestive upsets or obsession and therefore disinterest in dog kibble. In her own RV, Mandy could break any rule she wanted as long as no one would find out.

With Lyle snuggled on the couch now, Mandy lint-rolled her black pants. Despite her earlier efforts, fur had managed to cling to the black slacks. She boarded the Jeep for the trip to the funeral location, the town church. Mandy hadn't made church a part of her life, choosing instead to follow the philosophy that spiritual connections were best made all around instead of channeled through a church. She knew enough of the rituals to not make a fool of herself but nowhere near enough to teach Sunday school.

There was a fairly large gathering of cars and people outside the church. The denomination of the church was unclear. Since it serviced the entire community, being the only church in 100 miles, it was likely not a strict sect. Mandy entered the receiving room and signed the guestbook; even though she hadn't actually met Buck Dawson, she wanted to pay her respects. She let the greeter take her coat and made her way into the viewing area.

The church was brimming with people and it was big enough for the crowd that Buck's death had drawn. Obviously, this church was a major part of the community here based on its size and impeccable up-keep.

In the background, there was a nice display of photos of Buck and his involvements throughout his life. Dart championship, pool league, and shooting range trophies lined the back of one whole table. No target would have been safe from Buck's steady shot. The remembrance collage had a few pictures that Mandy recognized from the yearbooks she had seen at Anna's. One photo that she hadn't seen before had Buck, Anna, and Dennis, confirming her theory that they had been a trio of friends at one point.

Mandy waited her turn in line to pay her respects at the coffin. Buck looked far more peaceful than the morning she had first seen him. She shivered a little, remembering that morning. Out of the corner of her eye, she saw Dennis and decided to approach him.

"He was so young. This is such a tragedy," Mandy said to Dennis.

"Indeed it was. We knew each other in high school. I lost touch with him but I remember him being a decent guy," Dennis said, as he looked down at his shoes. Mandy took the opportunity to study his shoes, in particular, their size. With his wide-legged pants, though, she could not tell whether his shoes were narrow or even get a feel for the size.

"I saw a photo there of you, Buck, and Anna. Were you guys good friends back then?" asked Mandy.

"We were fairly close. It seemed we always got involved in the same extracurricular activities, like the paper. It is a small town though so it's hard not to know everyone and work with them on something at some point."

"That makes sense. When was the last time you saw him?"

"It would have to be last year at the Christmas Mingler, I think. I don't come back this way that often. The way life seems to be going at the moment, funerals are what brings me back more often than not. I don't feel like I am getting older but maybe I am."

"You weren't here for Anna's funeral?" Mandy asked.

"I was. What a sad affair," Dennis answered.

"But, you didn't see Buck then?" asked Mandy.

"Is this an inquisition? I told you I wasn't very close to Buck. Now I have some questions for you," Dennis said.

"I don't think is the time or the place to discuss Anna's possessions, if that's what you are leading up to. We can arrange a time to do that," Mandy said, curtly.

"But…" Dennis started.

"I know, you are leaving soon. I will meet with you this

evening, say five thirty, at the clinic?" said Mandy. "Is that soon enough?"

"I don't mean to be a bother. Thank you. I will see you then," Dennis said and made an exit from Mandy's presence.

Mandy surveyed the room to see if there was anyone she needed to speak with or hadn't met yet. She spotted a man dressed in nice slacks and red suspenders with white stars on them. He carried himself with an air of confidence like he was the mayor of town, but she knew he wasn't. She was curious as to his identity and decided to try to engage in a conversation with him. She didn't want to be too obvious so she waited until he was at the refreshment table. While he was getting a cup of coffee, she sidled up next to him to do the same. When he put his stirrer down, she reached to grab some sugar and made eye contact with him.

"Such a shame. It's hard to see someone so young be buried," Mandy offered in condolence.

"So true. I wondered how you were doing, what with your, ahem, role in this and all," the man said.

"That was an unexpected and terrible way to start that morning. I see you know who I am. I haven't had the pleasure of meeting you," Mandy said, offering her hand to shake.

"Barney Saunders, owner of the general store here in town," the man said, returning her handshake.

"Ah yes, nice to meet you. I understand you and Buck and Jim had a bit of a competition going for the top shooter in the community. Bet you're going to miss Buck," Mandy said, fishing for a reaction.

"Aw, it won't be the same without friendly competition between us all. Life has it's way of coming on and so, too, does death," Barney said, re-adjusting his suspenders.

"Too right. Are you a bit of a hunter, or are you just interested in the target practice at the range?" asked Mandy.

"A bit of both. I go out West every few years for big game hunting. Mainly I just enjoy the camaraderie."

"Do you know anyone who might have wanted to squelch the camaraderie and hurt Buck?" asked Mandy.

"Now you just got here. I thought you were a vet. Are you a detective as well?" Barney asked.

"Not exactly. Just trying to help," Mandy answered.

"Well, I would suggest staying clear of this. It's not really your business. But if you must know, I wouldn't hurt a soul, unless it was a real buck with antlers," Barney huffed.

"I didn't mean to offend you. I just want to help."

"You can help by leaving it to the authorities."

"Thanks. And it was nice to meet you. Again, I apologize."

"That's alright. But I do recommend sticking to your own role in this town. Stepping on toes isn't a good way to start," Barney said.

"Thanks for the advice. See you at the general store sometime," Mandy said.

The viewing was ending and the procession was beginning to form out front. Since Mandy had paid her respects, she did not plan to join the procession. She quietly slipped out the back door and climbed in her Jeep to head on back to the RV.

As she drove the short distance back, her mind was reeling with ideas. While she hadn't cleared Barney of a motive or established an alibi, her gut told her she was barking up the wrong tree with him. She decided her next move would be to visit the rifle range and ask around out there. First, though, she needed to eat something and prepare to meet Dennis.

At the RV, she found a note taped to the door. She pulled it off and brought it in with her. Inside, she found Lyle still snuggled up on the couch. She poured some crunchies for her and put some water on the stove for some chicken noodle soup.

Homemade was always better at a time like this, but she didn't have time or the ingredients for that so store bought would have to suffice. She at least had chicken broth so she could make it taste a little more delectable. Having caught a bit of a chill in the Fall air, Mandy also craved some steaming hot coffee. She normally only had coffee in the mornings. As an adult, she could break the rules every now and then.

Mandy sat down at the dinette and sipped her coffee while the soup came to a boil. She opened the note. It was a warning to her to case her investigation. If she did not, the writer of the note said that harm would come her way, and her little dog, too.

"What am I missing, little Lyle? Who is threatening us? I must be getting close to the murderer if we are at risk. I won't stop." Mandy said. "Are you willing to put our life in danger to solve this murder?" she asked Lyle. Lyle responded by angling her head and staring at Mandy. "I'll take that as a yes." She tossed the note in the trash.

"So, the size thirteen shoes are a good clue and I have been eying everyone's feet that I see. Most men in this town do have large feet so I am not getting anywhere with that clue. Most everyone has access to a gun so that doesn't help either. It's tricky to narrow down motives and alibis because I just haven't been here long enough to know how to get answers from people. What's a girl to do?"

Lyle responded by yawning and flopping down sideways to stretch her whole body out.

"Thanks for your interest. Are you giving me the cold shoulder because I wouldn't let you come with me?" Lyle merely sighed and stretched her body out further.

The soup was ready on the stove and Mandy picked her favorite ceramic bowl to enjoy it in. She had a fresh package of saltines and crumbled some on top of the soup. She tossed one to Lyle as a peace offering. The good thing about soup, Mandy thought, is that you can't eat it too fast so you end up feeling full quicker.

Plus, it warms your soul from the inside out which is always a comforting feeling. She would need all the strength she could muster to meet Dennis and sort out what he needed, once and for all. She was so worn out and cozy from her soup that she dozed off, waking up to Lyle licking her face.

"Guess I need some caffeine," Mandy said to herself as she warmed some coffee from the morning.

Chapter Twenty-Nine

To finish her coffee and satiate her sweet tooth, Mandy grabbed a few chocolate chip cookies to nibble on as the clock approached quarter past five. She left the RV and went into the clinic to check Trixie and Ronnie. They were still doing well so she left them to rest. She would have to come to a conclusion with Ronnie over the next few days so she would call his owner in the morning to make a plan. Lyle had been following her diligently while she made her rounds to check on patients until she veered off toward the lobby. Through the front window, Mandy saw Dennis pull up in Fred's VW beetle.

"It must be 5:30 already, Lyle," Mandy said to Lyle as she let Dennis in.

"Hi, thanks for meeting with me," Dennis said. "I know you are a busy lady these days."

"That's ok. I do have a bit on my plate. Even still, let's see if we can't get you a resolution."

"I'm glad we have a chance to be alone. I wanted to impress upon you how important it is that you keep your nose out of the murder investigation. I may not live in Crestview anymore but I know how this town is. They don't take kindly on outsiders butting in."

"You're entitled to your opinion. I have to do what I have to do. What is it that you are looking for anyway?" As she was asking the question, Dennis was pulling something out of his back pocket.

Before he could answer, Gerry came rushing through the door. Mandy was startled both by Gerry's entrance and by the way Dennis was pulling something from his pocket. When Dennis saw Gerry, he let go of whatever he had his hand on behind his back.

"I'm so sorry to barge in. I saw the lights were on. Reggie is howling in pain. I don't know what's wrong," Gerry said as he placed Reggie on the counter.

"I'm sorry, Dennis. This looks like an emergency. Duty calls. I don't know how long I will be so you can wait or we can try again tomorrow," Mandy said.

"I think I'll head on back to Fred's. I'll stop in tomorrow," Dennis said, clearly not impressed.

"Ok," Mandy said. She turned her attention back to Gerry and Reggie. "Talk to me. How did you find him?"

"When I got home from the funeral, I found him in front of the litter pan just yowling. I scooped him up and brought him here. That's all I know."

"Did you change the litter back to what you were using before?" asked Mandy.

"Yep."

"Have you been able to give the antibiotics?"

"Yep," said Gerry.

"Ok, let me have a look at him." She transferred him to the exam room table and felt his abdomen first. "Oh my, his bladder is enormous. I'd say we have a blockage in his urethra."

"What does that mean?" asked Gerry.

"Well, even though we found a slight infection and we're treating it, it seems he may have some sludge made of crystals that has blocked his ability to pee. I won't know for sure until I try to pass a catheter. I can say that his bladder should not be this large. First, I am going to give him some pain medication."

"Yes please."

"Once I have him more comfortable under mild sedation, I will try to pass a catheter and if there is a blockage, I will unblock it. We need to get his bladder empty quickly or it will stretch too far and not want to contract normally. Also, they can get toxic from not being able to excrete urine," said Mandy.

"Ouch. That all sounds horrible."

"It is. It's also not uncommon, especially in indoor male cats. I'm afraid he will need to stay with me for a few days. And we will be changing his food to try to prevent this problem in the future," said Mandy.

"I will leave you to it, unless you need a hand." Gerry placed a hand on Mandy's shoulder as a thank you. Lyle had been watching him closely and promptly snarled her lip.

"What is that about, Lyle?" asked Mandy. Lyle just looked from Mandy to Gerry with intense eyes. "I should be alright by myself. Thanks."

"Looks like Lyle would like it to stay that way, too," Gerry said, chuckling.

"She doesn't take kindly to anyone getting too close to me. She could finish my sentences if people only knew how to hear her. She is the yin to my yang."

"I understand. I am not here to intrude." As Mandy drew up

pain medication for Reggie and administered it, Gerry watched her intently, but from a distance. "Why was Dennis here anyway?"

"It seems he needs something that is in Anna's house. He has been trying to meet me to retrieve whatever it is. I have been busy so tonight was the earliest I could take him over to her house. He says he is leaving town shortly and wanted to get it before he left."

"I don't like the sounds of that. Next time, call me and I will be a chaperone. Correction, Lyle and I will both chaperone," Gerry said. Reggie was already starting to relax under the influence of the pain medication and sedation.

"Are you jealous?" Mandy asked.

"Me, no. I am just worried about your safety. There is still a murderer on the loose and we don't know who it is. Are you having any luck in your sleuthing?"

"I did just get an anonymous warning to keep my nose out of it. So, I must be getting close."

"As in a threat?"

"I suppose," answered Mandy.

"I don't like the sounds of that at all. Where is this note?" asked Gerry.

"I have thrown it away. Don't worry. I'm not phased," said Mandy.

"You best let me handle any threats to you. We can't allow anyone else to get hurt or worse."

"Point taken. Back to the investigation. I feel like I am missing something. I keep zeroing on a suspect before find out something that changes my mind. So, no, you?"

"We are still following leads. But we don't have a top of the list yet. We certainly don't have the makings for a warrant to arrest yet," Gerry answered.

"I am thinking of going out to the rifle range tomorrow to see what I can find out there."

"Be careful Dr. Bell. We have already investigated out there, but do let me know if you come across something important," said Gerry.

"I shall. I will also give you an update on Reggie. I better prepare a cage for him. My hospital ward is getting full," said Mandy.

"There's nothing wrong with being popular," Gerry said.

"True."

"Well, I will leave you to it. Call me."

"You have my word."

"Oh, and please be safe," Gerry warned.

Chapter Thirty

Mandy gathered the instruments and materials she would need to unblock Reggie and transferred him to the surgery area. He was now adequately sedated so she could proceed with her treatment. First, she administered a numbing agent to his urethra. She opened a sterile pouch of lubrication and attempted to pass the urinary catheter. Sure enough, there was a noticeable blockage which prevented the catheter from entering the bladder. Mandy drew up some flush in a syringe and attached it to the catheter. While moving the catheter in and out, she flushed with the syringe. Unblocking a tom cat can be as much finesse as scientific. She patiently kept repeating the process, being careful not to be too forceful or she could damage the urethra. As she concentrated, her glasses slid down her nose.

She leaned back and stretched her back and then repositioned her glasses. Reggie was comfortable under anesthesia so she was safe to keep trying. Finally, she was able to push the catheter and a fountain of blood-tinged urine swished out into the basin she had ready for this hopeful occurrence. She saved a pipet of the urine to test and potentially send off for a culture and sensitivity if the infection persisted despite the antibiotics he had been receiving.

Mandy filled several syringes full of flush and rinsed the interior of the bladder through the catheter. Once confident she had emptied the bladder, she sutured the catheter in place to ensure good flow until she could pull it for good. It would remain in place to allow urine flow for at least a day so she could monitor for additional blockages. Many cats objected to an indwelling catheter so she put an Elizabethan collar on his head to prevent him from pulling the catheter prematurely. She administered some subcutaneous fluids to Reggie since the poor guy had been unable to pee, and therefore, hadn't consumed much water, leading to dehydration. She also administered a drug to help the bladder muscles start to contract again since they had been stretched severely under the pressure of the urine. She gave another medication which would prevent the urethra from forming a stricture under all of the inflammation. Finally, she gave Reggie a strong dose of antibiotics before settling him in his cage for the night.

"When it rains, it pours," Mandy said out loud to herself, standing back to look at all of the sick animals she had collected over the last 36 hours. She checked Trixie's glucose again and was happy with how it was stabilizing. She would be able to release Trixie to her owner soon. Ronnie was lying on his side, wagging his tail. He had started to chew at his bandage on his leg so Mandy fitted an Elizabethan collar on him. He clearly was not impressed with this contraption and had his head rammed in the corner of the cage.

"If you had left it alone, you wouldn't have to wear the cone of shame," Mandy said, shaking her finger at Ronnie. "Alright you guys, I need to take a break to eat something. Everybody looks happy or as happy as they can be. Good night, all," Mandy said to her patients.

Emma whizzed around the corner, her feet hitting the floor with such gusto that she sounded like a herd of hyenas. "Mrrraw," Emma said loudly. She rubbed on Mandy's legs as Mandy attempted to walk.

"Ok, a little water for you," Mandy said and turned the faucet on. She gave Emma and Jimbo a few crunchies in their bowl and waited for Emma to get her fill of water before turning off the faucet.

"Now I am going to go get something to eat, you needy children!" Mandy laughed.

She went back out to the RV and Lyle climbed up to sprawl out on the dashboard to watch birds as the sun set.

The soup Mandy had eaten earlier hadn't kept her feeling full. She made herself a grilled cheese sandwich on the stove. Lyle jumped off the dash and sprang into action when she heard the sound of the cheese being unwrapped. She sat with the cutest, most irresistible expression on her face that Mandy rewarded her with a corner of cheese.

After eating, Mandy tried to get some rest. Half of her head was swimming with ideas of what to look for at the rifle range during lunch the next day. The other half of her thoughts were consumed by her patients. Even though she had been a vet for many years and had seen just about everything, she never became complacent. She often pushed herself to learn more and do better with every case. She was paranoid that she might miss something and get sloppy like many over-confident vets did in their mature years.

Numerous cases had resulted in restless nights due to her need to check on them through the night. She had learned to listen to the subconscious voice that awakened her during these occasions. In fact, more than once, the angle of the case she had been missing had come to her while checking the patients in the wee hours of the morning. One case, an elderly pug with liver failure, proved how this intuition could be the catalyst for a different treatment. This pug had been in her care for almost two weeks, on IV fluids, antibiotics, anti-nausea medication, the works. She knew it was liver failure due to uncontrolled diabetes but she could not figure out why the dog's nausea was so uncontrollable. She had been offering all kinds of different foods in an attempt to get the little guy to eat something. She could see that he was wasting away in front of her. She would back off the intravenous nutrition to try to encourage the dog to eat but to no avail. Finally, during a late night check up on her patients, Mandy got an idea. She had read once upon a time that eating liver could actually help a liver. She started boiling some up to entice the pug. In addition, she had tried every single anti-nausea combination except plain old Benadryl. She remembered that people who get motion sickness sometimes use that in a pinch for their dizziness. She administered the Benadryl while the liver was cooling. She knew she had better get to bed since she had a full load of surgeries the next morning so she left the liver for the pug to try on his own. The next morning, she found an empty bowl and a hungry pug. Mandy never knew whether it was simply time for the case to finally shift directions on its own or if her squirrelly late-night ideas were the cause, but she was always so thankful when things took a turn for the better.

Tonight, she would try not to wake up to check on her patients, but if the feeling came, she would honor it with a visit to the clinic. Lyle was curled up with her head on a pillow and her body pressed up against Mandy. The sound of Lyle's breathing was so soothing that she finally dozed off to sleep.

Chapter Thirty-One

Morning came far too soon. As usual, coffee helped reverse the damage of a sleepless late night. Even though she hadn't woken up in the middle of the night, she didn't sleep well. Today she would be heading over to the rifle range to investigate during the noon hour. After sufficient caffeine, she checked on her patients and they were all doing well. She gave each of their owners an update. Since Trixie was handling her insulin and change of food well, she would be discharged in the next few days. Ronnie's owner, Doug, opted for surgery and she would work that into the schedule this week. He also agreed to meet with her at the range today. Reggie was peeing well and eating so she pulled his catheter. If he continue to pee well, he could be discharged later in the week. Mandy made sure Emma and Jimbo were happy with fresh food, clean water, and scooped litter boxes.

Mandy could have scheduled for Gillian to come in to do the

morning chores, but with so many patients in the clinic, it was really better for Mandy to just do it while she was checking on them all. The clinic had a little fenced-in area in which to walk ambulatory patients. They didn't board animals but the clinic could be quite full with just patients alone.

Mandy returned to the RV and had a hearty breakfast of frozen waffles with peanut butter and sliced cheddar cheese. Although a strange combination, she found it kept her satiated for a long time and she would need it for her plans today. She also didn't enjoy traditional breakfast items like eggs and bacon. She detested sweet food early in the morning, opting to have something savory most of the time.

The morning appointments were seamless, with the help of Gillian and Lyle. They had a coon dog with a thorn in his paw, a cat with an upper respiratory tract infection, a bulldog with an ingrown dewclaw, and several routine vaccine appointments. Mandy and Gillian took one tea break in between the appointments and suddenly the morning was over. Gillian had kept the afternoon fairly light so Mandy could take a long lunch to go meet Ronnie's owner at the rifle range.

Mandy checked her patients and then went out to the RV to have a light lunch before heading out. Lyle really got jumpy around guns and gunshots so Mandy opted to leave her home while she went out to the range.

"I'm sorry, girl. We will go for a nice long walk when I get back. I'll bet you a dollar to a donut that you'd rather be here," Mandy told a very disappointed Lyle. She hopped in her Jeep, leaving a sulking Lyle in the chair by the door.

At the rifle range, Mandy had trouble finding a parking spot because it seemed to be a popular place in Crestview today. She hoped that she would still be able to interview Doug Reed for clues despite how busy he might be. She spotted him leaning against the partition from the main room to the break room. His mustache was moving wildly with each word he spoke to the person he was standing beside. The two people were in an animated discussion, so Mandy took the opportunity to look around.

On the wall was the Rifle Range Hall of Fame. Apparently, they had competitions for most consistent deadly shots in the paper models of perpetrators. There seemed to be different categories, but Mandy wasn't completely sure what the differences were among them. She had never actually been to a range before. It seemed a lot more complicated in person than she had imagined. There were a few different courses, some with stationary targets, and some with moving targets and obstacles. She always thought the point of a range was to keep one's aim fresh for hunting season. Clearly, there must be some other added benefits. Socializing was likely among the perks because the place was full of people.

Doug spotted her and made his way over. "Welcome to my humble range," he said.

"This is hardly humble. Bustling, more like. Thanks for taking time to meet me," Mandy said.

"Let me show you around," Doug said. He led her back to the front door. "This is the entry area. We check all FOID cards on entry. We have safes over this way where people can store their weaponry here instead of bringing it back and forth from home. Only I have the key to these safes so people must sign in and out through me for their guns. We also store supplies in here. I am pretty tight with security since I am liable for any issues here."

"That does seem like a foolproof system. Do many people store their guns here?" asked Mandy.

"Quite a few. Some people have one at home and one here. Some people bring theirs here. We like to make it easy for whatever option they choose. Many residents of Crestview have a gun of some sort. It's part of living in rural Illinois."

"I see. It sure makes it hard to solve a murder that was caused by a gunshot."

"Indeed it does. I can't tell you who has a gun out here, but I can answer yes or no, if you know what I mean," Doug said.

"I see. Does Dennis have a gun here?"

"No."

"Does Aaron?"

"Yes."

"Does Jim?"

"Yes."

"Well I can see that this probably isn't going to help. Just about everyone has means, some have motive, most have an alibi. Let's move on."

"I can show you our different range areas. The outdoor section is not open at this time. We are doing some maintenance. Clay shooting is one of the popular areas out there. Our three indoor areas include the typical stationary targets. Our newer area has moving targets and is a bit of an obstacle course. People are really enjoying it so we may have more of that sort of thing in the outdoor area as we re-format it."

"It seems nice. What can you tell me about The Hall of Fame?" asked Mandy.

"We have a competition once a year among the community members. I started it just as a way for people to have some fun. It has turned into quite the focal point and a great source of income right before Christmas. The competition is pretty fierce. Buck and Jim tend to be the main winners."

"I saw that on the wall of plaques. Do you know of any unfriendly blood between Buck and anyone in particular?"

"Not really. As I said before at the clinic, he owed a lot of people money. Although you'll probably find the number of people he owed money to is about the same as the number who have guns. I don't know how to help you there."

"Thanks for trying. This is just such a mystery."

"Anytime. I am going to do my rounds and check that everyone is content. Here are ear plugs to protect your hearing if you go into the shooting rooms. Make sure to stay behind the line painted on the floor at all times. I will talk to you later this week to check in on Ronnie," Doug said.

"Thanks to you, too."

Mandy looked around a little more. She didn't find anything out of the ordinary that would help her so she decided to head back to the clinic. She still had most of her lunch hour left. Perhaps she would pay Sonya, the librarian, a visit. Even though the library wasn't open during lunch, Mandy knew where Sonya lived and she could check on Bubba at the same time. She stopped by the RV to check on Lyle on her way there. Lyle was content but still holding out for the long walk that had been promised.

"Soon, sweetheart. I have one more errand to run and then I'll be back," Mandy said to Lyle.

Chapter Thirty-Two

Mandy drove out to the library and parked. Sonya lived in a little cottage out the back with Bubba and her cockatiels, Zen, Zac, and Zoey. Mandy drove since the clouds looked like they might be holding back a rainstorm. She knocked on the little arched door at the front of the cottage, although she hardly needed to announce her presence since Bubba was in the window barking before she even made it out of her Jeep.

"Hi, Dr. Bell. Come in. I was just going to have a rest myself. I have been cleaning all morning in the library. Can I get you a cup of coffee?"

"That would be fabulous. I had a late night and I couldn't sleep," Mandy said.

"Poor lass. What's got your panties in a bind?" asked Sonya.

"Well, I had an emergency last night. Even when I finished that, I just couldn't seem to rest, knowing the murder has not been solved. Hi, Bubba," Mandy said as Bubba snuck onto her lap and nudged her hand for some attention. Sonya was in the kitchen getting coffee and cookies together and appeared around the corner with a tray.

"Here, have a fresh cup of coffee and tell me all about it," Sonya said.

"Thanks so much. This smells lovely," Mandy said, taking in a long sniff of coffee.

"I never skimp on coffee. I get my fresh roasted beans in the mail. It's my one major luxury."

"That is a very good idea. I should try that. Not all coffee is equal, that's for sure," said Mandy. "Before I forget, I am going to have a pile of books to donate to the library from Anna's house. I haven't finished sorting yet."

"Oh, that would be wonderful. How is it going with Anna's house? What are your plans with it?" asked Sonya.

"I am slowly getting through it. But I did have a few questions for you."

"Sure, how can I help?" asked Sonya.

"Well, I wondered if you could tell me more about the Anna, Buck, and Dennis triangle."

"That brings back memories. We all had such fun in our younger years. It's hard to imagine that two of them are no longer with us."

"It is a tragedy. They were so young."

"I don't know very much about Dennis. Buck, on the other hand, kind of turned into a bad seed. In high school, they were all so normal and well-adjusted. Buck seemed to have more trouble as the years went on. He was always in search of easy money, working from scheme to scheme. He could have just settled down and had a steady job like everyone else. That wasn't his way."

"Did you know anything about Dennis and Anna buying a house together?"

"No, I can't say that I do. I knew they were an item on and off for quite some time but they never showed that kind of commitment. Then Dennis left town. He kept in touch with Anna for a while. I never saw him come to visit. That doesn't mean that he didn't. Meanwhile, I secretly think that Buck was trying to get his finances squared away so he could win Anna once and for all but he never could get there."

"Did he ever borrow money from you?"

"Look around. I clearly don't have much so I think he knew I wasn't a good option. He never asked. It's one of the perks of appearing to be a homely little librarian. I hate drama, except in books where I can close the book when I need a break," said Sonya.

"I can relate with that mentality. It seems to me that it is too much of a coincidence that Buck was murdered while Dennis was in town. I keep thinking it is somehow related to their relationship and feud over Anna. The problem is that I have no proof."

"I could see Buck murdering Dennis, just not the other way around. Now I haven't spoken to Dennis in a long time and didn't even know he was in town. I just can't see him doing that."

"In truth, nor can I. Do you know what he might want from Anna's house? He keeps pestering me that he needs to get something before he leaves town. I just haven't had a chance to meet him," said Mandy.

"I can't think what it would be. Maybe it was something special he had given her as a token of his unending love and he wanted it back?"

"You should write romance novels. I can see in your eyes that you could get carried away in that thought," Mandy told Sonya.

"I have thought about it but I have never actually done it." They were each finished with their coffee and cookies.

"If you ever do, I would help you edit it."

"Thanks. I will keep that in mind."

"I should go back to the clinic and check on my patients. Plus, I promised Lyle a walk, though the rain may change that," Mandy said.

"I'm glad you stopped by. I needed a break from cleaning, though I don't think I was that much help."

"You were. I just need that final little clue and it will all come together."

"I wish you luck. Please be safe," Sonya said.

"I will. And I will bring those books by for you sometime. I may need to come to the library to scour the town's history for clues in this mystery, too."

"Anytime. I can help show you our search engine and the microfilm system."

"Thanks," said Mandy. She left Sonya's cottage to get back in her Jeep. It was just starting to drizzle so the long walk would be only a short sprint with Lyle. She needed to air out her thoughts and a promise is a promise.

She arrived back to the RV to grab Lyle and a light raincoat. Lyle was so excited to be out of the RV that she bounced through the puddles starting to form. They wandered through town, Mandy deep in thought, and Lyle happily prancing. The air was chilly enough that they had to keep a brisk pace to stay warm.

Despite the coffee break at Sonya's and snack before the range, Mandy worked up a little appetite and they needed a break from the cold drizzle. They entered the Inn and Merv greeted them. At the same time, the smell of something fabulous welcomed them.

"What is that I can smell?" asked Mandy.

"We decided to have some beef stew ready since the weather started to turn chilly. Would you like some?" asked Merv.

"Count me in. Can Lyle have a small tidbit of something?"

"Coming right up."

Merv delivered the steaming hot bowl of thick stew and some freshly made dinner rolls for dipping and soaking up the gravy. Lyle's snack consisted of a smaller serving of roll drenched in gravy.

"What are you two doing out walking on a day like today?" Merv asked.

"I've been running errands over the noon hour and Lyle was getting stir crazy since she couldn't be with me."

"I see. What errands?"

"I was following a few leads on my investigation."

"Any luck?" asked Merv.

"Not so much. I won't give up, though."

"Larry was in earlier and the police don't seem to be getting anywhere. My opinion is that it was someone who had planned this carefully and had a substantial motive. I don't think they are the traditional murdering type."

"That's pretty much the conclusion I have come to. I just need them to make one tiny little mistake so I can penetrate the mystery."

"Better you than me," Merv said. Mandy was enjoying each spoonful of stew while Lyle had already eaten her portion. Lyle was thoroughly cleaning her bowl with delicate licks. "She's such a good dog. What is her favorite tid-bit?"

"She prefers anything dairy-based; cheese, milk, ice cream, anything creamy and milky. She also has quite a sweet tooth, although I don't encourage her to eat people food often. It's just a treat every now and then."

"We all need a little something now and then."

"Thanks for having the perfect comfort food to provide nourishment for us after our jaunt. I didn't realize how hungry I was," said Mandy.

"You came to the right place for that. Can I get you any dessert?"

"No thanks. I need to go check on the patients in the clinic. And if I keep eating like this, I will need to expand my wardrobe in a bad way."

"A vet's work is never done, eh?" Merv said, completely ignoring Mandy's comment about weight gain.

"You've got that right, especially this week," Mandy said. Mandy and Lyle left the Inn, feeling much better with warm stew in their bellies as they walked back to the clinic.

Mandy checked on Trixie, Ronnie, and Reggie. All was well so she went to the front of the clinic to check with Gillian.

"Any messages?" Mandy asked Gillian.

"Just the lawyer called again wanting to know if you found the deed," said Gillian.

"Oh yes. I did find that. What's her number and I will call her to arrange a time to drop it by," said Mandy.

"Here you go. Other than that, no messages. It's been relatively quiet here, with the exception of Jimbo and Emma meowling for an early lunch."

"That's not surprising. They have quite the personality," Mandy said, taking the number Gillian gave her for the lawyer. "Since it's so quiet right now, I will go in the office and do a little work."

"Sounds good. I will man the phones," said Gillian.

Lyle and Mandy trotted down the hall to the office. Mandy started by calling the lawyer whose secretary patched her through.

"Yes, this is Dr. Mandy Bell. I understand you require a copy of the deed to Anna's property. I have just located such a thing. Can you come by the clinic to get a copy. Ok. Perfect. I'll see you in an hour."

Mandy felt good that she was getting something checked off of her list of to do's, even if solving the murder wasn't one of them.

Chapter Thirty-Three

Gillian's face poked around the corner.

"Anything I can get you?" asked Gillian.

"I am good. Just trying to fit some pieces together. The lawyer is coming by in an hour. You may as well go home. We have no other appointments and I will have to check all of the animals this evening."

"Are you sure? Trixie's mom brought in some cookies for us. I'll put them on the counter in the back."

"Wonderful. A cookie might be in order in an hour or so. I'm still full from lunch. You have tomorrow off anyway so think of this as an early start to your day off."

"I really appreciate it. I will be able to get the house spick and span. We've been pretty busy lately. I've been doing a few hours after work driving tractors for of the big grain outfits on the edge of town to save up a little."

"You are a major help around here. I hope you are not working two jobs because you don't get paid enough here."

"No, I just seem to always be a little behind with surprises that suck up money. Last month, my shower flooded. I'm not complaining. I just do what needs to be done," said Gillian.

"I hear ya sister. I'll call you if the whole town suddenly comes in. Otherwise, I'm going to do some paperwork while I wait for the lawyer."

"You have my number. I will go clean my humble abode."

"And, Gillian, have a good day off. You have earned it."

"Thanks," said Gillian.

Lyle repositioned herself on the floor while Mandy got out her list. She decided to use the internet to search for any clues of connections she was missing. First, she checked her email. There was another threat in her inbox. The sender had clearly fabricated an anonymous email so she couldn't track it back.

The email made it clear that she should not continue to pursue her investigation.

She shrugged it off. She looked at her list. Howie was someone that she needed to check into more. She also needed those leaves raked up at Anna's. She decided to give his parents a call. She arranged for him to come out the next day. She would be able to talk more to his parents while they dropped him off.

Before she could transport herself into her mind, she heard a car door. She looked up at the clock and an hour had already passed. Lyle jolted up at the sound of the front door.

"Hi, you must be Dr. Bell," said a tall, slender woman. "I'm Lucy Vanderbeek. I am representing Anna's estate."

"Nice to meet you. Sorry to meet you under these circumstances," said Mandy.

"Indeed. Anna was a great woman and an asset to this community," said Lucy. "I am terribly sorry for your loss. I understand you were quite close."

"We were, despite the long distance. We had one of those friendships that we could pick up where we left off no matter how long it had been since we'd seen each other. It's strange to be here in this town she had talked about so much," said Mandy. Lyle, meanwhile, had crept up to Lucy's lap and was licking her hand. "Lyle, down."

"She doesn't bother me. My dad used to raise hunting dogs. I love animals. You can't live in this town and not love animals and the outdoors," said Lucy.

"It's such a shame that this murder shattered the innocence of Crestview," said Mandy, probing for a reaction. She wasn't sure if Lucy even knew Buck. At the moment, anyone she met was a potential suspect or source of information.

"It is indeed. I went out with Buck once upon a time. We just weren't right for each other. In a town this small, unless you marry your high school sweetheart, you end up dating anyone who is eligible. I'll miss the old brute," said Lucy.

Mandy could see in Lucy's eyes that she was genuine. She trusted Lyle's judgment of people explicitly. For Lyle to like Lucy immediately, Mandy had a feeling that she could trust her.

"I think I have what you have been looking for. The deed to Anna's house was tucked up in a closet. Here it is," said Mandy, handing over a copy to Lucy.

"Interesting. That's what I needed to know," said Lucy.

"What?" asked Anna.

"For some reason, the original copy of this in the courthouse is missing. I needed to know if it listed just Anna or anyone else. See, the first deed to the property has Dennis on it. He was laying claim to the property based on that first deed. But when I went to the courthouse to verify his claim, the property was listed nowhere. It was odd," said Lucy.

"That is strange. So, at some point, Anna had bought him out without him knowing?"

"He would have had to sign documents so he knew that it had happened. The courthouse had a fire a few years back. The documents may have been destroyed in that. Who knows? The important thing is that we have the proof that Anna was the sole owner. Since she left everything to you, you are now the owner, with no room for formal contest," said Lucy.

"I had no idea that any of this was being contested," said Mandy.

"There was no need to involve you until I had proof one way or the other," said Lucy.

"That makes sense. Thanks," said Mandy. A howl could be heard from the kennels. It sounded like an animal in distress. "I better go see what that's about. Excuse me."

"I can let myself out. That is all I needed. Thanks for your time. Welcome to Crestview," said Lucy.

"Nice to meet you, Lucy," Mandy said.

As Lucy headed out the front door, Mandy and Lyle went to the kennels to see who was upset. Ronnie was whining as they approached his cage. He had peed and was vocalizing to indicate that his cage needed cleaned. Mandy transferred him to a clean cage and disinfected the original cage. She checked on everyone else. All was well so she returned to her office to work on the case, stopping to get a cookie on her way past the kitchenette.

Chapter Thirty-Four

The brainstorming was interrupted by a knock at the front door.

"Hi, I'm sorry to bother you. My Basset here seems to have a problem," said a man with a wool plaid shirt and torn carpenter jeans.

"Oh, come on in," said Mandy, opening the door. She led him into the exam room. Before she could even ask him what was going on, the Basset hound threw up foam. "I see he is throwing up. How long has that been going on?"

"Since yesterday. He doesn't normally do this. And he's so mopey. Something is really wrong."

Mandy proceeded to kneel down on the ground in front of him. She checked his gums which were a brick red, instead of pink. He seemed a little dehydrated, judging by the tackiness of his gums. If he had been throwing up for twenty-four hours, that would make sense because he would have a lot of fluids. She smelled his breath which had a rancid undertone. Already, she had a theory but she had more animal to examine. She listened to his heart. It was normal in rhythm although slightly elevated. His lungs sounds were unremarkable. She listened to his abdomen with her stethoscope. He had increased noise in his intestines, like a gas bubble moving. She felt his abdomen with her hands, carefully placing one hand on one side and one hand on the other. She applied pressure using both hands to capture organs in her hands. This technique allowed her to feel the consistency of his intestines, spleen, bladder, and colon through her fingers. Next, she took his temperature. It was elevated and there was no stool on the thermometer.

"When was the last time he ate?" asked Mandy.

"Yesterday afternoon. He wouldn't eat breakfast."

"And have you seen him poop?"

"We live out in the country so I don't reckon I have seen him. That's not unusual though."

"I see. Have you fed him anything different recently?"

"Nope."

A loud bang came from the back, startling them both.

"Excuse me. I just need to check on that. It's just me here today," said Mandy. Gillian had to take Hamish to a doctor's appointment. Mandy headed to where she thought the noise had come from, the kitchenette. She found Lyle inhaling the sugar cookies that Trixie's mom had dropped off. "Lyle," Mandy said with a stern voice. Lyle backed away from the cookies, finishing her last bite. "I knew you were being awfully quiet with a client coming to the door. I should have known. You are a perfect dog but you cannot resist a cookie. Such a sweet tooth. You get a pass since I am the one who put the cookies on the counter where you could reach them. Just try not to get a bellyache." Lyle sat, listening to every word Mandy said. The look in her face said that she would do it all over again even if she gets a bellyache. "I can't handle two dogs with upset bellies in on day. Cookies are not safe around you." Mandy returned back to the front.

"Sorry about that. Lyle, my collie, helped herself to an entire plate of sugar cookies. Your Basset won't be the only one not feeling too well today. So, Mr. - um, what is your name, sir?" asked Mandy.

"Mr. Hoffman. Call me Nolan. And this is Chester."

"Ok, Nolan, it seems Chester has eaten something that he shouldn't have. I can feel something about the size of a gumball in his intestines that shouldn't be there. I think we should take an x-ray."

"Money is no object for Chester. Anything you need to do, ma'am. He's my daughter's dog and I will do anything for her."

"Fair enough. I will need your help as Gillian is off today," said Mandy.

"I'm all yours."

Mandy led Chester and Nolan to the x-ray room. She set up the specs and the film. They suited up in the lead aprons and thyroid protectors. They held Chester on his side and engaged the x-ray beam over his abdomen. Mandy stepped out to develop the x-ray and came back to put it on the viewer.

"See this little lump here. That is what I can feel. It's not a rock or bone because it is not showing up white. It's something a little less dense. Either way, it needs to come out. He is throwing up because nothing can get past it. He is blocked."

"Little stinker. I bet it's a calf bud. We were debudding calves a few days ago and he was with us. He probably stole one."

"That could be it."

"When will you do the surgery?"

"The sooner, the better. Are you squeamish? Think you could give me a hand?"

"Sure thing. I have helped with cow c-sections. I should be ok, as long as you tell me what to do."

"Alright. Here we go. First we will need to give him a shot to make him a little sleepy. We can get everything else ready before we put him under," said Mandy.

From the lockbox, Mandy pulled the drugs up into syringes that she would need and then locked the box. She gave Chester a shot of pain medication as a pre-medication. Then, she got busy setting up the surgery. She would need the large surgery pack and drape and two sets of gloves. Since Chester was a large dog, she changed the anesthetic breathing circuit to a bigger tube and bag. Nolan just sat with Chester, watching Mandy as he petted his Basset who was starting to get very groggy.

"I think we are ready to go," said Mandy. "Are you sure you can be my assistant?"

"I'm ready. Just tell me what to do."

They lifted Chester up to the table and Mandy administered the induction drugs via his front leg vein. Chester immediately went flaccid on the table. Mandy directed the light to his mouth and inserted the endotracheal tube. She hooked him up to the oxygen and turned on the gas. She put the pulse oximeter on his tongue and the steady beat of his pulse was the only sound. Lyle was sitting at the door to the surgery, waiting to see if she could help in any way. Mandy turned Chester over on his back and tied his legs down. She shaved a large area of his belly and vacuumed the fur off. She scrubbed the area to sterilize it

"Ok, Nolan, I am going to show you how to scrub your hands and put gloves on. I won't need you to do that until I am in the abdomen. You will be helping with the anesthesia until I can get the blockage exposed," said Mandy.

She patiently showed him the art of scrubbing and gloving up. She only had gloves that were her size so she knew that he would have trouble with them but it was the best she could do. Nolan watched and asked questions so Mandy was confident that he could do it. Mandy placed the drape on Chester and made her incision. She worked quickly and methodically. The blockage in the intestines was easy to find. She pulled it out and examined the blood flow. Luckily, Nolan had noticed Chester was sick quickly which meant that there was no damage to blood flow. She would not need to remove any necrotic intestine.

"First, give Chester a few puffs by pressing on that bag on the anesthesia machine. Turn the dial on the machine down to one and a half. Then put a little water from the sink on his tongue where that little light is on the sensor." Nolan followed directions perfectly. "Ok, now I need you to scrub and glove up." Nolan did as he was told. The gloves were a tight fit for him but he manage to get them on.

"I'm ready," said Nolan.

"Hold your hands up and don't touch anything. Walk over here and place your hands on the drape where mine are. Now take your thumb and forefinger on each hand and pinch off the intestines on either side of the blockage. I want you to hold it tight enough that nothing can seep through but not so tight that you are cutting off the circulation. Whatever you do, do not let up until I tell you. Got it?"

"Yes ma'am."

Mandy made an incision right over the bulge in the intestines. She removed the culprit, which was indeed a calf bud. She sutured the hole in the intestines with tiny suture and tidy little knots.

"You will need to let go now. Now, place your hands on the drape. I am going to check for leaks," said Mandy.

She picked up the syringe she already prepared to puncture the intestines. She depressed the syringe, releasing saline into the intestines. To her delight, no saline leaked from the incision. She squished the fluid around to make absolutely sure. No leaking.

"Good job. You can take your gloves off now. I have a bag of fluids warming in the sink over there. Cut off the top with the scissors next to it and, without touching anything, pour it into the abdomen as I hold it open for you. We are flushing the abdominal cavity to cover our tracks and in case there had been any infection starting. Perfect. You can leave the rest in the sink. I will clean it up later. Now let's turn his anesthesia down to one. I will suture him up and he will be awake shortly," said Mandy.

Mandy went into a trance as she sutured the three layers she had cut. She took such pride in her suturing. Her goal was for the incision to heal as if nothing had ever happened. She had found over the years that people judge your external sutures more than they judge what you actually did so she had learned to be very precise.

"Let's turn him off the anesthesia and just let him have oxygen."

Nolan turned the dial to zero. Mandy removed the drape and

cleaned the area on his belly. Overall, it was a straight-forward surgery and there had been no complications. She placed all of the instruments in the sink to soak. She checked Chester's vitals manually and was pleased. She untied the stays from his legs and rolled Chester over to his side. He started to cough. She deflated the cuff in his endotracheal tube and let him breathe room air. He started to swallow so she pulled the tube. They carried him into the surgery ward and he immediately started to sit up. Mandy gave him another injection for pain as well as some antibiotics.

"The hard part is done. Your were an excellent assistant. He should be able to try eating soon and, as long as he does that, we can send him home. Let's let him rest and go back up the front to make sure I have your number."

Nolan gave Chester a heartfelt hug and covered him with a blanket. Chester responded with a big sigh. Lyle was waiting for them at the front of the clinic behind the desk. She relaxed into her chair when she saw them both come back calmly. She knew everything had gone well. If the outcome was euthanasia, Lyle somehow always knew to become a grief counselor and comfort the owner.

"Jot down your details on this hospitalization form and I will keep you posted." Nolan wrote down his phone number and address as instructed and handed it back to Mandy.

"I see you run a business. What is your line of work."

"I do a little of this and a little of that. Mainly I run big machines for concrete, excavating, bulldozing, anything like that. I do some salvage. It's the big jobs that keep my machines paid for."

"I see. Do you know much about Buck?"

"I hired him at one stage to be a hand on bigger jobs. He was useless. Never showed up on time. He seemed to think he could come and go as he pleased. He didn't stay long."

"Did you notice anybody coming to see him on jobs or anything like that?"

"Are you asking because you want a hand in solving the murder?"

"Maybe."

"I wouldn't recommend sticking your nose in it. If you're asking my opinion, I'd focus on women. He was always talking about a new woman. He'd used up all the ladies in this town and was starting to go further afield. Somebody must have a broken heart somewhere."

"Thanks I will look into that."

"No no, thank you, Dr. Bell. You are a miracle worker. You saved little Chester."

"You are the astute owner who noticed something was amiss."

"Well, thank you again. I look forward to hearing from you."

Chapter Thirty-Five

Mandy woke up a little early in order to do morning rounds on her patients and still have a head-start to the day. Todays was Gillian's actual day off after finishing early the day before. Mandy thought it was important for her to have some time away from the clinic. They had been working fairly hard since Anna passed. They would have a full morning of surgeries the next day but this morning there were no appointments on the books. Mandy would take the opportunity to check into more leads.

Mandy had her oatmeal and coffee and Lyle had her kibble. They went inside the clinic and found Jimbo and Emma snuggled up together. After giving them their breakfast, Mandy went around the clinic, watering the plants. She was humming peacefully. Today she wouldn't overdo it. The emergency the other night had disrupted her normal sleep pattern and she had been working double time to try to solve the murder. Then she had that surgery yesterday afternoon. She was exhausted.

She did a quick check on the patients, administering medications and checking progress. She had made arrangements the day before to meet Howie and his parents at Anna's house. She locked the clinic up and boarded the Jeep with Lyle at her side. They just needed to meet to exchange the plan for what exactly Mandy wanted cleaned up. It wouldn't take long to meet them and interview Howie's parents. Then she could head back to the clinic to follow up on the theory she was forming.

They had beaten her to the house and were already starting to unload Howie's gear. He had all of the equipment to run a professional lawn service. Since it was Fall, she didn't need lawn mowing services, but rather leaf clearing and tidying in preparation for the coming winter.

"Hi there. I hope you haven't been here long," Mandy said.

"No, ma'am. We always try to be early to all of the appointments," said Howie.

Mandy smiled and then showed Howie what her intentions were.

She didn't have any bags for leaf collection. Luckily, Howie had come prepared with everything and would take all of the debris away in his trailer. While Howie started to work, Mandy sidled up to his parents.

"He seems like such a fine young man. You must be very proud," Mandy said.

"We are indeed. He does well for himself, despite his potential limitations," Aaron said.

"It's nice to see that he has a busy schedule. You guys are quite dedicated to help him load and unload for all of his appointments," said Mandy.

"We wouldn't have it any other way," said Pat.

"It seems like you would protect him from harm like a mother bear," said Mandy.

"I'm not sure what you are implying. But, yes, I would," said Pat.

"I'm not implying anything. I'm just -"

"Nosing around Buck's murder, aren't you?" asked Aaron.

"I am trying to piece it together. It seems so out of character for this community, or what I know of it so far," said Mandy.

"I can assure you that we had nothing to do with it. We keep to ourselves mostly. Not that I need to have an alibi, but I can say that we were all at home the night of Buck's murder. The three of us can vouch for each other's company. We were watching a nature documentary and then went to sleep," said Aaron.

"I understand. Thanks for your cooperation. I know it's a touchy subject. I will leave you guys to it. Here is the money that we agreed upon. Please come by the clinic and let me know if it takes longer than you anticipated and I will pay more," said Mandy.

"Thanks. Howie will have this place ship shape for you. I know you are trying to help. My advice is to stay out of the murder investigation," said Aaron.

"I better get back to the clinic to check on my patients. The house is unlocked if you need anything, Howie. Make yourself at home," said Mandy. Lyle had been sitting at the base of one of the large trees. She was eying a squirrel. In her Border collie way, she was willing the squirrel and any other squirrels that wanted to join to come down from the trees. The only movement of her entire body could be seen in minute changes to her eyes. The poor squirrel was in a trance.

"Lyle, come," Mandy said. Lyle broke her stare and bounced over to join her human. They drove back to the clinic, leaving Howie, Aaron, Pat, and the squirrels so they could get back to work.

She would take some time to sit at her desk to work on the case. She would also work toward discharging Trixie and she would have to wait until the next day when Gillian was back to do Ronnie's surgery. Chester was sitting up in his cage and gulped down the slurry that Mandy offered him. She would try him on hard food later in the day and if he pooped, he could go home.

Mandy checked Reggie whose litter pan indicated he had peed in the night. She picked him up and placed him in a clean cage so she could clean where he had been. He dribbled a little urine on her wrist and watch when she was moving him so she went to the sink to wash it off. She removed the watch and cleaned it carefully before leaving it to dry. With the watch off, she washed her hands, noticing her tan line around her wrist from all the sun she had gotten at the softball game. Suddenly, she had a thought. She left a message on Gerry's phone that Reggie was doing well but that she would be making a trip out to the McMurphy Farm to do some investigating. He could come in later that day to pick Reggie up when she got back to the clinic.

She checked the messages and Dennis had again left a message that he needed to catch her before he left town.

"Ok, ok. You'll get your stuff, whatever it is. But first, I have other things to do," Mandy said out loud.

Mandy let Lyle out so she could hop in the Jeep and put a note up in the window that she would be closed until after lunch. She wanted to use the morning to follow a lead she had thought of. She called Dennis and left a message with Fred that she would be gone for the morning but could meet with him that evening after work. While she was on the phone with Fred, she figured she could follow up on the lead from Nolan about Buck's trail of broken hearts.

"Fred, while I have you on the phone, I wondered if you could help me out."

"Sure thing, sweetheart."

"I've heard from a few people that Buck had some trouble with the ladies. I wondered if you had heard of anyone since I last talked to you whose heart he broke hard enough that they might want him off the face of this planet."

"Hmmm. A lady was in the day before the funeral to get her hair done. I hadn't seen her before as a client. We got to talking and she seemed a little jilted by Buck. She was getting herself done up so she could show off at his funeral what he missed out on. I don't know if she would hurt anyone but someone sure broke her heart."

"Do you remember her name?" asked Mandy.

"I don't. She got color done so I will have a note card with her information on it. Let me grab it for you," said Fred. He must have put the phone down because Mandy could here his steps walking away from her.

"Here it is. Lucy Vanderbeek."

"Thanks. I think she is the lawyer in town," said Mandy.

"She didn't mention that so I don't know."

"I will look into it. Thanks again and don't forget to tell Dennis I called," said Mandy.

Chapter Thirty-Six

She checked the patients. All was well there. She just couldn't seem to sit still in her office. She wanted to follow up on the hunch she had. She and Lyle got into the Jeep. As she started the ignition, she visualized the route to the McMurphy Farm. She had been so shaken up the last time she was there that she had to concentrate to remember the way. She recalled it with some effort and they headed down the road.

The rain from yesterday made it feel like winter was coming. There was still frost on the areas of grass that hadn't come into the sunlight yet. She turned into a gravel road about a half a mile before the entrance to the yards at the farm. She parked the Jeep behind some shrubs to hide her presence here. She left Lyle in the Jeep and cracked a few windows for her to be comfortable.

"Now sit and stay. I will be right back," Mandy said.

Mandy walked through the drainage ditch to stay below the horizon in case anyone was watching. There was a remnant of a turtle shell that a coyote must have eaten recently as the shell had not yet faded. This was a reminder to Mandy that there were predators out here so she needed to work quickly.

Her walk took her to the entrance to the yards. She retraced her steps from that fateful day to the sight were she had planned to innocently use nature's little girl's room. It had been a week since the murder. The yellow tape was no longer surrounding the crime scene. The police had combed over the whole area for clues and hadn't come up with much. But, they missed one spot. She reached down into the bushes around the gate leading to where the shooting had taken place. She got down on her hands and knees and kept feeling around.

She had pieced together that they had to have missed the one clue that would lead them to murderer. She found what she had come for and slid it into her pocket. Before she could stand up, she heard a voice coming and quickly hid under the thickest shrubs she could find. The voice was definitely heading her direction. She felt like she was in the poem by Edgar Allen Poe about the beating heart. She hadn't even done anything wrong and her heart was beating so loudly she was sure that her hiding spot wouldn't last.

"It has to be here somewhere," a voice said. "This whole silly town wouldn't know something if it hit them in the face," the voice said, finishing his sentence with an eerie cackle.

She recognized that it was Fred. Before she could make a plan as to how she could get out of this situation, Fred leaned down and tapped her shoulder. Try as she might, her hiding place didn't hide her fuzzy hair. He must have seen her in the bushes.

"Fancy meeting you here," Fred said.

"Um, I ..." Mandy stuttered.

"Well, I suppose if you are here, that means you have figured it out," Fred said.

"Not everything. I just had a hunch I wanted to check up on,"

Mandy said.

"So, do you have what you came for?" asked Fred.

"What?" asked Mandy.

"The watch," said Fred.

"Oh, that," said Mandy. "Yes, I found it. I'll just give it to you and then you can make your escape. I don't really have everything figured out so there is no need to do anything to me."

"I don't think so. I don't like loose ends so I have no choice but to remove you from the situation," Fred said, pulling a gun from behind his back to point it at her. She couldn't tell what kind of gun it was but she did recognize that it had a silencer equipped to the end of it. She knew that meant he was planning to remove her from the situation silently.

"But, I really don't know anything," Mandy pleaded.

"What don't you know?"

"Why did you do it?"

"I have always loved Dennis deeply. I wanted him to live happily ever after with me."

Mandy had a hunch that this was the truth behind it all. It was not satisfying to hear it straight from Fred in these circumstances, however.

"I decided that if I couldn't have him, he needed to be happy and I knew Anna was perfect for him. Plus, it would bring him back here closer to me. I even grew all kinds of species of cacti to make him feel as if he was out in the West when he came to visit." As Fred spoke, he led Mandy at gunpoint further and further into the woods beside the yards. Mandy knew it would be hard for anyone to find her. She was trying to come up with an escape plan, but Fred was keeping a very fast pace.

"I couldn't believe that Buck made it so difficult for Dennis to be happy with Anna. Buck spent years tormenting Dennis over Anna. I couldn't watch it anymore," said Fred. "I tried to keep you from getting stuck into the middle of this. I sent you two written warnings to which you took no heed. I even tried pointing you on wild goose chases. You are just too stubborn for your own good," Fred said.

"I couldn't let Anna's town be blemished by an unsolved murder. Anna meant too much to me," Mandy said.

"She meant something to all of us. She was supposed to make Dennis happy since I couldn't. But then she ruined the plan by dying."

"Why now? Why kill Buck now?" asked Mandy. Mandy could tell that Fred's grasp on reality was a distant thread. Still, she was curious as to his mindset.

They continued their pilgrimage to parts unknown of the woods. Mandy's heart was beating so hard it was pounding in her ear drums. Her palms were sweaty. Fight or flight adrenaline was in full throttle mode. She tried to remain calm and think on her feet. It was a little hard with the cold tip of a gun jammed in her back. Fred was making her keep her hands in the air which was hard to do for this long. Her arms were starting to ache.

"I knew that Dennis was coming to town and I didn't want him to have to face the man who stole happiness out from under him. So, I had to kill him before the Halloween Hoedown where Dennis would surely see him."

"Why the McMurphy farm?"

"It was a place I figured no one would be able to find him until his body was unrecognizable from the coyotes. If it wasn't for the nosy vet who had to pee, it would have been months before anyone found him. They just would have thought he left town again on some crazy scheme. No one would have missed him. And Dennis could have moved into Anna's house and been close by me."

Mandy thought about the coyotes. If only that had been her only worry now. A coyote might be easier to defend herself from than a crazed hairstylist with a gun.

"So you thought he was still on the deed? You didn't know that Anna had bought his share out from under him?" said Mandy.

"I wasn't sure and neither was Dennis. That's what he needed to find from Anna's house. He had asked the lawyer to get it from you, but you hadn't been able to find it. He thought he would know where it was. Now I have a question for *you*. How did you know about the watch?" asked Fred.

"I had seen the tan line on Dennis's hand and knew he was missing something like a watch. Being from out West, his tan line was so obvious and I just kept thinking about it and how he reacted when I pointed it out. Then I saw the way you looked at him. I thought maybe you had taken it as a memento of him. And then, I knew it would be too loose on your wrist since you are more petite than him. I figured that when you opened this gate it would have fallen off or you took it off so it wouldn't have gunshot residue on it. I thought it was strange that it hadn't shown up again on Dennis's hand so I knew you had or he gave it to you and then you misplaced it. It was a long shot. I had

been trying to piece together the triangle between Dennis, Anna,

and Buck. I was missing a piece. Then I realized that piece was

you."

"I'm impressed Dr. Bell. It's too bad you won't live to tell

anyone of your cleverness. You should learn to mind your own

business."

They had made it so far from where they had started that even if

Mandy was going to try to run, she didn't know which direction

to go. The clouds were covering the sun so she couldn't even tell

which way was north.

"It's not in my nature to stay out of things. I just can't believe I

shared gummy bears with you."

"I put on a good act. They said I could have gone to Broadway."

"Why let all of this ruin the rest of your life? If you confess to

the murder, you can plea bargain and get off light. You can

follow your dreams. You are still young."

"You're not talking me out of this. You have to go, now," Fred said with an evil voice that Mandy couldn't believe was coming from such a fashionable, seemingly well-adjusted man. "Now turn around and face forward."

Mandy did as she was told. She was startled by the change in Fred's face. He was clearly not well.

Chapter Thirty-Seven

Mandy didn't imagine her life would take this turn of events. Though she never planned to settle down, she didn't plan on an early departure either. She focused on her breathing to remain calm. She had already tried talking Fred out of it with no success. She thought of one more idea.

"Don't you want to say goodbye to Dennis and explain that you have done this all for him? If you kill me, you will be caught and he will never know the truth about how you felt."

"I am going to kill you and then kill myself. This world is not ready for what I have to offer," Fred said.

Having tried that approach, the only thing left to do was try to knock the gun out of Fred's hand. He had obviously grown up in Crestview and had an aiming stance that showed that this was not his first exposure to a gun and he would likely shoot with accurate determination. There was not even a waiver in his grip. He was ready to do the deed he believed to be the correct next move.

The world was suddenly very still to Mandy. She could hear
every bird chirping in the woods and even thought she could hear
pine nettles brushing against each other in the wind. She always
figured that the last moments of a person's life would be marked
by a fast forward movie of their life's memories. She was not
experiencing that. The tunnel of light people describe was not
present in her consciousness either. All she could focus on was
her breathing while her eyes were fixated on Fred's maniacal
countenance.

As she was deep in thought about how to get out of this mess,
she heard a loud bang. She thought for sure she had been shot.
The adrenaline must have shielded her from the pain because she
felt nothing but numbness. She fell to the ground and the world
became a black hole in her mind. She felt a warm sensation over
her face. It was like she was being baptized. The warmth turned
to wetness. She thought this was a rather strange way to start an

afterlife, if there would be one. She then felt pressure on her shoulders as if someone was digging at them.

"Ruff, ruff, whimper," cried Lyle.

Suddenly Mandy's eyes popped open to find Lyle licking her and pawing at her. She could see a blurry version of Gerry in the background as well.

"Are you ok?" Gerry asked. He had one hand on her head and the other was checking her pulse. Lyle was torn between licking Mandy and growling at Gerry for being so close to Mandy.

Mandy realized that, in fact, she was not dead. She felt dizzy and confused. Her version of Heaven might include Lyle, but it surely wouldn't feature Gerry.

"I think so," Mandy said with a tremor in her voice. "What happened?"

"I got your message that you were coming out here and I didn't want you to be by yourself. I must have arrived just after you did. I found your Jeep hiding in the bushes down the road with Lyle in it. I let her out and since there was no sign of you, I knew you were in trouble. Luckily, Lyle here led the way. She's not just an eye dog. Her nose works pretty well, too," Gerry explained.

Lyle sat obediently by Mandy's side. She was still licking her. Now she had moved from her face to her hands, softly nudging her as she licked. Her bushy black and white tail was swaying back and forth to show her appreciation of one more day with her beloved human.

"She led me all the way over here. I could see I only had a split second before I was too late, so I took that shot that I could get. The ambulance is on its way. I called them in when Lyle and I were in pursuit," Gerry continued. "I am just so glad we got here in the nick of time. Are you sure you're ok?"

"I appear to be unscathed. All of a sudden, I am very cold," Mandy answered.

"I haven't seen any wounds. I'd say that you are suffering from a bad case of shock," said Gerry.

"Fred?" asked Mandy.

"The shot I took looks to have been fatal. I could only get a clear chest shot."

The ambulance EMTs showed up, having following the trail of yellow tape that Gerry had tied to branches here and there as Lyle led him through the woods so the EMTs could find their way. They checked Fred over first. He was indeed deceased. Mandy, on the other hand, was fine. They gave her a blanket and some hot tea.

Larry arrived shortly after and took Mandy's statement. He would get the rest of the story from Gerry back at the station. They loaded Fred into the ambulance and decided the rest of the formalities could wait. The murder had finally been solved. Night was coming in and it was time to get Mandy back to town.

"Would you like to accompany me to the Inn?" Gerry asked Mandy.

"Is this a date?" asked Mandy.

"Nope, just a gentleman looking after a lady in distress," Gerry retorted. "The town will want to thank you as well."

"Thank you for saving my life, by the way," Mandy smiled back.

Despite Gerry's help in saving Mandy, Lyle wedged herself in between them when he gave Mandy a hug.

"Jealous, eh?" Mandy said, looking down at Lyle. "I can take a hint," she said as she backed away from Gerry.

Chapter Thirty-Eight

"What a couple of weeks," Mandy said with a sigh. "I never thought Anna's little quiet town of Crestview would have a murder and a Hoedown in the same week."

"I hope this doesn't cloud your view of our quaintness. Now that you are the town hero and all, I'd suggest you stick around a while and at least enjoy the fruits of your labor," Gerry said to Mandy with a nudge. Lyle darted over to them and squeezed herself between them to cut off the nudge.

Myrna and Merv delivered a feast of roast turkey with all of the fixings to the table. There was sweet potato casserole with marshmallows, green bean casserole, mashed potatoes, dressing, gravy, fresh rolls, cranberry sauce, and a steaming hot mound of freshly cut turkey off the bone. The Inn was toasty warm and packed full of people. The Halloween decorations had been removed and in their place was a plethora of Fall decorations. There were all the colors of Fall represented in various shapes of leaves suspended from the ceiling and bar area. It created the illusion of feeling of being outdoors in the forest while staying warm inside.

"This meal is on the house, ladies and gentlemen. Thanks to Mandy, Crestview is back to normal. With any luck we can convince her to stay on as our vet slash sleuth," Merv said.

Around the table were Rhonda, Doc Tom, Gillian, Hamish, Mandy, Gerry, Larry, Dennis, Pat, Aaron, and Howie. The rest of the Inn was filled with more locals, all enjoying the early Thanksgiving meal.

"We will see about that. I have enjoyed myself here, but I never planned to settle in anywhere," Mandy said as she started to load her plate with the dishes that were being passed around on the lazy Susan in the center of the table. "I think I will stick around for the Christmas Mingler and then see what happens after that. That should give me sufficient time to sort through Anna's affairs."

Since Lyle had played a huge part in solving the murder and saving Mandy's life, she had an extra special spot on the floor at the foot of the table. Merv had placed a nice plush pillow for her comfort.

"Poor Lyle is feeling left out so I made her a special treat. I understand she is fond of dairy so I made her a cheesecake to show our appreciation," Merv said. He lifted the lid on the serving tray he had carried from the back and placed it in front of a very excited Border collie. She wagged her tail with a newfound happiness and started to gently lick her reward.

"Wow, that is very sweet of you, Merv. Thanks so much," Mandy said.

"You know, Mandy, if you stick around, Hamish and I can teach you how to ride a quarter horse so you and Lyle can really start to work some sheep," Gillian said.

"We'll see, you guys. For now, let's enjoy this meal. A toast to a wonderful meal with lovely company," Mandy said, as she raised her glass to the others.

"And to the future, and whatever possibilities it may hold," Gerry added to her toast, giving Mandy a cheeky wink. Lyle promptly stopped eating her cheesecake to give Gerry a disappointed stare.

Before everyone could dig into their meals, the phone rang.

"Who would interrupt this?" asked Merv as he walked to the bar to answer it. "Hello. Yes, she is here. I see. Let me get her for you." He set the phone on the bar counter and asked Mandy if she could be so kind as to take the call.

"Hi. This is Dr. Bell, how can I help you? I see. Hmmm. Are you sure. Ok. I can meet you at the clinic in a few hours." She hung up the phone and turned to the table of people waiting in anticipation.

"What is it?" asked Gillian.

"It seems that a baby orphaned bobcat has been found in the

outskirts of town. A citizen brought it inside and warmed it up. It seems to be hurt and someone had said that I had experience with wildlife," she said as she winked at Gillian. "So they are going to bring it to the clinic for assessment."

"How cool. I've never seen a bobcat," said Gillian.

"Me neither. And, depending on how young and how sick it is, you guys may all get your wish. I've always wanted to rehab and release a bobcat and I have never had the opportunity. The whole process could take months," said Mandy.

"That is wonderful news! For now, let's all sit down and have a meal together," said Merv.

No one needed a second nudge to start eating. All that could be heard was the clanking of serving forks and spoons on serving dishes as everyone piled their plates high. After such a dramatic day, Mandy was certainly famished.

"Tell us the whole story," said Rhonda. "We want to know how you managed to figure it out and save the town all in one day. Of course, in between bites of this delicious spread thanks to Merv and Myrna."

"Well, I knew that there was something we were all missing. I just kept thinking about the day that I went to have my haircut and how odd Dennis acted. See, I had seen a tan line on his wrist as if he was missing something - a watch, bracelet, or something like that. I asked him about it and he became very cagey when he answered. He said he must have just misplaced it. He acted so weird, though. Then, I was going through Anna's things and kept finding a link between Anna and Dennis. All evidence was pointing to Dennis. He had just come into town and Dennis was a wild card to everyone. I couldn't get much information about him. I kept trying to find a motive for him. I found out some discrepancies with the deed to Anna's property. And he kept hounding me for something from Anna's house. He just seemed like the perfect fit."

"So, how did you get from Dennis to the cattle yards?" asked Gillian.

"First of all, I had studied Dennis's feet. I knew that size 13 shoe prints were found at the murder scene. Dennis, on the other hand, had size 14 shoes. I managed to sneak a peak at an impression of his shoes in the sand at the softball game. While someone could have worn bigger shoes to throw off the investigation, Dennis would never have been able to squeeze his feet into a smaller shoe and walk all the way out there."

"I'm so glad that the murder has been solved because everyone keeps giving me very strange looks," said Dennis.

"We know you are innocent but Mandy did have some interesting reasons to suspect you," said Gillian.

"Well, if everyone must know, I am the one who gave Fred my watch as a token of appreciation for him letting me stay at his place. He had always admired it. I only acted odd because a man giving another man a watch is a little strange and then he went and lost it anyway."

"Oh, he didn't lose it. That's why I went out to the cattle yards. The image of the murder scene was ingrained in my mind and I kept going over it and over it for clues. I knew I had seen something shiny that was out of place and it took me a while to put it altogether. I knew I would find that watch there. Fred wouldn't lose the watch. He cherished it. He had taken it off to avoid gun powder residue and then forgot to pick it up or it fell out of his pocket or something. He couldn't go back out to get it until everybody started going about normal business and not loitering around the yards with the investigation, so he was waiting," said Mandy.

"I still don't understand how you knew it was Fred," said Rhonda.

"Bear with me. I'm getting to it. I had been digging around in Anna's things, trying to find an heir to Anna's estate. I also perused library archives. I came across Dennis and Anna's relationship from years ago. But what we had all missed in that relationship was a jealous third party. In all of the years of information I went through, I never once found any special someone in Fred's life. All along, he had been waiting for Dennis. He couldn't handle that Dennis wouldn't love him back but he still wanted Dennis to be happy. Buck had always been the undoing of Dennis and Anna ever getting together. Fred was trying to protect Dennis from the heartache of seeing Buck again so he murdered him before they crossed paths again."

"Whoa. That is all very convoluted," Dennis said.

"Indeed. The other missing factor to consider is that Fred was mad as a March hare. His form of logic was clearly not linear nor sane. While love can do a lot of strange things, I'm guessing Fred's secret life was hard for him his whole life. He just snapped," said Mandy.

"That is absolutely dreadful. We may be a small town but we certainly don't judge people's choice of love, even if it is unrequited," said Rhonda.

"Very true. We accept everybody here. Poor guy," said Gillian.

"There's one thing I still don't know the answer to," said Mandy.
"What on earth was so important for you to get from Anna's?"
she asked Dennis.

"I just wanted to get a few odds and ends, a sweatshirt I gave her
when we were back in high school, a few pictures. I did want to
check the deed to make sure we were all square," said Dennis.

"You sure made it seem like the earth would end if you didn't
retrieve the items you wanted," said Mandy.

"Sorry about that," said Dennis.

"So, Gerry, how did you know to go rescue Mandy?" asked
Rhonda.

"She had left me a message on my phone that she was going out
there to check something. I didn't anticipate how much danger

she would be in. I just didn't want her to be exploring anything on her own. Unfortunately, I was too late and Fred had already led her out of eyesight. I knew she was around somewhere because her Jeep was there. Lyle led us to her so we could save the day," said Gerry.

"I'm so glad everyone had their Sherlock Holmes sleuthing caps on, including Lyle," said Gillian. "Perhaps life can get back to normal now, or as normal as it ever was around here!"

"I hate to eat and run. It's about time to meet the lady with the bobcat. A few hours just flew by," said Mandy.

"On behalf of the town, thanks for your bravery today. You have helped to restore Crestview to the safe, quaint town it was supposed to be," said Gerry.

Mandy rose, bowed with a wink, and left with Lyle by her side.

Chapter Thirty-Nine

Mandy and Lyle returned to the clinic stuffed to the gills with the wonderful meal. They fed Emma and Jimbo, giving them a little moist kitten food as a treat.

"Nobody should miss out on the feasting today," said Mandy.

As they were making the rounds to check on patients in the hospital, Gillian and Hamish joined them.

"You sneaked out rather fast. You didn't think we were going to miss the bobcat," said Gillian.

"I wasn't trying to sneak. I am just so excited about this bobcat. I am convinced that it will be just a Maine Coon kitten or something like that. Plus, with all of the excitement today, my patients haven't received the care they deserve from me."

"Hamish and I checked in on them before dinner. I think everyone is doing well," Gillian said.

"Thanks for doing that. Yes, I think we can discharge Trixie and Reggie tomorrow. We can do the amputation tomorrow, too. We need to clear out this hospital to make room for the next onslaught of patients. They tend to come in waves. Let's get a few things ready for the new addition. Fluids, a heating pad. Do we have any kitten or puppy formula?"

"I have some of each in the freezer. I'll go grab it," said Gillian.

"Great. We may need to mix them together because neither is perfect for bobcats. I will set up a cage in my office. I don't want it exposed to the hustle and bustle of the clinic or the diseases of other animals," Mandy said, almost skipping as she went to her office.

"They're here," said Gillian, as she opened the door.

Karen and Ted walked in with a box draped with a wool blanket. They set it on the table and stepped back. They were the town trappers, living way on the outskirts of town. They looked the part, almost like they had stepped out of the wilds of Alaska.

They each had on neutral toned clothing that become naturally camouflaged due to the years of dirt and wear. Their hats were made from offcuts of fur from various mammals. They smelled fragrantly of a combination of pine, dirt, animal fat, and grease. Their eyes were completely focused on the little box.

"So, what do we have here?" Mandy asked rhetorically as she opened the box.

"We were trapping out West of town and came across a mama bobcat in one of the traps. We didn't aim to trap her. We have been out there trying to relocate some coons that have been wreaking havoc. We use a small live trap so that we don't catch things like bobcats. This mama must have been desperate from the drought for food that she got in and got captured," Karen said.

"Unfortunately, she panicked and broke her neck. We found her deceased with little kitten trembling beside her," said Ted. "We couldn't bear to see it not make it and we heard you have the know-how to get the little guy back to the wild. We searched for others and there was only this one kitten, if that's even what you call them."

"It's unusual to have a litter this late in the season so I'm not surprised there was only one. Poor mama. It happens though and you did the responsible thing by bringing it in," said Mandy.

She pulled the little ball of fur out onto the rug she had on the table. She examined it thoroughly and found no wounds. Its little ears were still flat against its head. Its eye were barely starting to open. She checked and it was a little boy. He seemed very weak and dehydrated. She got him on the heating pad after she weighed him at 320 grams. Even though he was so small, he was clearly not a domestic cat. His markings were designed for him to be invisible in the Fall ground cover. He had little stripes along his back and sides and a smattering of dots along his belly. His fur was dense, almost like a goat or sheep, instead of a cat. His claws were already gigantic compared to a normal cat. One of them inadvertently hooked into Mandy's skin as she checked him over. It was definitely a bobcat.

"I can't make any promises here. I always take wildlife day by day. We will get him warmed up and on some fluids and then see about starting some formula tomorrow. Poor guy has had a harder day than me, and that's saying something," said Mandy.

"Oh, we heard about your day. Thanks for your bravery, Dr. Bell. And thank you for giving this guy a go in life," said Ted.

"And if you need anything, please call us. Gillian knows how to get a hold of us. We can help arrange food if you need fresh meat. And we can help with release when the time comes," said Karen.

"That's great. We won't need meat for quite a while but fresh is always best," said Mandy.

Gillian led Karen and Ted back out. She raced back to the table to get her own close-up look at the new patient.

"That is truly amazing. They are built to be athletes from birth. Look at those feet!" said Gillian. Hamish was staring wide-eyed beside her. People can live in Illinois their whole lives and never see a bobcat, much less a baby one. This was a real treat for everyone.

"Rule number one. This is an animal that should be afraid of people. We have to do our best not to imprint it. No loud talking around him. We wear leather gloves when we handle him. We do as little handling as possible. Ok?" said Mandy.

"Aye, aye, captain. What can we do to help?" said Gillian.

"Let's get some fluids into him. We can do shifts through the night. I'll take the first few nights to get him stabilized and then you guys can take a few nights. He will need to be fed several times through the night. For tonight, I will just do electrolytes until we correct his hydration status. We'll get a portable cage set up so we can transport him without changing his environment. We'll need a stuffed animal for him to bond with and a little clock for him."

"A clock?" asked Hamish quietly.

"The ticking helps mimic the heart beat of a mama. They find it soothing," said Mandy.

"That's clever," said Hamish.

They gathered around while Mandy gave some fluids under the skin. He was so weak that he made no attempt to swallow when she tried oral fluids. He didn't even fight when the needle went under his skin for the fluids.

"Rule number two. Try not to get emotionally attached. Wildlife is very hard. Sometimes they don't make it. We all need to be prepared for that and take it day by day," said Mandy.

"We are on board, Dr. Bell," said Hamish. Lyle had been through this drill before but she sat at attention listening to every word Mandy had to say. She was an indispensable nurse in the first few weeks of care for an infant animal. She kept Mandy company during the late night checks. She also helped wake Mandy up if she overslept one of her shifts.

"Let's all get some rest now. It's been a long day. I will bring him to the RV with me tonight and check him in a few hours for more fluids," said Mandy.

"I'll be back bright and early to get the hospital patients taken care of and the surgery ready," said Gillian. "Anything else we can do?"

"Grab the doors for me and get some rest," said Mandy. They all filed out of the clinic. It seemed fitting that a new adventure should begin before the previous one had ended. Never a dull moment at a vet clinic.

The End

Acknowledgments

I would like to extend gratitude to friend Vivian McGeehon for her continuous encouragement to finish the book that was started as a few chapters five years ago. Without her guidance, this book would have remained a fruitless hobby. In addition, a big thank you is in order for Chau Schroeder who inadvertently volunteered to edit the first book in the series about Dr. Mandy Bell. Cheers to Kane Deuel for crafting the perfect bumble bee costume for Lyle to bring the book's description to life. And, thanks to Britt Bailey whose photographic talents allowed the creation of an eye-catching book cover, featuring none other than Lyle. Lastly, thanks to Lyle for being my soul mate. We have been through thick and thin together and you continue to inspire me. Dogs are in fact the center of my universe.

A portion of the proceeds from the sale of this book will go to Clay County Animal Rescue and Shelter, one of the author's favorite causes. Visit them at the website at:

www.claycountyshelter.com or check out their Facebook page.

Book Two

Keep an eye out for book two of the Mandy Bell Series, Pasture Post-Mortem. Check out the Mandy Bell Series on Facebook for updates.

35198159R00246

Made in the USA
Lexington, KY
02 September 2014